I0580462

Crashing the Net

CEDAR RAPIDS RACOONS

LASAIRIONA MCMASTER

DRAMA LLAMA PUBLISHING

Dedication

*For anyone who has ever had to give up on a dream, or fight like
fuck to hold onto it.
This one's for you.
And for Fancy, because Fancy Fucking Says.*

Content Warning

This book contains certain subjects that some readers may be sensitive to, including but not limited to: injuries as a result of a major (on page) car accident, depression, anxiety, trauma and PTSD.

As with every book with content warnings or potentially sensitive subjects, please be cautious when undertaking this story and take care of your mental health.

CHAPTER 1

Edith

(DECEMBER 26TH)

Working out beyond exhausted and with a carb hangover was not my best idea ever. I'm on the struggle bus, and there's a sixty-five percent chance that I'm going to puke. Maybe even seventy. As I finish my last set of leg presses at the gym, I regret the decisions of past Edith.

It's all Apollo's fault.

It's always Apollo's fucking fault.

It was his stupid Christmas party last night that led me here.

The grumpy bastard himself grumbles at the free weights he's lifting across the room. His teeth are gritted, exertion clear on his face, a thin sheen of sweat coating his biceps and seeping through his tank top. Despite the permanent funk of body odor lingering in the gym, I can't help but admire the lines of my ripped best friend.

I hate him.

Usually, he keeps his festive celebrations to a single Christmas Eve party, but this year one shindig wasn't enough for the prince of darkness and his fancy-pants siblings. So I ended up breaking my own rule and staying out late two nights in a row. I rarely drink, special occasions only. But I did go a little crazy with the carbs over the past couple nights, and my body really doesn't like me for it. In fact, let's go ahead and make that a seventy-five percent chance of puking.

There's no room in my life for vices, only dancing. And apparently my best friend, Apollo de la Peña, local hockey god with the name of an *actual* god. He counts as a vice too. Because something about him prevents me from saying, "No, Apollo. I'm staying home tonight with a hot bubble bath and a great read."

The man in question stands about twelve feet away from my machine doing arm curls next to the weight rack in front of the mirror.

I've known him for years. He's like an annoying brother, but even I can appreciate the definition in his arms as he raises the weight up and down. He also has the perfect hockey bubble butt. The shiny tech material of his shorts stretches across his ass, and I'm in the perfect position to ogle.

Ballet boy butts are similar to hockey butts in being excessively muscled, but ballet butts are a little sleeker, a little more heart-shaped from the way they work. Also, dance belts and tights means it's all butts all day in my world. I'm generally blind to the ballet butts but something about *his* hockey bubble butt catches my attention in those shiny short shorts.

He pauses his set, cocking his head, a couple stray beads of sweat dripping from his nose. "You checkin' out my ass?"

And the rest of him, but I'd never tell. He'd never let me live it down. Plus, it's kind of weird letting my eyes linger on any piece of him that's currently exposed and rippling with exertion. I shrug, bring my knees up toward my chest before pushing the plate back to the machine.

"What can I say? I know a fine ass when I see one, Señor de la Peña."

He glares at me, muttering something to himself as he wipes down the weight and replaces it on the rack. Picking up his bottle from the floor, he tips it at me. "Almost finished? Or should I do something else?"

Sure, he's sweaty, but he's chipper and seemingly ready to do another workout without missing a beat.

Jerk.

"Almost dead, you mean." I wince. It's best to quit while I'm only a little behind. "My insides hate me. There's every chance I'm going to throw up in your way-too-extra car on the way home."

Despite being a fancy-pants rich boy, his life is relatively normal. That is, until it comes to his apartment and his vehicle. We live in the most expensive building in downtown Cedar Rapids.

There's no way I could afford the apartment I live in by myself. My parents, on the other hand, are loaded and spend most of their time sailing the world on expensive yachts and drinking Champagne that tastes like paint thinner.

Not together, however—never together. The last time my parents were in the same room together there was a shift in the earth's tectonic plates that caused rumblings across three continents. Mom's on her second marriage, and Dad likes the carefree life and women barely older than me. But who am I to judge?

When I told them where I wanted to live, they didn't bat an eyelid. In fact, less than a week later I had the deed to the apartment with my name on it in hand, and the key to the place across the hall from my best friend.

Is it guilt money? Or more that they just have so much of it that they don't care what they do with it, or what I do with it either? Regardless, I'll take it.

"No one forced those garlic knots down your throat,

princesa." His intense stare bores into me. But his grumpasaurus ass doesn't scare me.

I don't even bother to roll my eyes at the more-than-a-decade-old nickname. When we met, it was Halloween, and I was dressed like a Disney princess. He's called me princess ever since. It grates on any woman he dates which makes me love it just a little bit. But I'd never tell him that out loud either.

Jabbing my finger in his direction, I scowl at him. "Lies. You did."

He smirks at me with a shrug. "You need to learn to let your hair down every now and then."

Yet again, I don't dignify him with a response. He knows how I feel. We're both semi-professional athletes in our prime. And by semi-professional, I mean not-at-all professional but working toward it. That's the end game for both of us.

Despite being a Neanderthal hockey player, Apollo gets it. He understands why I'm strict with my diet, why my body is a temple, and why even on the day after Christmas, I'm at the gym.

He *really* gets it. It's why we fit so well together as best friends. Since everything in the entire universe is designed for couples, we get a meal prep box delivered once a week and take turns cooking dinner. Every Sunday, we batch cook our lunches for the week ahead, and when we hit the gym, we almost always go together.

I wipe down my machine, swipe my water bottle from the floor and follow him toward the exit, pausing over the trash by the door as my stomach lurches.

"I hate you," I grumble, holding out my bottle for him to take while I clutch the sides of the garbage can.

He waves my drink at me. "Hydrate. Mind over matter. Let's go home and get some food into that stomach."

At the mention of food, my stomach heaves, and I spew like the kid from *The Exorcist*. Apollo grunts behind me, shuffles—probably to put the drinks down—before he rubs my back. "Lightweight."

I can't help but laugh, despite the acid burning a trail up my chest. He knows I'm anything but. Ballet dancers might look beautiful and fragile on stage, but underneath all that delicate tulle is nothing short of a gladiator.

His warm—albeit sweaty—hand rubbing concentric circles on the small of my back is soothing. But ugh. I fucking hate throwing up. This is one more reminder that binge eating is not worth the carb hangover. Or the bloating. Or the shits. Or the constipation.

"Never again." I say it every time.

But bread tastes so damn good.

"You said that last time." He chuckles, removing his palm from my spine. "Let's get you home. Window open and a bag in your lap. No puke in my new car."

He didn't need a new car. In fact, the matching SUVs he and his brothers all drive are barely, what, a year old? But he "felt like a change," so he bought a sporty... something. He claims it's not sporty. He says it has a five-star safety rating, it's built for comfort not speed, but when girls and cops see him driving by, they totally think he's a little boy racer. It turns heads nearly as often as his ego does.

The only person in Cedar Rapids to get pulled over more than him is his older sister Athena. And that's because she rarely drives at speeds less than a hundred. I'm only exaggerating a little, too. The woman is terrifying.

I'm now regretting his choice of vehicle. He opens the passenger door for me, and I groan. The seats are practically on the ground in this thing. It was leg day. My legs are like fucking jelly. How the hell am I supposed to squat and get all the way down there?

"Maybe I'll walk."

"*¡Ay! Princesa.*" He shakes his head as he pulls his door

open with a growl. "So fucking dramatic. It's like you're a performer or something."

I give a flourish with my hand before flipping him off.

"You belong on the stage."

"I belong in the fucking shower. I stink."

"Yeah, but I didn't want to say."

If I had something to throw at him, I would. But I don't, so I grunt and groan as I lower myself into the bucket seat. "You're pretty stinky yourself, you know."

Before he moves, he points at the water bottle. "Hydrate."

"Shut up and drive, rich boy." Reaching for the radio, I elbow him. Thankfully, we have the same taste in music, so there's no argument over who gets to listen to what. We have one rule when we're together in the car, and that's if we sing, it's loud and proud.

As I reach for the volume button, his phone rings in the cup holder. The name "Papá" appears on the screen. I can almost hear Apollo's eye roll. He stares at the phone, indecision flickering across his face.

"What's his problem this time?"

Apollo shrugs, his stare not moving from the screen.

I silence his ringtone, give his thigh an *I've-got-you-boo* pat, and crank up the tunes. He starts the car, his shoulders softening. I've been around long enough to know that *el príncipe de las tinieblas*, the prince of darkness, and his father have a challenging relationship. And sometimes that means I run interference, for everyone's sake.

The bass rattles through my seat as Apollo starts nodding his head in time with the music. I don't recognize the song, but that rarely stops us from singing along. We're epic at making shit up. Confidently.

He lowers the volume enough to be heard over the thumping music. "Did you go on that date last week? You never said anything."

I never said anything because when I tell him I've been on a date, he spends his time dissecting it and telling me what went wrong. What I did wrong, how I scared the guy off, or how the guy is an asshole, or how the guy would end up being an asshole.

For once, I wanted a minute to enjoy a nice date, with a nice guy, without Apollo going all *He's Just Not That Into You* on me.

I've seen the old movie, and while it would potentially make my life a hell of a lot easier if Apollo was criticizing all my dates because he was secretly in love with me, he really isn't. He enjoys being a dick. A grumpy dick at that. And rude. A grumpy, rude dick. How am I even friends with this man? I'm a fucking delight.

For someone so perfect to look at, he has a list of crappy qualities a mile long. He's lucky I love him.

Sighing, I nod. "I did." I move to turn the music back up, bumping his leg in the process, but he nails me with his infamous side eye.

"Not good?"

"No, it was good."

"Not great?"

I shrug but stay quiet.

"Where'd he take you?"

I smother a laugh. "The Taco Depot."

He slows the car to a stop at a red light, and if life was a Gif, right now he'd be the Latina woman "gasps in Spanish" because his hand flies to his chest as his mouth drops open. "You're shitting me?"

Like I said, he's so fucking extra.

I can't help it—I'm all out laughing at the disgust painted across his dark features. "He'd never been to Guac 'n Roll and didn't want to try somewhere new." I shrug like it's no big deal. "I really wanted tacos." It's totally a big deal. Abuelita de la Peña makes the best tortillas in the entire world, and let's not even start on her tres leches cake. None of these things I should eat, but every now and then I can't help myself. I guess he saved me from myself, but even then Abuelita's mofongo is delicious.

He answers with a grunt, drumming his thumbs on the steering wheel. "How was it?" His question is begrudging, cautious, and laced with contempt. His family-owned Guac 'n Roll is a local institution in Latin cuisine.

I love rattling him, though, so I lean into it. "Fucking delicious. Best I've had."

His jaw drops, his head spins to me, and I reach over to push his chin up so his mouth closes. "I'm kidding, el príncipe de las tinieblas." I drop my voice. "If you tell Abuelita I even joked about that I'll kill you in your sleep."

When he started calling me princess, I returned the favor by asking his twin brother, Artemis, how to say prince of darkness in Spanish. Apollo pretends that it bothers him, but he loves it. It suits his life vibe. Tall, black hair, dark brown eyes, and brooding. Lots and lots of brooding. Like a Latino Derek Hale from *Teen Wolf*.

"You know nowhere beats your Abuelita's tortillas."

He nods, the light changes to green, and he pulls forward into the intersection. The screen of his phone lights up with another call from his father, but we both ignore it. He doesn't need that ball ache right now.

Blinding lights catch my attention out the passenger window, but before I can process what's happening, or react, they charge into us at speed.

Glass explodes into shards as the metal frame of the car buckles, searing pain envelops my entire body, and somewhere in the distance someone's screaming. By the time I realize it's me, everything's going dark.

CHAPTER 2

Edith

I might be dying.

Bright lights tease the edges of my awareness drawing me back to consciousness. Everything's blurry, blinding, and hurting so fucking badly.

The pain isn't a dull ache, it's a sharp stabbing, a deep burning, an all-consuming body ache that hurts so bad even breathing causes pain.

I'm cold. I think I'm still in Apollo's car, but I'm not sure. It doesn't feel right. Liquid trickles across my forehead, and I can't move to check whether it's water, gasoline, or blood. I don't think I want to know.

I move my mouth to speak, but no sound comes out.

Something shifts to my right, and pangs of white-hot pain radiate down my leg.

The faint sound of sirens in the distance call to me. Are they real sirens? Or metaphorical sirens signifying my dwindling time here on earth?

I don't know. From the pain south of my waist, it could be either. There's a metallic taste in my mouth so whether or not the sirens are real, the blood certainly is.

Then the darkness takes me again.

Apollo

~

My head is throbbing. Pressure building behind my eyes like I'm on a rollercoaster, flying upside down at high speeds through the air. Except we're not moving anymore. At least I don't think we are. But from the way gravity is pulling my body, we might be upside down.

I don't think I'm really hurt other than the ache in my temples and at the back of my skull. My leg is trapped under the crumpled dash, but I can wriggle my toes, my fingers, and other than something dribbling down the side of my face, I think I'm good.

Fuck. Lady luck was clearly on our side tonight.

Flexing my fingers once more, I nod. Yeah, I definitely think I'm good.

The seatbelt chafes on my neck as I turn to Edith.

Fuck. My blood freezes in my veins. No. No, no, no, no, no.

There's blood all over her face, her eyes are closed, and her whole side of the vehicle is buckled in on her.

No, no, no, no, no, no, no, no.

A bolt of pure panic shoots up my spine, stealing the breath from my lungs.

This isn't good. *She's* not good.

"Edith?"

Nothing. Not a wheeze, a whimper, a sigh. Zero.

Fuck.

I yell her name, and when she doesn't reply, I scream at her, louder this time, desperate to wake her up, but it doesn't work, and I can't twist myself in my seat enough to reach for her. I'm helpless. And I fucking hate it.

Focusing on her body, I search for any telltale signs of life, but her chest doesn't rise and fall.

An icy, consuming dread threatens to suck me into panic.

Edith

I can't breathe.

My teeth chatter as I shiver. Someone's mumbling something next to me, but I can't hear what they're saying. Am I under water?

Where's Apollo? Wasn't he with me?

Oh my god… is he dead?

I try to move, to turn to see if I can find him, but all that greets me is bone-deep agony. A scream rips from my raw throat before my eyes roll back, my head lolls… darkness.

A cold hand slides into mine but doesn't squeeze. "Edie?"

Despite the shivering, warmth spreads through my limbs. I'm not alone. My prince of darkness won't let me die alone.

"Edie? Can you hear me?"

I don't think the noise I make is anything resembling

coherence, but it seems to prompt excited movement, which only makes everything hurt more.

Another scream. I think it's mine.

Apollo

~

Tears course down my cheeks as I stare at the busted screen on my phone. I can't reach Edith's either, but I bet hers is fucked up too.

We're upside down in the middle of an intersection. Sirens wail in the distance, closing in on our position, but unless someone else called 9-1-1, they aren't for us.

I swallow down the bitter-tasting panic at the back of my throat and risk another glance at Edith. She made a noise a couple seconds ago, and her fingers flinched when I held her hand. She's not dead, but how much longer can she hold on for? With every second that passes, her life hangs in the balance.

A juddering sob escapes from me, and I cram my fist into my mouth in a vain attempt to silence my fear. It doesn't work, though the bite of pain through my muscles is comforting.

I should be strong. I should be calm. I should step up for

her in this moment. She needs me. But I think my best friend is dying. And if she dies, part of me will die too.

Another sob seeps out between my clenched knuckles as her fingers curl around my hand.

"Apollo?"

"*¿Sí, princesa?*" My blood chills at the anguish in her voice as she says my name, while relief unfurls in my shoulders that she's still alive and breathing. She's speaking, that's a good thing, right? And she at least remembers my name. Also good.

"I'm here."

"Don't leave me." Her heavy, terror-filled eyes meet mine, as my heart slices into pieces in my chest. "Don't let me die alone."

My mouth moves, telling her she has to stay with me, telling her she's not going to die, and that she has to fight, to live. But it doesn't look good as her eyes roll back in her head. My mouth might be telling her one thing, but my stomach sinks, and my rational brain kicks in. I'm not sure I believe the things falling from my lips to comfort her.

She's bleeding, her eyes are glassy when she can open them, and she's so fucking pale I can almost see through her skin. She really might be dying.

And there's literally nothing I can do to stop it.

CHAPTER 3

Apollo

"I'm fine."

"Mr. de le Peña, I need you to sit still so we can check you over and make sure you're not injured."

"I said I'm fine." I swat the nurse's hand away as she tries, yet again, to take my blood pressure. "I was in a car wreck. My best friend—" My voice cracks along with the final piece of the veneer that's been covering the truth all this time.

Edith Fisher has never been *just* my best friend. She's the love of my fucking life. And I might never see her alive again.

The admission to myself swells in my chest, consuming every cell in its path, controlling the rhythm of my heart, the oxygen in my lungs and veins, and shaking the foundation of everything I thought I knew and held true.

Something catches in my throat as I attempt to clear it. "I'm going to guess my blood pressure is through the roof, so that machine isn't going to tell us anything we don't both already know." Clamping and releasing my jaw, I scowl.

She looks at me like I'm a five-year-old who won't take a nap. To be honest, a nap sounds pretty damn good right about now, but I can't. I need to know. I need to see Edith. I need to hear her beautifully pitched voice, I need to stare into her grey eyes, and I need to sweep that piece of golden-honey hair out of her face that annoys her when it falls from her messy buns.

I need all of her.

The nurse's eyes soften. "I'm sure—"

"Don't." I hold up a hand. "You can't possibly know whether she's going to be fine or not." I drag my fingers through my sticky hair, wincing. "Look." I blow out a heavy breath. "What's the bare minimum you're going to let me get away with before I can walk out of this room?"

"This isn't a negotiation." A smile ghosts her lips.

"I'm about fourteen seconds away from signing myself out against medical advice. I'm an athlete—I know what the signs of concussion are and how to treat it." I fold my arms. "I can't stitch up my own face and scalp, and I can't see through my leg to make sure the bones aren't broken. Stitches and X-ray, then I need to go find my girl."

I want to feel shitty for being a dick. This nurse is only doing her damn job, trying to make sure I'm okay, to provide medical care because it's her career, and also trying to make sure my family doesn't sue them if I get up off this bed and collapse in the corridor.

But none of that matters.

Nothing matters if Edith doesn't open those sparkling gray eyes and call me the prince of darkness with her snarky grin ever again. So I'm fine being an asshole right now.

After a long, hard stare, the nurse relents. "You'll still have to sign an AMA form if you don't let me do everything I need to do."

Clenching my teeth again, I jerk my head. I don't care.

"You know they won't let you in to see her if you're not family, right? You're better off staying put until she..." The sight of my resolve must give her pause.

That car crash ignited a fire inside my soul. It ripped the

protective casing away from my heart and revealed the message perfectly stamped across it: *Property of Edith Fisher*.

How have I not noticed before now? I'm such a fucking idiot. My stomach swooshes.

I'm in love with Edith.

I *love*, love her.

Fuck. *Love,* love. Like want to marry her and have babies with her kind of love.

An almost hysterical sounding laugh slips out between my pursed lips. It doesn't feel nearly as silly an admission to myself as it probably should. That's how I know it's real. Have I been in denial about her this whole time?

The nurse sighs, muttering under her breath about punk-ass kids thinking they're invincible and a snicker about young love. I don't bother to correct her. I don't think I'm invincible, though. In fact, I'm completely vulnerable. Edith is my vulnerability.

I am Clark Kent, and she's my Kryptonite.

I am the Joker, and she's my Harley Quinn.

I am god of the sun, and Edith is my night.

My Achilles heel.

It's an excruciating wait to be x-rayed and stitched up. I lose count of the number of paper stitches Nurse Ratched puts on my face and wince as she uses the real ones on my scalp. It almost seems as though she's enjoying herself at my expense. Serves me right for being an ass.

When she's done, I let her take my blood pressure for good measure, scrawl my name across her precious AMA, and burst through the doors with only one thing on my mind—finding my girl and telling her I love her.

"I'm sorry, sir. We can't give out that kind of information if you're not family."

It's the third time, and the third person who has given me the same answer to the same question I've asked each of them.

My blood is on fire with frustration, and my head is still throbbing. That one's my own fault though, since I stupidly told the demon nurse I didn't want pain meds.

Apparently I can't tell Edith I love her with a clouded head. I need clear focus, which currently feels a lot like white pokers stabbing into my face. Good job, Casanova.

I grossly underestimated how much I was going to ache all over after my car got crushed like an empty cereal box. Apparently my athletic conditioning doesn't quite stretch to being prepared to be "rammed by a truck," and not a single one of the almost seven hundred muscles in my body are happy.

I can't lose my shit. I can't get myself kicked out of here. That won't do anyone any good, and I'll still be in the dark. So instead of lashing out, I do the only thing I can do—pace. With every step I take, my body groans under its own weight. The doctor said my pinned leg is just bruised, as is what feels like ninety four percent of the rest of me.

I'm going to need a few ice baths for sure. I don't know how long I trail back and forth across the linoleum floor, clenching and unclenching my fists with each stride.

The door to the waiting room bursts open, and my reflection stares back at me, stricken. My twin brother's pale face is creased with agony, and his red-rimmed eyes are wide, his cheeks tear stained. His chest heaves, like it's physically painful for him to draw breath. His shoulders are tense, and a muscle feathers in his cheek like he's gritting his teeth so fiercely tight together that his jaw might crack. Or his teeth. Or both.

Artemis doesn't say a word. He storms across the small room, throws his arms around me, and pulls me hard against his chest. Which one of us are the hiccupping sobs coming from? Maybe it's both of us. For almost an entire minute, I let myself fall apart in his arms.

He clutches me, without words or judgment as I get my shit back together. Wiping my face on my sleeves, I take a step back from him. He searches my face, his eyes raking over each stitch holding my skin together and lingering on what I can only guess are the already blooming bruises on my temple and down the side of my cheek.

He holds my stare for a long moment, so much unspoken passing between us in those heavy seconds. Sucking in a loud breath, he squares his shoulders. "What do you need?"

I sink my teeth into my quivering bottom lip, afraid I'm going to fall apart all over again. Artemis grabs me by my arms, though I don't know if it's to hold me up or focus my attention.

"*¿Qué es, hermano?*"

What is it, indeed? My throat is dry, scratchy, and tears burn my eyelids as I blink them away. *"La quiero."* The words burst from me on a fractured breath as I tell my brother I love my best friend.

His face softens, sympathy etched in his features. *"Lo sé."* He pops my shoulder with his fist. He knows. "It took you long enough to figure it out." Then he winces when he must realize that I hurt all over.

The weight on my chest doesn't ease with his attempt at lightening the mood. "They won't tell me... I don't know... I can't..." I grab my hair, ignoring the bite of pain radiating through my scalp and start to pace all over again.

Artemis grabs me again, shaking me until I stop muttering and moving. Everything fucking hurts, especially my heart.

"Why won't they let you see her?"

Casting my gaze over his face for signs of humor, I swallow. "I'm not family."

"You didn't tell them you were her fiancé or something?"

I press the heel of my hand to my temple, the pounding in my ears almost too much to bear. I definitely need meds, even if they fuck me up and make me spacey. He's right, I should have made something up, but in the moment... I guess I was too tangled up in panic and fear to come up with a plausible story to get me inside the room. Terror and logic aren't the easiest combination of things to navigate.

I'm clearly not the twin you should want in a crisis.

Shaking my head, I swallow again, the stubborn dryness in my mouth refusing to abate.

"Then let's go tell them that *I* am."

Hell no. I'm not letting him get through those doors before me. I'll tell them I was in shock or something, convince them I really do belong in the room with her.

I follow Artemis for a few steps before my feet stutter to a stop. I can't. I... tendrils of terror coil around my ribs, crushing my chest and squeezing the oxygen from my body. What if she doesn't wake up?

My hands shake by my sides.

What if she's already dead and no one has found me to tell me?

What if—?

Artemis's palms cradle my cheeks as he forces me to look at him. "She's alive, do you hear me?"

I try to nod, but he didn't see her, he didn't hear her screams as they cut her from the crumpled body of my car.

"Apollo, I know you're scared." His eyes meet mine, his hands shaking as he holds my cheeks. Sadness is heavy in his features. He can relate to my fear in this moment. When he got to the hospital he probably had no idea whether I was alive or dead, either. "Trust me, I know." He shakes his head as though trying to upend a memory he doesn't want to linger on. "But she's alive, and she needs you."

The door swings open and my other two siblings shove into the room, launching themselves at me before Athena bursts into a string of Spanish cusswords as she berates me for almost dying on her. For all her bravado and badassery, my sister is soft for only three things in this world, and we're all standing around her in this room.

I can count on one hand how many times I've seen her this emotional. She grabs my hand, threading her fingers between mine and squeezes. I've also never seen Ares this quiet. It's unnerving. He keeps casting furtive glances in Athena's direction but doesn't say anything out loud.

He's got a bug up his ass about something. My Spidey sense tells me it has nothing to do with the fact someone almost killed me and my very alive, not-at-all dead, and soon-to-be-girlfriend-slash-wife earlier tonight. Athena shakes her head at me when I catch her attention. It can wait, her face says. It's not important. And I trust her judgment, especially when my own is impaired.

She takes a step back and surveys me, head to toes and all the way back up again. "Damage report?"

Artemis snorts. "Yes, Lieutenant. Give the Captain a status report, would you?"

"Cuts and bruises." Jutting my chin out to her as if to prove a point, I crack a smile that hurts all the way to my core. "I'm fine, Hen. I'm okay."

She narrows her gaze like she doesn't believe me. I don't blame her since I don't quite believe me either. "And Edith?"

My whole body tenses, threatening to burst apart at the seams. Every muscle aches with the behemoth effort of holding myself together. Shrugging, a weird noise is the only answer I can give my sister.

"They won't let him in. He's not family."

"*¡Puta madre!*" Her eyes flare, hotter than the sun. I know that look. She's going to scorch the damn earth until someone gives her the information she needs, and I bet she won't so much as break a nail while she does it. I'm pretty sure she has a titanium rod where her spine should be.

"Let's go." She turns toward the door, pausing I guess

when none of us make a move. "What is it?" She eyes me, waiting for an answer as to why there isn't an Apollo-shaped hole in the wall from me trying to find out about my girl.

Tears burn then trickle down my face. I can't form the words to enunciate the grief rattling at the back of my throat. I should be stronger than this. I should be able to straighten my spine and go find out what I need to know, but I'm paralyzed.

What if the answers that lie outside that door are answers I'm not ready to hear? What if I don't get to share the discovery of my heart with the woman I love? What if I never hear her laugh again? Or see that single brow raised in exasperation at my grouchy ass?

What if she never even speaks again? Can I live for the rest of my life without ever hearing her voice?

Athena marches toward me, an accomplishment in itself considering I'm only a few feet away from her, but she's most definitely marching. She grasps me by both shoulders and squeezes while she shakes. Don't these people know I fucking hurt all over?

"Shelve it."

I open my mouth, but she glowers so hard my mouth snaps shut.

"I know you've had a traumatic experience, and you're sore, and tired, and scared, but right now..." She swallows. *"Lo siento, hermanito.* But this isn't about you. You love her, right?"

Fuck's sake. Did everyone know but me? I nod, mute.

"Then you've got to step up. I know you're falling apart inside. I know it's scary and consuming, but you've got to stand up straight, loosen your jaw, and walk out there like you own this place. You need to tell them you *are* her family, convince them, and then go to her. You need to sit with her and hold her hand through whatever shit storm she's facing *because* you love her."

I don't know where I was on the day they handed out strength to my siblings, but I seem to have been at the bottom of the pecking order. Chin still trembling, hands still flexing by my sides, I follow my sister out into the corridor, not really ready to ride into whatever war I need to so I can lay eyes on Edith.

Athena's right. I can't fight a battle I can't see. So I walk right up to the nurse's station, give Nurse Ratched my most charming smile, and ask, once again, about my girl.

CHAPTER 4
Edith

I can't open my mouth.

My lips are stuck together, and my mouth is so dry I'm scared if I force it open, my face might crack and break into millions of pieces.

A ringing sound invades, sending a dull ache thrumming through my body, and without opening my eyes I can tell I'm in a hospital from the scent. That freakishly clean, bordering on death smell that lingers in the air.

Panic snakes up my spine as I try to remember what happened, what brought me here. I was in the car with Apollo, dangling upside down, fire raging through my muscles, and someone screaming.

Was that me? Is that why my throat is so raw?

I try to clear my throat, but a groan comes out instead.

"Edith?"

My body relaxes into the sound of Apollo's pained voice saying my name.

Apollo. Did he tell me he loved me? I could have sworn he told me he loved me. There's more chance of an alien invasion than my best friend saying the L-word.

He says it sometimes, but it's always followed by "butt face."

Or in a sibling love kind of way. But the way he said it in my dream, that was... it was... definitely *more*. Has to be the drugs, though from the pounding behind my eyes they may be wearing off.

I struggle to open my eyes but it's so cozy here in the quiet darkness.

"It's okay, *princesa. Sueña.*"

Dream. Apollo's right. Nothing hurts when I'm asleep.

~

"How are you feeling Edith?"

I don't recognize the voice. Is she the one holding my hand? I still can't find my voice or open my eyes. Maybe I don't want to. I'm scared of what I'll find if I do.

~

"Why isn't she awake yet?" Apollo's words are so visceral, so laden with emotion that my throat clogs.

I want to reach out to him, to comfort him, but everything's so damn heavy. I'm so fucking tired.

"The doctor said it would take some time, *hermanito.*" Athena sounds so tender with him. It's a far cry from their usual bantering back and forth or her threatening to kill him. "Be patient. She'll wake up when she's ready. She needs to rest, to heal."

Someone sniffs. My gut says it's Apollo. I don't know what to do with that. I've never seen him cry. We've been friends since we wore diapers, and I've never once seen him lose control. I've never once seen him bested by his emotions.

I think he's crying for me. It must be bad but I'm not ready to find out.

"Apollo?" My voice is croaky. The room is dark. The hum of machines fills the air, and someone's here, bustling around my bed.

"He went to get something to eat, hun. He'll be right back. Your boyfriend hasn't left your side since you were brought in."

I could have guessed that he wouldn't leave me without telling me, but it still makes me warm inside. It's who and what we are. Ride or die. Found family. He's my person. An act of a god I don't believe in couldn't pull me from his side if it was him in this bed, and in my heart of hearts, it's the same for him. He's literally the best. But he's not my boyfriend.

"He's such a sweet boy."

Is she talking about the same Apollo? Grumpy, smoldering, acerbic wit? Perhaps she got him confused with Artemis. He's the sweet one. He's the one everyone *thinks* is grumpy but once you talk to him you realize he's actually kind of adorable.

Apollo, sweet? Maybe I woke up in a parallel universe. Maybe in this multiverse, Apollo's not a cantankerous shithead.

"Humph." It's the only answer I can manage.

"That boy loves you."

I love him, too. He's the bestest best friend and chosen brother a girl could ask for. I hope he's okay, but I'm too tired to ask.

Pain.

Pure unadulterated agony searing through my veins, my bones, my teeth... even my skin hurts. Why does everything hurt so much?

My eyes snap open, taking a second to adjust to the harsh, fluorescent lighting in the hospital room. "It hurts." I claw at the hand holding mine, my voice coming out scratchy and broken.

"She's awake."

I don't recognize the voice, but I want to yell at him to shut the hell up, my head hurts. Why is everything so damn loud?

"They dialed back your pain meds." Apollo soothes me with both his voice and his hand stroking mine. I can't bring myself to look at him yet. I'm too scared of what I might see when I do.

"Wh-what happened?" My mouth still feels funny, like my tongue is too big for the space it's in. I try to swallow, again and again, but it doesn't help.

Apollo's hand leaves mine, and he stands. It's only when he presents me with a cup of water and a bendy straw that I finally meet his eyes. "Small sips."

Bossy fucker. I'm almost tempted not to drink just to spite him, but my lips are so chapped and dry it feels like I swallowed sandpaper. Or regular sand. All of it. All of the sand in the whole world.

"Come on, Edie. Hydrate. You'll feel better."

Hydrate. He said that to me in the car, right before... before what? Did we crash? It had to have been a crash.

Wait.

Did he just call me Edie? He never calls me Edie. Edie is for special emotional breakdown occasions, like when I didn't get through to the final round of my auditions.

Edie is kid glove territory.

Edie is "she's going to cry until she pukes over a bad breakup" territory.

Something is wrong, really, really fucking wrong.

My gut sinks as his face softens with sympathy. He has cuts and bruises all down one side of his face. Dark circles underline his eyes, and he looks so damn pale. We aren't hugging kind of friends. Well, I am, but he's prickly, so I generally respect his boundaries and keep my distance.

Right now, though, I want to reach out to comfort him, even though I'm the one in the hospital bed. He looks... broken.

After three small sips of blissfully cool liquid, I try again. "What happened?"

Apollo's brows pull together like he's afraid I'm going to freak out and lose my shit if he tells me what happened.

"*Pollo*?"

He hates when I call him chicken, when anyone calls him chicken. His scowl darkens, his nostrils flare, and he sighs. "We were in a car accident."

His admission isn't as much of a surprise as it could have been. I've pieced a few bits of the jigsaw back together. And if I let myself remember, I can feel the impact, hear the smashing of glass, the crushing of metal, and smell blood. I think it was mine.

I lift a tentative hand to touch my head but stop when I see the cast. It's bad enough that my arm is wrapped up, but my dominant arm? Ugh. This is going to create problems. Like wiping my ass. Or rubbing one out. Guess I'm gonna need new toys.

I almost laugh. Almost. I don't know why that's where my head went, but it is. Let's blame the drugs.

Switching to my other hand, relief seeps into my muscles. It's not in a cast. I can handle a broken arm. My hand drifts to my head. Quietly assessing my injuries, I let my fingers wander through my hair, confirming that I, too, have head and facial injuries like Apollo does, probably some impressive bruising as well.

I suck in a fractured breath. From the length of the cut in my scalp, mine's worse.

But that doesn't explain why I'm in this room, this bed. Do they want to keep me under observation for concussion? Or my arm? Or... Oh... no. No, no, no, no, no. Nausea sweeps through me like a wildfire, my stomach lurching at the sight part of me has been avoiding.

While my fingers keep tracing the damage to my head and face, my eyes scrape over the elevated cast my leg is in.

Panic seizes my entire body as I focus my attention on Apollo. There's a dull throbbing back in my head, and it's as though making eye contact with my leg reminded it that it should hurt too.

A sharp pain shoots into my chest, and I'm not sure if it's real or if it's the abject terror of what he's about to say coursing through my veins. My eyes widen.

"Apollo?" My hoarse voice is barely a whisper.

His eyes never leave mine. *"Sí."*

"How bad is it?" My jaw trembles, and hot tears are already spilling down my cheeks. We both know the implication of an injury to my leg. How bad the break is will determine how long I have to recover, how long I have to rest and not dance. A *really* bad break could impact my entire future. Even a minor one could derail my plans. I don't have time to watch my classmates surpass me from the sidelines.

His knuckle slides under my chin, sending a shiver skating across my face. "Try not to panic. A nurse or doctor should be here soon to talk to you, to tell you about your injuries."

"No." I smack his arm away from me, my stomach bubbling. I don't want his comfort, his warm, smooth hands caressing me like I'm fragile. I want the truth. "Just tell me."

He sighs, catches Artemis's eye in the corner of the room. He has been so quiet I didn't even know he was there. Yet I'm not surprised. As much as Apollo and I are like siblings, nothing comes close to the twin bond he shares with his brother. When Apollo hurts, Artemis hurts as well.

Artemis looks much better than Apollo—his clothes aren't wrinkled, he's clean shaven, and despite the frown creasing his face, he looks well rested. At his nod, something unknots in my chest.

If I'm getting bad news, I'd rather it be from someone who really cares about me than a stranger who cares for me because it's their job.

"The accident broke your foot in four places. You have a trimalleolar fracture in your ankle, your fibula is shattered, and you have two separate breaks on your tibia." He rattles it off in a monotone, like he's been memorizing it, repeating it to himself over and over, because he knew it'd be the first thing I asked when I woke up.

The accident broke my foot. Not "You broke your foot." The subtext in his words says that it's not my fault. Or his. His eyes plead with me not to blame him for what he told me. I don't think I could ever blame him.

Unless the accident was his fault, but I've been riding shotgun with him for years. Despite owning fun cars, he's never driven recklessly, and he keeps on top of servicing his vehicles. I can't see how it could be his fault, yet from the pain written clearly across his brown eyes, he blames himself.

"That doesn't sound good," I choke out through my still-falling tears. Maybe I don't want to know what happened. Maybe I don't want to know the full extent of my injuries. Maybe if he doesn't say it, it won't be true.

He rolls his lips between his teeth, and a sob escapes me as my body starts to tremble. That's his tell. That's his *really* bad news tell. That's his *Edith, you might not dance again* tell.

Something inside me breaks.

"They took you to surgery for your foot right away. Your wrist is broken in two places but should heal on its own." It's as though he added the last bit as a consolation prize. Your foot is mangled, but your wrist isn't quite so fucked up.

"Edie..."

"Don't. Don't say it, Apollo. Please, please don't say it." I scrunch my eyes closed and shake my head, willing my best friend not to destroy my dreams.

"It's bad, *princesa*. I'm so fucking sorry. If I could take these injuries from you I would."

"Please don't say it."

"I have to. You need to know the full extent of your injuries. Out loud. We're always honest with each other, remember?" His voice softens. "Even when the truth hurts."

I already know what he's going to say. It's cruel of him to put me through listening to the words, even if he feels like he has a reason to crush my soul in this moment. Perhaps he's trying to punish himself by absorbing my pain, or maybe he's trying to spare the doctors from having to tell me themselves. Either way, a teeny tiny piece of me hates him right now.

His hands cup my cheeks, turning me to face him. "They need to wait for the inflammation to go down before they can fully diagnose you. But it's possible you might never dance again, Edith. They say chances are slim. Your injuries are too extensive."

Apollo's face pales as my chest cracks open, baring my anguish for both of them to see as a grief-charged wail rips from my body. I knew what he was going to say, but somehow hearing it out loud shreds my insides.

His grip on me tightens as I fall apart. "It's going to be okay, *princesa*." His voice is firm, full of conviction I doubt either of us are feeling. "We're going to get through this, together. You and me."

Only one of us needs to get through anything, and it's not Mr. Both-my-legs-are-working-just-fine. The room spins, my chest constricts, and I can't keep up with my sobs and tears. This can't be happening to me.

"Edith." Apollo's sharp voice pulls me back to him. "Whatever it takes. We'll get nurses to come and stay at the apartment. We'll get you through PT."

He's saying "we" to make it seem like I'm not alone in this. But the more he talks the more I want to punch his perfect fucking face. There is no "we" here and now. There's only me. I'm the one with the fucked-up leg, I'm the one whose career is slipping through her fingers like grains of sand fall through a timer.

Rationally speaking, that's a big jump without any doctor or nurse to back up this claim, so I hold on to that. Until the doctor comes in and reemphasizes Apollo's words. It's early days, he tells me, but to keep things realistic, it's not looking good. Apollo wasn't simply lowering the bar for my expectation, he was keeping it real.

Before I woke up I was destined for spotlights and critical acclaim.

Now, I need to learn how to walk all over again.

CHAPTER 5
Edith
(JANUARY 3RD – DAY 7 POST OP)

"Where's Apollo?" My best girlfriend, Penelope, peeks her head around the door to my hospital room. "Did you send him away?" She steps into the room, smiling when her eyes land on me. I'm dressed—if you can call it that—and ready to be discharged from this clinical prison.

I'm not exactly sure how I'm going to manage around my apartment, but I'm sure I'll figure it out. I nod at her. "Yeah. He was starting to stink up the place."

She snorts.

"And Movember was months ago. There was no charity benefiting from his wild and unruly facial hair. He was approaching mountain man-level beard. I was afraid woodland creatures would take refuge in there..." I try to shift my weight, but everything's heavy. "He, uh, left for Belfast yesterday."

Her eyes widen, jaw dropping just enough to register her surprise before she snaps it shut. "He left?"

Discomfort nestles deeper into my chest. I didn't want

him to go, but he had to. I did us both a favor by forcing him to get on that plane without telling him I was being released today. "He did. The team needs him. *He* needed to go. It's an exhibition weekend, but they have scouts in Ireland too." Gesturing at the vase of flowers next to me, I smile. "He brought me flowers."

"Still. I can't believe he flew to Ireland to play the Blizzard when you're..." She waves a hand toward me.

I can't help but defend him. "He didn't want to leave. I made him."

She snorts again. "Babe, no one makes those de la Peñas do anything they don't want to do. He could have stayed."

I dunno, maybe. I'm not convinced. I was pretty mean to him when I told him to get out of here and chase his dreams. "He left the day after the rest of the team. He stayed for as long as he could."

The team left on New Year's Day, but he followed behind on his father's private plane on the second, landing this morning. I can't imagine how he's going to play—jetlag is going to kick his ass—and he'll be dragging on the ice, but when I pointed that out to him he told me that was his problem.

"Has he fully recovered?"

I nod, but I'm not sure I'd know if he hadn't. He's been keeping his own complaints away from me. I guess he thinks he can't grumble about his aches when I'm so banged up.

If I'm honest with myself, it was my bitterness, my jealousy, that kicked him out of my hospital room and onto that plane. It didn't come from a place of kindness or because it was best for him. I couldn't stand to watch both our futures circle the drain.

Yeah. I don't like myself very much right now.

"Did he organize a nurse to go home with you?"

My cheeks burn.

"Edie?"

I pinch my lip between my teeth, refusing to meet her probing stare.

"Apollo said he'd get you a nurse for the apartment. Is that set up?"

I shake my head. "I told him I'd be fine, that I don't need a nurse."

She opens her mouth, from the creases furrowing her forehead she's about to scold me. But the door opens again, and Simon—the guy I went on one date with—steps in. What the hell is he doing here?

He twists his hands in front of him as the door swings closed. "Hey, Edith. I... I, uh, hope you don't mind me stopping by." He casts his stare to the floor. "I know we just had that one date before your accident, but when I heard..."

He meets my eyes again. "I wanted to come see you, to see if you needed anything." His gaze flicks to Penelope, which must be how he knew where I was and how to find me. "I figured you might need some help getting home."

I don't know whether to laugh or cry. This guy... he's adorable really. Blond hair, cheek dimples, bright sparkly blue eyes, and a heart that's clearly bigger than Iowa, but he doesn't set my heart racing. I need to tell him thanks but no thanks, but when I open my mouth to do just that, he stops me.

"Please let me help get you home. Please?"

The nurse comes in next, papers in her hand, and I'm hoping they're my escape route out of this place. Twenty minutes and a behemoth effort from Pen, Simon, and the nurse later, I'm stretched out in the back seat of Simon's car. Penelope's classic VW Beatle isn't big enough to accommodate my immobile leg.

By the time I unlock my front door and get settled on the couch, my back is drenched with sweat, and I'm ready for a nap. Penelope had to take off for class, so it's only Simon, me, and the vase of fresh flowers sitting on my coffee table.

De la intruder strikes again. I'd threaten to take my "in case of emergency" key back from him, but I fucking love fresh cut flowers, and he knows it. I read in a book once that the hero made a "pick a vase and always keep it full" pledge. Every week when the previous flowers died, he'd replace them for her.

How Apollo remembered such a throw away detail from a million years ago is anyone's guess, but seeing the brightly colored Gerber daisies ignites a bubble of warmth in my chest. It's such a little thing, but it makes me glow. Both the fact that he remembered, and the burst of vibrant color in the room.

I have to say, I didn't appreciate the freedom I had to decorate my own space until I spent a week in a bland, beige hospital room. I'm getting a bucket of bright paint and coating some of the walls in here as soon as I get this fucking cast off. These casts.

"Nice flowers." Simon jerks his chin at the vase like I might not know what he's referring to as he places the flowers from my hospital room next to them.

"Yeah."

"From someone special?"

I almost choke on my saliva. He thinks an admirer left flowers for me? As if. I can't stop myself from coughing, and by the time Simon hands me a glass of water and some pain meds, my chest burns and my eyes sting.

After I take a few measured sips, I shake my head. "He's my best friend." There was nothing romantic about the gesture, though I can see how it might seem that way.

Simon doesn't look convinced, but it's not my job to put his feelings at ease. I've told him the truth—if he doesn't believe it, that's his problem. Not mine. Plus it was one average date. I don't owe him a damned thing.

"Can I get you anything else?" He pulls my wheelchair closer, like I have much chance of getting myself mobile with a shattered leg and a broken arm, but I like his confidence in me.

I bite down the bitterness bubbling on my tongue. I hate being dependent on anyone, for anything, and ever since I woke up in that hospital bed I haven't been able to do a damn thing for myself.

Ignoring my headshake, Simon fluffs the cushions behind me before disappearing. He returns with two pillows. As he slides them under my leg, the front door bursts open.

Apollo dumps his kit bag at his feet before striding across the room, pausing when he clocks Simon, who quickly backs away from the brooding hulk of a tall, dark, and blazing man staring him down.

He's supposed to be in Belfast, playing hockey with his team. But he's standing here, shoulders heaving with determined breaths. Apollo is a man on a mission. What that mission is, I have no idea. At least not until he leans over me, glides his thumb across my bottom lip, and before I can breathe, think, or register what's happening, his lips are on mine.

Ew. I'm kissing my brother. I mean, *ewwww*, am I right?

Except it's not *ewwww*. It's not *ew* at all. In fact it's kind of the best feeling in the entire world, and I find myself sinking into his kiss. My lips part. I'm not sure if it's on a sigh, a gasp, or because I need my best friend's tongue in my mouth, but when our tongues collide, my world shifts on its axis.

Sweet baby Jesus in the manger. Where has this come from? Apollo's kissing me with such depth, such tenderness it brings tears to my eyes. For a moment I forget that he's my childhood best friend. I forget that he's the rich guy next door, the hottie who shares girls with his twin sometimes and all the fucking lines we're crossing right now. Hell, I almost forget that pieces of my body are broken and let him kiss me.

The prince of darkness kisses like he's claiming every single one of my kisses forevermore, like he's claiming *me* right down to my very soul.

Our kiss has barely begun before it's over. He pulls back, his eyes raking over my features like he's expecting me to be someone else. Is he mad? Excited? Aroused? I have no idea because his intense stare is un-fucking-readable as always. Except usually I have some idea what he's thinking but this... huh.

We're off script with this one.

He doesn't say anything for a long minute, and I'm pretty sure I've stopped breathing. He kissed all my breath away, and now I'm suffocating, waiting for something, anything to tumble from those pretty, pouty lips of his, or for him to kiss me so I can breathe again.

He glances at Simon but doesn't otherwise acknowledge him, or show any signs of guilt, remorse, or embarrassment. Instead, he glides his thumb over my cheekbone, plants a kiss on my forehead, and stands upright.

"I'll wait for however long you need me to."

Then he's gone. I stare open-mouthed after him as he picks up his hockey gear and closes the door behind him.

What the actual fuck just happened?

My fingers ghost my lips. Did he really kiss me?

The look on Simon's face tells me it not only happened, but he's not all that surprised by it. Well, I fucking am. That was so out of left field I can't even pick through my thoughts for a coherent sentence right now. But I think I'm mad.

No. I'm definitely mad. Super mad, in fact. So mad my blood's fizzing and hissing in my veins. Vibratingly mad.

Simon rubs the back of his neck with his palm. "I guess I should, eh..." He points at the door. He shrugs. "I'm not getting in the middle of that."

"There is no *that*," I splutter. That's a lie. There is most definitely a *that*. *That* might be new, but there is absolutely, positively now a *that*.

The sympathetic smile Simon offers me is like scratches on my skin. "Okay, well give me a call if you want to hang out, or if you need anything, or..." He shrugs again, and even though it's not my fault, I feel bad. I feel like I've kicked a puppy.

I thank him for everything, and the second the door clicks shut behind him, I have regrets. First of all, I regret letting him leave. Panic clutches my throat as I look around the room. The walls don't close in on me like they did while I was in the hospital. No, instead they expand, making the space too big and everything in it too far away.

My next regret is that I didn't let Apollo figure out a nurse for me because my glass is empty and while my wheelchair feels so far away, the kitchen is most definitely further. I guess this is where I die, right here on my couch.

Punching the sofa cushions at my sides isn't enough to let off some of the frustrations coursing through my body. I pick up a pillow to my side and throw it. The reward for my adolescent behavior is the corner of the cushion catching the vase of beautiful flowers and sending it to the floor with a crash.

"Motherfucker!"

Grinding the heel of my not-casted hand into my eye socket to prevent my tears from falling, I swallow down gulping breaths, letting the anguish wash over me in waves. The music from the last piece I performed tinkles in the back of my mind, getting louder with each note.

Before the crash, we'd finished up our performance of *The Nutcracker*. It's always *The Nutcracker* for Christmas. I was in a quick recovery window before prepping for audition season for a summer attentive and our spring show in school. I hate my lamé gold unitard with a fiery passion, but right now, I'd give anything to wear it again if it meant I could dance.

What have I done to deserve this? It must have been really

fucking bad because I can't imagine a worse fate than being stuck here, on this sofa, when all I want to do is get up and dance. And all the while knowing that might never happen again.

CHAPTER 6

Apollo

What the fuck was I thinking? Flying back from Ireland, barging into her space, and laying one on her like she belongs to me.

I spin back toward the door to my apartment, striding at it, hands tangled in my hair. Turn, walk, pivot. I guess pacing back and forth is my thing now.

Like she belongs to me.

But that's just it, isn't it? She *tasted* like she was already mine. The way she melted into my touch, the way her face sat perfectly against mine... We didn't bump noses, there was no awkwardness, our teeth didn't clatter together. It was consuming, it was emotional, it was life changing.

It. Was. Everything.

Tipping my head back, my eyes flicker closed as I relive the best moment of my life to date. I could get drafted by an NHL team and win the Stanley Cup, and I doubt I'd ever feel like this again. I drop my head against the door with another thud.

A really huge part of me wants to go back over there, to kick what's-his-face out onto the street, and kiss her again.

Maybe it was a fluke. Maybe it was an in-the-moment chemistry that fizzled out as soon as I pulled my lips from hers.

My groan echoes around my apartment. My lips still sizzle from the contact.

It wasn't fucking fake.

It was the kiss to end all kisses.

My last first kiss.

That kiss rattled me all the way to the deepest, darkest levels of my heart. I have no idea why I walked away, why I didn't keep kissing her...

Blowing out a whoosh of air, I bang my head harder against the wood. Perhaps it'll knock some sense into me. Or perhaps my head will thump a hole into the door that I can fall through because even though I'm only around fifty feet from where she is, it's fifty feet too fucking far.

Now that she has me in her orbit, I need to go to her, to be with her. I need to wrap my arms around her and hold her until she's strong enough to stand on her own two feet again. Christ, how dramatic?

Who the fuck even am I?

I bang my head again. This is Nora Roberts shit. Romance and butterflies flitting around in my chest. Can't get the girl out of my mind. This isn't me. I'm not that guy.

Except after that kiss, I want to be that guy. Fuck. I'll be anyone she needs me to be.

I hate the desperation coursing through my system. I've had my first taste of her and all I can think of is how stupid I am to have waited this long, to have given guys like *Simon* the chance to win her heart. Fucking *Simon*? Fuck that dude. Fuck every dude who isn't me.

That shit stops here. Her heart has been mine for as long as mine has been hers. It has to have been. We just didn't realize it.

I never in a million years thought I'd be a walking cliché,

but when the truck hit my car and flipped us upside down, I saw my life flashing before my eyes. I saw Edith. Really saw her, like for the first time with wide open eyes.

And now I can't unsee it. I can't unsee her, or us, and even if I could take back that kiss, I wouldn't.

I'm in. With two fucking feet, I'm in this thing. And I sure as shit hope she's right there with me.

A door opens and closes in the hall. My desperate ass launches at my own door, pressing my ear against it before squeezing my eye to the peephole. Simon stands outside her door, dragging his hands through his hair before turning away.

He pauses, indecision etched across his face, stares at my door, takes two steps toward me, and stops again.

His shoulders sink, he shakes his head, and he makes his way toward the elevator.

Chicken shit.

What crossed his mind in that moment? The hurt-her-and-die speech? The she's-mine-leave-her-alone speech? I almost snort. I'd like to see him try it.

I'm being a dick, I know. But I can't help myself. There's this… possessive force rattling inside my ribcage, and even the thought of him being closer to her than I am makes me grind my fucking teeth.

I should be taken aback. Should feel confused, uncertain, hesitant, nervous… but I've never seen so clearly in my entire life. There isn't a trace of indecision in my body, only resolve.

My phone vibrates in my back pocket, making me jump. It's going to be Papá, and I don't want to talk to him right now.

He sent me some paperwork for a deal he wants me to close next week and is probably calling to talk it through even though I should be in Europe playing hockey.

The weight of his expectations threatens to ruin my buzz. If only I could find my balls and tell him outright that I don't want to inherit the family business. What I want is to play hockey. He'd laugh in my fucking face if I even suggested I hang up my suits and my successorship instead of my skates.

Edith's date has had enough time to get the hell out of our building. Squaring my shoulders, I nod to myself as I open the door, those damn butterflies flapping in my stomach as I cross the hallway and let myself into her apartment just in time for her to toss a pillow across the room.

¡Ay! There go the flowers. *¡Dios mío!* So fucking dramatic.

Okay, while she can be dramatic, that's probably not fair at this particular point in time. Shit's hard for her, and her tear-stained, flushed face turns to me with distress carved into those delicate features.

Hurrying over to her, I crouch at her feet. "It'll be okay, *princesa*. One day, one hour, one minute at a time, okay? I swear, you're going to get better and we're going to do everything we can."

She shakes her head, tears flowing faster now. Rolling her eyes like I'm the world's biggest idiot and have no idea what I'm talking about, she sighs. It's all I can do not to kiss her again. *Coño.* My fingers tingle with the urge to reach out and sweep her beautiful golden hair out of her face.

Her brows dip, her forehead wrinkles, and I know I'm about to get my ass handed to me a split second before she opens her mouth. "What the fuck did you do that for, Apollo?"

Huh. I guess she's not down for the kissing thing.

CHAPTER 7

Edith

Dude's giving me golden retriever energy right now, and I have no idea why. Doesn't he know what he's done to me? To us?

Why is it that when men think they've got a great idea, their dicks just run with it?

Like, on what planet did he believe kissing me was a good plan? I... Ugh. And he's still looking at my lips like he's going to take another bite out of them.

I'd be lying if I said I didn't want him to. But I can't. We can't. Even if every friends to lovers couple I've ever known of hadn't turned to shit, his timing couldn't be worse.

He thinks that right now, after an almost life-ending and potentially career-ending car accident, when my life got literally flipped upside down, is the perfect time to declare his undying love for me? He thinks this hot garbage on a summer's day that is my life is the right moment for me to embark on a new romantic relationship?

Okay, fine. He hasn't said either of those things, and I'm ignoring the little flutter in my chest at the idea that he might want to declare his undying love for me because now isn't the time.

It's not.

Is post-accident love-struck-ness a thing? Like PTSD but without the trauma and with a boner instead? That's what this is. A post-traumatic stress boner. He saw the light at the end of the tunnel, that end-of-life montage you get with scenes from your existence set to a badass eighties backing track, and now he thinks he needs to act on it.

Idiot.

I have no idea how men run the world when their dicks are almost entirely responsible for their thought processes.

Maybe he's scared of dying alone. Or it could be a guilt thing? He blames himself for our accident and throwing himself at me is his method of penance?

He's just staring at me, head tipped to the side like an honest to god excitable dog waiting for a scratch behind the ears. His beard has been trimmed, his dark locks are slicked back, and I can't tell if it's with hair product or because he's run his hands through it enough times that it's stuck.

"I love you, Edie."

And there it is.

I should be flattered, right? Or at least not blood-boiling level mad when my best friend, my neighbor, and the boy who taught me Spanish and pushes me to be the best version of myself confesses his love to me. But all I feel right now is rage, and I'm doing my best not to smack that love-sick look off his beautiful fucking face.

It's tempting, though.

Idiot!

"I see that look on your face, *princesa*. This is real, true. I mean it. I love you. I think I always have."

A chink appears in the armor on my chest, and my breath stutters, but I won't be deterred. I won't. I can't.

It's a stupid idea.

Don't make life-changing decisions after trauma. That's the rule, right?

Well, if it isn't, it damn well should be.

"Apollo..."

His fingers cover my mouth, and I want to bite them. In a not kinky way.

Fine. In a kinky way too.

It's infuriating that he'd consider kissing me right now when I'm hurt, fucked up, and so fucking scared of what the future holds for me. It's audition season, and I've already missed two auditions. What the hell do I do if I miss them all?

But he kissed me. And part of me is even more terrified to even consider exploring whether or not there's something between us.

I could lose my best friend.

That's too high a price to pay for dipping my toe in the delicious el agua de la Pena.

I've seen the girls he hooks up with—they're nothing like me. Plus, we'd never work out. And if the relationship fails and we broke up, well, then I'd lose the most important person in my life.

Friendship is simpler, less fraught and not doomed to fail.

And selfishly, I'm not strong enough to face this mammoth recovery alone. I need him. Sure, his super soft lips against mine felt phenomenal. And yes, maybe I wanted to slip my fingers under the hem of his shirt and trace the pale skin I've stared at as he's paraded around both of our apartments half naked damn near every day. But I couldn't. I can't. I won't.

I need to stay on team #hellno and #whatthefuckareyouthinking because I refuse to lose my dream and my best friend all at the same time.

So I guess now I gotta kick the puppy.

CHAPTER 8
Apollo
(JANUARY 4TH – DAY 8 POST OP)

She's so fucking stubborn.

She's been home for less than twenty-four hours and already we are verging on killing each other. It's not quite the happily ever after I've been dreaming of every night since the accident.

That's a fucking lie. Every night I close my eyes, I'm plagued by her lifeless body next to me in the car. I'm trapped and can't get to her. Fear grips me in its clutches, and I wake up drenched in sweat with tears running down my face.

Mierda.

It should be easier with her living across the hall from me. But it's not. Nothing short of having her in my arms at all times so I know she's safe will help cure this ball-crushing terror that I'm going to lose her.

I wish she'd let me help her. I've done the reading. For the first two weeks, it hurts like hell to stand up. She's got a cast from her toes to her knee, and a forum on the internet tells me that every time she stands up, blood rushes down, bringing a wave of incredibly painful pins and needles. Like her leg has fallen asleep, only far more excruciating.

I ended up on her couch last night. I was in and out of her apartment so often that it made more sense to camp out here. But she won't let me move in. She won't let her bestie Penelope move in either. And she still won't accept a nurse.

I'm at my fucking wits end with this woman.

I get not wanting to be a burden, but she literally can't do a damn thing by herself right now, though that's not stopping her from trying. I have to bring her food, water, pain meds, help her get to the bathroom, help her get out of the bathroom. I'm not complaining about helping her, it's what I want to do, need to do, but she's so resistant to any and all help that it's exhausting watching her struggle.

My phone vibrates on my chest just as my eyes are drifting closed. I bolt upright, ready to spring into action for whatever she needs.

Papá.

I'd better get this over with before he shows up on my doorstep.

"Hola, Papá."

"You left Belfast?" He spares me a greeting, launching straight into his first criticism of the day. At 6am, it's earlier than usual, but from the sound of his voice he's already been up for hours. The man never sleeps.

"I should never have gone to Belfast. I'm still having some trouble with my leg, my head isn't on straight. I wouldn't have given it my all."

He sighs, disappointment floating down the line between us. "You want me to take you seriously when you say you want to play that silly game, *hijo.*"

Son. I don't think that word means what he thinks it means.

"How can I take you seriously when you don't follow through? Either you want to play that game or you don't. This flaky attitude, this lack of commitment, it doesn't bode well for handing the business over to you."

Then don't do it. Give it to someone who wants it. Give it to Artemis.

It makes my tongue scratchy to keep those words inside.

He launches into a diatribe about how I'm letting him down every time I fail on a commitment, how he's depending on me, how I need to step up and show him I'm worthy of inheriting the family business.

My head's throbbing, and I need to check on my girl.

"Are you listening to me?"

No. "*Sí, Papá.* You want me to call Mamá."

The line goes dead without as much as a goodbye. He didn't once ask how I'm recovering after the accident, never mind Edith. He's worked with Edith's father since we were little. He should give a shit.

But Alonso de la Peña doesn't do trivial things like become invested in someone other than himself.

Ugh. Bitterness before breakfast isn't good for my digestive system. I attempt to make us omelets in Edith's kitchen. It takes me almost twenty minutes to find everything I need, then another twenty to make something that vaguely resembles scrambled eggs. It all went terribly wrong on the flip.

Trying a bite, my teeth hit something hard and crunchy. *¡Dios mío!* It's an egg shell. I can't feed her this. She's depressed enough already without adding broken teeth to the mix.

Grabbing my phone—which is now covered in gooey egg and pieces of cheese—I wipe it off on the thigh of my sweats and pull up DoorDash. Once breakfast is ordered, I open the app for the meal prep service we use and pause our order. We're going to be eating at home full time for the foreseeable future, and left to my own devices isn't always the best plan.

A quick search shows a place that does home cooked, ready to reheat healthy food that goes straight into the oven or a pan on the stove. Our lives need to be as simple as we can possibly manage over the coming weeks and months. From what I've read, recovery isn't going to be fun or easy. My freezer is damn near empty, and after a quick check in hers, I guesstimate how much we can handle, place an order, and am rather smug at the fact I'm inflicting my help on her whether she wants to accept it or not.

A scream of pain pierces my moment of glory, draining all the warmth from my body. I bolt to the bathroom.

Edith is on the floor in the bathroom, her pajama pants piled on one foot. She's crying, her shoulders bouncing with each sob, and I'm pretty sure... yeah, she peed herself.

"Don't." Agony coats the single word as she holds up a hand to me. "Just... don't say anything. Don't look at me. Just... don't."

My strong and broken bird has no idea how resilient she is. She's embarrassed, frustrated, the inferno in her soul is in pain, but she doesn't see her power.

Her hair is twisted on top of her head in a knot. I don't know when it was last washed. I can't imagine how helpless and scared she feels right now, but all I see is strength. She needs help finding her way back to the badass, determined, take no shit best friend who got in the car with me that night.

Taking a step toward her, I shake my head when she glares at me. "Let me help you, Edie."

"No, Pollo," she spits at me.

There's my girl. The firecracker. That little flicker of spite and grit is enough to give me hope. She's still in there, and I'm not letting her forget who she is. I refuse to let her lose herself because she broke her fucking leg. The bones will heal, but her psyche might not if I don't stop that train of self-destruction she's intent on lying in front of.

"I'm moving in."

"The hell you are."

"*Princesa*, you're not exactly in a great position to negotiate. Either I move in, or we get a nurse like we agreed."

"You'll be travelling with the team." Her accusation sends an arrow straight into my chest.

"I'll leave the team if I have to."

Her eyes flex wide, mouth dropping open. It's as though I smacked her in the face. "You don't mean that."

"I fucking do. Try me. You're not alone in this, Edie. I'm moving in, end of discussion. Now, are you going to let me help you out of this mess, or are we going to do things the hard way?"

Her nose flares, eyes narrowing and crosses her arms.

Guess we're choosing violence today.

Closing the distance between us, I brace myself for the fallout of what I'm about to do before I pick her ass up off the bathroom tiles.

Ignoring her squeals of protest and her flailing limbs—for the record, casts fucking hurt when you get smacked with them repeatedly—I carry her from the toilet to the space between the his-and-hers sinks.

She's still scowling when I carefully set her down, but I'm undeterred.

"*Escúchame, princesa.*"

"No, Pollo. *You* listen to *me*."

Gritting my teeth, I push aside the fleeting idea of picking her panties up off the bathroom floor and shoving them in her sassy mouth to shut her up. I settle for covering her mouth with my palm.

"You can fight me all you want, but here's what's going to happen. I'm going to get the plastic bags Penelope brought over last night to cover your casts, and then I'm taking you to the shower where I'm going to get you clean, hair included. We're gonna get you dressed, breakfast is on the way, and I've ordered food for the next couple of weeks."

Her eyes sparkle with what I'm hoping is gratitude, but it might be murderous intent. I can't quite tell.

"If you need me to stay in the friend zone for the duration of your healing, that's cool. I will absolutely do that. But make no mistake that when you're ready to explore this..." I sweep my finger between both of us. "I'm here. I'm all the way in. Both feet. Whole heart. And I'm not giving up on the idea that we're meant for each other."

Her eyes narrow, and her mouth moves behind my hand, but I'm not done yet.

"This isn't trauma speaking, Edith. I don't care what you say. This isn't something new, or scary, or temporary. The accident woke something up inside me that's always been there. I'm in love with you. Accept it. Get over it. Live with it. And perhaps be open to the idea that you might be a little in love with me too. I'll wait."

The woman growls on my hand. It would be hot if I wasn't concerned for my junk.

"And since you're quiet, I have something else to say. While you're sulking that I have to help you out in the shower I'd like you to think about something else, too. Think about how fucking resilient you are. Maybe even be a little grateful for the strength you've built in your legs through your training."

Her eyes pop wide, brows shooting up in question as a muffled, "huh?" comes from behind my hand.

"I get that this is literally the worst thing you believe could have happened to you. But have you given a second to consider the fact that while yes this is awful, and exhausting, and you have such a long stretch of uncertain terrain ahead of you, that you're also in a really good fucking position to fight through it?"

She grunts. Good. She's still listening, even if she's pissy and seems to think I'm being ridiculous.

"This is going to be easier for you than it would be for someone who wasn't a dancer. Think about it, Edie. Your training means your legs are strong as fuck, and they're used to working independently. Over the coming weeks your good leg is going to take a lot of the pressure and stress to compensate for your broken one. But you're going to heal faster because you are tough, your legs are conditioned and robust. I know it doesn't feel like it but you've got this. And when you don't, I've got you until you do."

And I fucking do, too.

CHAPTER 9

Edith

I hate when he's right.

I need help, and I'm mad about it.

Sitting on the couch in my living room, and my bladder is aching. He's getting ready to leave for a double-header weekend with the Raccoons, and I'd be lying if I said I'm fine with him leaving. Except that's exactly what I told him. "It's fine, you should go."

Dude took it at face value, too, and he's leaving. Ugh. That's not entirely fair. He's caught between a rock and a hard place. He'd much rather be here with me, but his commitment to his team, his future, that's not something he takes lightly.

At least his team appreciates when he shows up. I yell at him for cleaning up my piss. He's even going late, again, to join them separately. They're already in Sioux Falls getting ready to face the Phoenix.

I've seen damn near every game Apollo has ever played, and watching him on the ice against the Phoenix might be my favorite. I'm not even sure why.

He's left the chess board within arm's reach, but it's no use, I'm utterly flummoxed. As usual. The temptation to *acci-*

dentally kick the board over with my cast consumes me. We've played chess together since we were teenagers. He's played daily since he was six years old and is basically a master.

My chances of beating him are slim-to-none. I can count my wins on one hand, in all the time we've played I don't seem to improve even a little, but he never lets me quit, and he always comes back for more.

Sadistic fucker.

It's not even an ego thing. He doesn't enjoy watching me flounder and fail. He told me long ago he's always pushed me to be the very best version of myself. How the fuck losing to him at chess twice a week does that is anyone's guess. But here we are.

"I'll tell him it wasn't an accident." Penelope's voice draws me out of my intention.

"It could be." Shrugging, I groan. "He'd believe you over me though."

"He knows you too well." She smiles, handing me a glass of water with a metal straw. I'm a fucking invalid. For so long I've prided myself on being independent, strong, capable, and here I am, stuck on this stupid sofa, unable to do the simplest of tasks.

A familiar ire slinks under my skin. I'm not this person, and I fucking hate it.

"Shouldn't he be gone already?" Pen is moving in for the weekend. I tried to protest, but neither of them would listen. Assholes. I'm sure I'd be fine by myself. Kind of.

Okay, so I can't stand up by myself, use the bathroom alone, or prepare my own food, but it'd be fine, right?

I have to stop myself from snorting. As fine as that gif where a dog sits at a table in a burning building.

Apollo tried to find me a nurse, but not even the mighty de la Peña name can overcome the nursing shortage in Iowa right now. I'm almost relieved about that, I'd hate to cut the line and get special treatment when so many other people are waiting for help they need far more than I do.

"Edie?"

"Hm?"

"Sir stomps a lot." She jerks her chin to the banging and swearing across the hall. "He should be gone already."

My face heats. "He's following behind."

"Again."

"Again." I can't look her in the eye, afraid she'll see the war waging inside of me. I wanted him to kiss me the other day, and I don't know how I feel about that.

Did this life altering experience make me acutely aware that I'm alone and could have died alone? Sure.

Did it also make Apollo think he's wildly in love with me? Yes.

Might I be attracted to my hot, funny, grumpy buttface best friend? Affirmative.

Am I going to pursue it and see what happens? Fuck no.

I can't risk going there. I can't. I can't take the chance that dating my best friend will go well when so many people cross that line, and it turns to shit.

Exhibit A: my parents.

Mom and Dad were best friends through their teenage years. High school sweethearts who got married early, had me early, and then split up because it didn't work out. My stepfather is a nice guy from what I can tell, but he and Mom are always gone and busy, so I wouldn't know if he wasn't. And their love story was far less adorable, and much more sordid.

He cheated on his wife with Mom and left his partner of twenty years, three kids, the white picket fence and two dogs to be with her and travel the world.

Call me selfish, but I need Apollo too much right now to let romantic ideations get between us. I don't know which way is up. Do I *actually* have a crush on him? Or do I need an escape from the potential fact that my dreams might be crumbling right in front of my face?

Who knows?

Certainly not me. I'm not about to risk a sixteen-year friendship on near death experiences and Disney dreams.

"Edith?" I snap my eyes up to meet Pen's questioning stare. "Are you in there? Pain? Do we need drugs?"

Definitely not. They make me floaty and weird, like my body isn't my own. But the pain gets pretty bad so I don't really have a choice.

Sighing, I blink back the brewing tears.

"What is it?" She sits next to me, cradling my hands in her lap. I met her in Bitches Brew, the campus coffee shop on the first day of my first semester, and the rest is history. We bonded over our mutual love of *Ted Lasso*, musicals, and Chris Pine—the most delicious of the Hollywood Chrises.

"Are you stewing? Do you need a distraction?"

There is no one with a purer heart than Penelope. "I need to dance."

Her throat bobs as she swallows a couple times before her eyes fill with tears, too. "It's been four days since you got home, E. You've got to be kinder to yourself. This isn't going to be magically fixed overnight."

I grunt. "Fuck patience. I can't afford to lose this time, Pen. You know what it took for me to get here. This is my last chance." It's not my senior year, so it's not quite my last chance to audition, my last chance to get a contract and make this a career. But it's close enough. If I'm not good enough now, when there are sixteen-, seventeen- and eighteen-year-olds who are already getting contracts, I'll never make it.

But I finally felt like I had a real shot. Last year the new artistic director really took an interest in me at my auditions and told me, specifically, to come back this year.

I don't bother to fight the tears coursing down my face.

Apollo offered to pay for a therapist as well as a nurse. I told him I didn't need someone poking around in my brain, but once again, he might be right.

Sometimes I hate him and his stupid rightness.

"Progress is slow, painful, I get that. It must be so frustrating for you to be cooped up in here like this. Especially when you love performing. But you're strong, determined... as much as I believe you're going to get through this." Her gaze turns sympathetic. "Edie..."

"No." The word lodges in my throat. She doesn't believe I can do it. Of the few people in my life I can rely on, I assumed Apollo and Pen would have faith in me, would push me through these dark days and help me get back on the stage. From the downturned curve of her lips, she's already given up hope that I'll ever dance again.

It crushes my heart like an aluminum can.

"The doctors said it'd be highly unlikely, E." She shakes her head. "You're determined, there's fire in your belly, but can we please focus on trying to walk again before you set yourself up for heartache? Please?"

A fresh wave of tears pours down my cheeks. "I'm going to get better." My voice shakes, but I try hard to inject confidence into my words. "I'm saying it now. Manifesting. The last audition of the season is in March. I'm going to dance on that stage." Shrugging, I bite my lip. "I put the sixty bucks for the audition in an envelope with the date on the front and pinned it to the wall above my bed. I'm going to make it happen, Pen." Sniffing, I wipe my nose with my sleeve.

"You have to pay to audition?"

"Savage, right?"

"I..." She shakes her head. "I had no idea. I figured you auditioned, got picked, and danced."

I snort. "Hot shot hockey players get paid to play while we dancers gotta pay to play. It is what it is."

She's quiet for a long moment, and I'm sure I've finally won her onto my side.

Worrying her lips between her teeth for a beat, she sucks in a deep inhale. "Okay, but." Raising both hands, palms out like she's surrendering, she holds my gaze with hers. "Devil's advocate. What happens if you're not well enough for the audition? What happens if you can't dance? In March, or ever again, Edith?"

"Don't be like that, please." Her soft voice makes everything worse.

I don't want her sympathy, her pity, I don't need her negativity, or her to play devil's advocate. I need my friend to believe in me.

"Please, Edith. I don't want you to set yourself up for failure."

"Forgive me if I expect my friends to help set me up for success."

She flinches as if I smacked her.

"To believe in me. To help me rally when my chips are down."

She opens her mouth to speak but I've gone from zero to sixty. I'm freewheeling downhill, picking up speed, and my brakes have failed. "I heard what the doctors said, Pen. I was there. I know the prognosis. But miracles happen every fucking day. People recover from far worse than a mangled leg in a car crash."

The words tumble from my lips, my tears turning from hurt to anger. I can't tell if I'm trying to convince her or myself, but either way I can't stop myself.

"I thought you understood. I thought you knew just how important this is to me. Dancing is my everything, my whole life, Pen. It's all I've ever wanted to do."

She tries again but I don't let her talk. She's said enough. Her face says enough.

"You should leave."

Her mouth drops wide open.

"If you're not going to support my recovery the way I need you to, you should go."

When she doesn't move, I angle myself away from her. "Now."

We both know she can't leave, not with Apollo traveling for hockey, but she gets up without another word and leaves. She's only gone into another room, but the silence that descends in her absence is stifling.

She doesn't get it, doesn't have the dreams I do. She's never wanted to dance at The Met in NYC. Or The War Memorial Opera House in San Francisco, the Kennedy Center in Washington DC, or Covent Garden in London. She's not as driven as I am, she doesn't know how this feels, this... uncertainty. She just doesn't get it.

It might be a moment later, it might be ten, but Apollo bursts into the apartment, his hair unkempt, sweatpants riding low on his defined hips, huge bouquet of flowers gripped in his hand.

"The old ones aren't dead yet."

He flashes me a bright smile. "Neither are you, *princesa*."

In some of my darkest moments I wish I hadn't woken up from that crash. But that feeling will pass. Right? It has to. I'll find my fight, my legs, my talent, and everything will be fine. It has to be, because I don't know what's next for me if it isn't.

CHAPTER 10

Trash Can Tattle with Tabitha

Hey, Trash Panda fans!

For those of you who are new to TCT, my name is Tabitha Tucker and I am your resident sports-blogger-salacious-newsletter-author extraordinaire, spilling the tea on all things hockey and hotties.

Trash Can Tattle is a regular column that falls somewhere between gossip and game, bringing you all the things in one convenient place – away from the excellent news, features, and opinions and interviews from the rest of the NCAA, right here at UCR (the University of Cedar Rapids).

This week I come bearing good news, okay, great news. By all accounts Apollo de la Peña is back in the game.

Despite flying back to Iowa in the midst of a team trip to Belfast, Northern Ireland, for exhibition games with what seemed like persistent injuries following an almost fatal car accident over winter break, the top scoring forward is recovering nicely.

The infamous *Prince of Darkness* himself went on record with yours truly, telling Trash Panda fans that while he's still not at full strength, he's well on his way to peak fitness. Great news.

Unfortunately, long-time Raccoon's fan, and friend of de la Peña who was also injured in the accident, Edith Fisher, is having a tougher time.

In his interview, Apollo told us she's resting at home, but her injuries are extensive.

Myself and all TCT readers would like to wish a huge "Get well Soon" to you, Edith. Keep scrolling for well wishes from the fan base. We look forward to seeing you around the Trash Can soon.

In other news, the UCR Raccoons are getting ready for tomorrow's game against the Cincinnati Vipers, and it's sure to be a barn burner.

We're closer to the end of the season than we are the beginning, and whispers of potential Hobey Baker award contenders are sweeping the NCAA community like wildfire.

In net, there are several goaltenders who are strong candidates. Our own Ares de la Peña (UCR) is well on his way to glory, leading the pack with a .943 save percentage and a second-place goals against average of 1.57.

Cincinnati's Thomas Joseph (grandson of 'CuJo' Curtis Joseph formerly of the Toronto Maple Leafs) is second in that category with a 1.50 GAA to go along with a .939 SV% coming in behind only de la Peña. Perhaps the two most valuable goaltenders thus far though are not even drafted prospects. Beskorowany is back in the starter's net for Kalamazoo and keeping the Kings in games with his third-ranked .927 SV% and top-ten GAA. Recent standout Dexter Holden of the Minnesota Snow Pirates unsurprisingly holds a top-five GAA and top-ten SV% as well. Both could draw interest from NHL clubs later this spring, a nice consolation if they aren't Hobey Baker finalists.

That's it for this week, hockey fans, don't forget to...

Dish the deets

Heard a rumor? Spied one of the delicious de la Peña brothers or any of the Raccoons out in the wild? Click here to contact Trash Can Tattle with Tabitha.

CHAPTER 11
Apollo

(JANUARY 14TH – DAY 18 POST OP)

The weight of the world on my shoulders is fucking heavy.

Since the accident, Papá has taken a greater interest in me for all the wrong reasons. Not because his son was injured and could have died, not because his business partner's daughter really almost died, but because I'm fucking up.

Or at least he says I am.

Coach seems pretty happy with the wins we've been racking up since the team came back from Belfast, but considering he's a *cabrón* at the best of times, it's hard to tell. He hasn't yelled at me in a while. That's as good as it gets.

I haven't dropped the ball on school work either. International business isn't an "easy" degree by any means, it's also not what I would have chosen for myself, but it is what it is, and I'm maintaining a decent grade point average in my sophomore year.

Papá's problem has been that I've stepped back from the family business. And that would never do.

I almost pull a muscle rolling my eyes as I lace up my skates. Tate Myers slaps me on the shoulder. "You okay?"

My eyes meet his, and he doesn't look away. Why wouldn't I be okay? Or more to the point, how does he know I might not be?

Nodding, I grunt, pulling the laces tighter. "I'm fine. Just tired."

"If you need more recovery time..."

Canting my head, I start lacing up the other skate. "I'm good, thanks though."

He hesitates. "I've been in a wreck like that, man." He scratches the back of his neck. "Fucked me up pretty bad. I'm just saying..." He winces. We're teammates, sure, but Tate and I aren't what I'd consider close.

"I appreciate it." I finish lacing up the second skate. "But I'm okay. Tired and worried about Edith."

Something flickers across his face as he nods. "I get that. Recovery is shit. If you need to talk, I'm here. Also... I have the number of a great therapist if that's your jam." He holds up both hands. "Sorry if that's an overstep."

It's actually refreshing, warming even that he cares so much he's going out of his comfort zone to talk to me about something so personal. Especially when my siblings don't know what to say.

Myers lingers for a long moment before nodding, as though he's done what he came over to do, and now he can leave. It's on the tip of my tongue to unload on him, to tell him how tight my muscles are with tension, how heavy Papá's expectations weigh on me every morning when I wake up.

How desperate the need to set myself apart from my family is. How badly I wish to take Edith's pain from her. How much I blame myself for her injuries, for the accident.

Edith's right and has been right for some time. I don't want to inherit my father's business. I thought admitting that to myself would make things easier, that things would feel lighter, but it made the walls close in further.

I can't *tell* Papá I don't want to inherit his business baby when he dies, because from the day and hour I was born, I was the chosen one.

It was fun at first, sticking it to my siblings that Papá loved me most like a smug little asshole, but I didn't realize that love didn't come unconditionally. It came with a price tag that in retrospect, I wouldn't have willingly paid. The price was, and continues to be, far too high.

Being groomed for corporate life from the age of fourteen hasn't been easy, especially since no one asked me if I even wanted it in the first place.

I thought I did. And some days I think I want to play a role in the business. But taking over? That's not for me. And if Papá bothered to pay closer attention, he'd not only know that, but he'd also know that it's Artemis who's not only hungry for the business, but he's so fucking talented, he could run Papá's affairs with his eyes closed.

Artemis is the only reason I haven't completely flared out and fucked up beyond repair. Speak of the devil, the man himself saunters over to the bench where I'm sitting. *"¿Estás bien?"*

"Sí. Estoy bien. Why does everyone keep asking me that?" By everyone, I mean two people, but that's two too many.

He surveys me, assessing. I can hide a lot of things from a lot of people, but my twin brother knows me better than anyone. His brows pull together as he checks around us, I assume for eavesdroppers. "Is she okay?"

Grabbing my helmet from the bench beside me, I grunt. "No, *hermano*. She's not. She's drowning, and I can't save her."

He shakes his head. "You know it's not your job to save her, right? She can save herself. Your role is to remind her of that."

Sometimes my brother is so sensible I want to spit. "Doesn't mean I don't want to rescue her, though."

He nods, like he knows exactly what I'm talking about. But he doesn't—he can't. Papá isn't breathing down his neck all the time. His best friend isn't sinking deeper into depression because she can't do the one thing she lives for. He doesn't have this... this... consuming, overpowering love fizzing through his body and the woman he loves thinking it's because he saw white light at the end of a dark fucking tunnel.

I need to get my mind in the game. Hockey is my happy place, the one space where, from the moment I first stepped out on the ice as a child, I've felt like I belonged.

Except from the second the first puck drops, I can't get my shit together. It's as though I left my brain in the locker room, and my legs.

Carajo.

Raffi sails the puck my direction. It's an easy pass, one we've made a million times before, one we could do in our sleep, and I miss it. Cincinnati turns the puck over and head back toward center ice as Raffi gives me a "What the fuck, man?" look before chasing after it.

I wish I could give him an answer, but right now I don't know "what the fuck?"

If I don't get my shit together, it'll be one more reason for Papá to give me a hard time when the game ends. Not going to happen. He has enough ammunition after the deal with the new avionics parts suppliers I was working on through the holidays wasn't as good as he'd have liked.

Turning on the ice, I hunt down the Viper who picked my pocket.

If daddy dearest wanted a better deal, perhaps he should have done it his fucking self. Excuse me if I don't want to gouge the shit out of people. It's not how I do business.

Checking the Cincinnati defenseman into the boards, I

take back possession of the puck, the crowd going wild at the impact. I'm not letting him ruin this for me.

Ever since I was old enough to skate, I've wanted to play in the NHL. Artemis plays because I play. Ares started out because he wanted to be like his older brothers, but he's got more natural talent in his pinky finger than Artemis and I combined, though I'd never tell him that of course. His ego doesn't need it.

All three of us started playing because of my dream. Theo Fleury always said that when he started skating, he wasn't dreaming of playing in the NHL, he was preparing for it. That's how it is for me—it's in my bones, my soul, the very blood pumping through my veins. I was destined to be a professional hockey player on the ice at the Meredith Arena in Des Moines.

It's a secret I've cradled in my chest for my entire life. Something I can never let Papá near because he'd destroy it. As long as he thinks it's a silly little hobby that I enjoy, it's safe.

I zip past Cincinnati's center, energy zinging through my muscles as I cross the middle of the ice and approach their blue line. This arena is my domain. Countless hours of skating under my belt. I've shot at the net from every single spare inch of the ice pad, some days blind folded, with the sole intention of improving my game. I want to be the best.

Re-watching goalie tapes is my hobby. I study them, fastidiously. So much so that even Edith has become familiar with some of them. The motherfucker staring me down right now as I approach the net? He's a cocky prick who tends to wander too far from his crease. I need to get him a little farther out, and there's a goal with my name on it.

An hour a day, minimum. When my papers are done for school, and Papá is placated with our twice daily calls, I learn every strength and weakness of every goalie on every roster in the NCAA, NHL goalies too.

As Sun Tzu says, "If you know neither the enemy nor yourself, you will succumb in every battle." I only know that because Artemis told me that's what Sun Tzu wrote in the *Art of War*.

It's almost too easy, the biscuit goes in the basket, lighting the lamp, and the crowd roars, but at the last second the Cincinnati goalie hooks my skate, bringing us both down in a heap in his crease.

Strong hands not wearing green and white haul me off the netminder, so I psych myself up for a scuffle when my skates hit the ice.

Before I can blink, I'm surrounded by members of my team. Artemis flanks my left, and Scott on my right. Staring down the defenseman who still has my shirt clenched in his fist, silently threatening him to start something.

Part of me wishes he would. My gloves are already inching toward the ice. If this asshole wants to punish me for his goalie being a dick, then bring it. I wave off my defensemen. This is my battle, and I'm prepared to fight it.

The refs intervene, but the defender and I stay squared off until we're pulled apart.

I pick up another two points on the ice before the game ends, but it doesn't cure the itching under my skin. Bands of frustration tighten around my chest making it hard to breathe as I skate off the ice and make my way into the locker room.

Before I get undressed, I dig out my cell.

Princesa: Great game, flyboy. You shoulda hit him [winky emoji]

Penelope: She barely ate. You might have more luck. I'm worried about her, Apollo. She's fading into obscurity, and I can't figure out how to pull her back.

"What's wrong with your face?" Ares toes my skate with his own as he walks past me.

Dropping my phone back into my bag with a grunt, I shake my head.

"*Ay, hermano. ¿Qué lo que?*" He glances over to Artemis who flanks my other side, probably protecting me from the questioning eyes of the team. Or them from me.

"Edith's struggling."

Ares nods. "Do you want my pig?"

Scott snorts behind Artemis, choking on water. Adolescent.

"What good would Bacon do?"

Ares clicks his tongue like I'm un idiota. "You've heard of emotional support animals, right? Bacon makes for a very good cuddle buddy. He could cheer her up."

It's a sweet offer, but right now I'm not sure whether Edith would cuddle the pig or cook him. Though I guess maybe I should find out.

CHAPTER 12

Edith

"Princesa, I'm hooooome!" Apollo steps into the apartment with a dramatic flourish, a grin on his face, pizza box in one hand and... Leash in the other? What the hell?

"You went to play a hockey game and brought me back a pig?" I pause mid-crunch on the floor.

Bacon the team mascot has a green and black tutu around his waist, he's got oversized diamanté studded shades covering his face as he walks toward me with more swagger than the three de la Peña boys combined.

Gotta admit, he's kind of cute.

The pig too.

"What the fuck are you doing?"

That didn't take long.

"Crunches, Apollo. I've seen your abs, you do them often enough to recognize what they are." Ugh. The snark is out of my mouth before I can stop it. It's happening a lot lately, and I'm not a fan. I don't mean to be such a salty bitch but everything's so fucking hard.

"You're pushing yourself is what you're doing. *Mierda*, Edie. You're going to hurt yourself."

Sitting up with a grunt, I scowl at him. "I'm being careful, Pollo. Scout's honor."

"You were never a Scout." He wags a finger at me while he ditches the pizza on the table and unclips Bacon, who toddles over to me for scratches and sniffs.

"I can take care of myself you know." I gesture at my injuries. "I'm not a complete invalid."

At his hard stare, I continue. "It's not like I'm doing pushups, or jumping jacks, or even walking. It's only a few crunches."

When he squats next to me, dropping to his knees, then butt, so we're sitting butt to butt. It's not uncomfortable, but it's awkward. I attempt to retreat. I'm soaked with sweat, and I stink. Sure, I'm taking it easy, but it's not really easy when your body is focused on healing injuries. Every minor exertion leaves me drained and doused in sweat.

The tenderness and care in his eyes steals my breath away, and my eyes fill with tears. "Why won't you just leave me alone, Pollo? I'm fine."

His fingers skim my jaw, sending shivers skating across my skin. He threads his hand underneath my messy bun, and the electricity hanging in the air intensifies. It was never like this before, the air never got thick with anticipation and need when he was this close. But he's also rarely been this close to me.

Dropping his forehead to mine, he sighs. Bacon nudges my hand because I've stopped giving him scratches. He grunts and wanders off. Apparently he needs more excitement than watching Apollo hold me captive with those eyes.

"I love you, Edie. I'm concerned about you, I care about you, and if roles were reversed you'd be as in my face as I am in yours." His breath tickles me as he talks.

My heart thrashes wildly in my chest. The intensity drilling into me from his stare freaks me out, and I stupidly cast my gaze to his lips.

As first kisses go, the one on the couch was pretty memorable. Has he considered repeating it? A sneak peek at his eyes tells me all I need to know. He's thinking about it right this very moment, and every reason I've had in my head not to let him has suddenly dissipated. How convenient.

The urge to lick my lips is strong, but if I lick my lips, I might lick him, too. And I'm not sure that's the signal I want to send.

I don't know when I started crying, but he's brushing tears away with his thumb. Between delicate kisses pressed to my forehead, he mumbles to me in Spanish about how I'm not alone, how strong I am, how I'm going to get through this.

I'm powerless.

No strength in all the world is potent enough to resist a beautiful Latino man caressing your brokenness and whispering about how everything's going to be okay.

He doesn't instigate, he doesn't even pressure me, but the draw to his lips is unyielding. I need to kiss him, for both our sakes.

"I stink."

He nods, his nose brushing against mine. "You do."

My chest heaves, weighty with each intake of air.

"No me importa." His voice is strained, like he's fighting his urges, and I'm glad it's not only me feeling this... whatever it is.

It's clearly not important to him since he's right... there. Can I get past my fear of losing him enough to actually be with him?

Do I need to decide that right now?

Need thrums through my body. The closer he is, the

quieter the doubts get. Heady, demanding, consuming desperation claws at my body as his thumb strokes my face.

"Apollo." More tears trickle down my cheeks.

Fighting on all fronts is exhausting. Would it be so bad to give into it? Aching for comfort, closeness, guilt tugs in my chest. I don't want to use him, but he's offered to give me whatever I need. In a moment of weakness, I'm tempted.

I'm losing my mind. Since the accident I'm either yelling or crying, sometimes both simultaneously. I can't figure out how to balance my anger, fear, and pain, and a huge piece of me is afraid that one more snide comment, or one more dismissal, will be the straw that breaks the hockey player's back.

Except none of that matters right here, right now. Nothing matters but how he's looking at me, eyes filled with guarded adoration, patience, and understanding.

"I'm scared."

He nods again. *"Lo se, princesa. Lo se."*

"You're not?"

"No tengo miedo."

I guess I'm afraid enough for the two of us. "What if it all falls apart?"

"¿Y si no es asi?"

He's right, what if it doesn't?

Fuck it.

CHAPTER 13

Apollo

The moment she decides to kiss me her breathing shifts, her shoulders relax, and a smile ghosts her lips. I've wanted to kiss her again every single second of every day since our first time on the couch and our second time in the bathroom. My body may explode with relief as she closes the final few millimeters between our mouths and presses her lips to mine.

I let her set the pace, not wanting to spook her. Uncertainty is clear in the tiny wrinkles in her forehead and the hesitation with which she moves as if holding onto reason, sense, the past... with everything she has.

She has no idea it's already too late.

That accident forced us across an invisible line, and there's no turning back. Even if we wanted to.

I don't want to.

I want her to be mine, body, mind, heart, soul, for the rest of our fucking lives. She's just taking a little longer to figure it out, and I'll be ready when she does.

Her lips part on a sigh, and I make my move. If I'm on a limited number of kisses with this woman, I'm going to make each one count. My tongue finds hers, caressing it with confident sweeps, enjoying the moan I pull from her.

"Apollo." Has my name ever sounded sweeter?

She wants to remind everyone that she's strong, all the while feeling helpless and weak, broken inside. Every fiber of my being yearns to take care of her, but it's my place to show her she's not fragile. I tangle my fingers in her hair, tugging her head back so I can deepen the kiss, and she gasps again.

The kiss is passionate, demanding, toeing the line of *more*, and when we pull apart to catch our breath, I trail my lips and tongue down her neck. She shifts next to me, and I feel her need in my bones curling around my own. Dragging my fingers up her inner thigh and over her toned stomach, I pause at the waist of her pajama pants. She almost cried when we took a pair of scissors to the thighs of some of her pants for easier cast access, but I promised we'd replace them once she was all healed up.

I won't do anything she doesn't want me to. She might regret it in the morning, but if I can give her even a moment of bliss, a second of distraction from the tormented past, the painful present, and the murky future, I'll do it.

"Apollo, please."

It's the first and last time my girl will ever beg.

My fingers walk under the band of her pants while my eyes hold hers, locked together in a decision we won't be able to come back from. Her breath stutters. We both know this is the turning point for our relationship and all that might entail. The thought alone energizes me, spurring me forward, sparks dancing under my fingers as our skin connects.

She has a little hair covering her pussy, but if I was a gambling man I'd say she's usually bare and hasn't waxed since the accident. It would make sense with being a ballerina, what with "unsightly" hair poking through the leotard.

She arches her back, tilting her hips toward me on a sigh.

But she doesn't reach for me, she seems content to let me do my thing. And I intend to.

My already straining dick weeps into my dress pants. Fucking hell. A few weeks ago I'd never given a single thought to Edith's pussy, and now I'm sliding my fingers between her slick folds, enjoying every mewl, every stuttering breath, every connection between us unfolding on her living room floor.

She shivers when my finger sweeps across her clit, and I savor the reaction as my dick gets harder, something I wasn't sure was possible. Her body is beautifully responsive. Sweat beads on her forehead, her nipples press against her sports bra, and her teeth pin her lip in place like she's afraid to truly give in to what she's feeling.

A la mierda eso. Fuck. That.

Picking up speed, I swirl my fingers over her clit, cradling her neck as her head tilts back against the couch cushion. She's fucking glorious. Perky tits pointing at the ceiling, flushed face, tendrils of hair falling from her hair tie. I might come in my fucking pants.

Holding her gaze with mine, I take my time, selfishly wanting her to see, to really fucking see what I'm feeling as I hold her. She's a fucking goddess, and she's given me the honor of touching her. I don't take that lightly. These emotions spinning in my chest aren't because of the accident. And I'm not wasting my chance to prove to her we have chemistry.

If she doesn't feel it now, she never will. I'll figure out a way to respect her choice and remain her friend. But if she is feeling it and she's fighting it, *that* I can help her through. And I'm a patient man. I'll wait for as long as it takes, even if it takes forever and a day.

Her body jerks, muscles twitching, and she moans. Her

nails dig into my forearm, gripping me, hips bucking as she chases her release.

As her eyes roll back in her head, she pants. "Apollo... please, please don't stop."

She's adorable and clearly doesn't know me as well as she thinks. "Not going to happen, *princesa*."

Her lips part like she's about to talk again, but I'm done waiting for her to get out of her own head. Squeezing her clit between my finger and thumb, I gently twist, and she falls apart.

Watching her orgasm at my hand is the most sensual, sexiest damn thing I've ever experienced. Her features are serene, a sheen of sweat covers her face and chest, and her limbs soften as she starts to come down. But I'm not done, and from the hungry look in my girl's eyes, neither is she.

Dropping my face to hers, I kiss her over and over, nipping at her lips and exploring every inch of her mouth before I move lower. The more my lips travel over her skin, the more she reacts to me. Panting, her skin pinking. After a long moment with my teeth grazing her nipples through the fabric, she tugs up her sports bra with her cast-free hand, giving me access.

Soy un hombre afortunado. A very lucky man. It's like all my Christmases came at once. Sucking one of her pert nipples into my mouth, I skim my teeth over the hard peak. She shivers before hissing out a long breath. Something hard butts into me from behind and my teeth slip, sinking into the supple flesh of her breast.

She gasps as I unlatch, then giggles. A soft grunt behind me suggests I've been cockblocked by a potbellied pig, but the smile on her face is hard to be mad at.

"Maybe he's hungry?"

He's not the only one.

She smiles again as I ghost my fingers across her nipples.

Her eyes roll closed, her back arches, and she moans. I love that sound. I'd give my right ball for the privilege of making her make these noises every fucking day. Maybe my left one, too.

I'm painfully hard. It's going to take a minute before I can move. She tugs her sports bra back over her tits, and a piece of me dies. When I finally peel my gaze away from her chest and land on her face, cold dread skips through my muscles.

Tears course down her beautiful face all over again, and my stomach sinks. Does she regret this already? Fuck. Did I hurt her?

"Edie?" Should I touch her or leave her the fuck alone? The desire to haul her onto my lap wins out, and I'm hoping that if she's uncomfortable with the physical touch she'll speak up.

Instead of pulling away, she buries her head in the crook of my neck and shoulder and sobs.

"Ay, princesa." I stroke her arm from fingertip to shoulder as she cries. Her tears soak through my dress shirt, which only makes me hold her harder.

"I hate being so miserable," she manages between broken sobs. My heart fractures with every sniffle and wail. Before the accident I'd never seen her so damn sad. She was the sunshine to my darkness. *Ella es el sol a mi noche.*

Bright, vibrant, happy, so full of joy the air around her shimmered because she couldn't contain it all inside. I haven't seen much of that woman since the wreck, but she's in there somewhere, and I'm even more determined to help her resurface.

"Edie, when was the last time you were outside?" She stills in my arms but she doesn't answer. I need to help her remember who the fuck she is. Silently telling my dick he's going to have to wait, and promising I'll deal with him in bed later, I scoop her up onto the couch.

"What are you doing?" She wipes her eye with her free hand, lifting her cast, I assume to wipe the other but she pauses, growling at it like she keeps forgetting it's there.

"Giving you a ride."

If I don't ignore the flush deepening in her cheeks, I won't let her leave the couch. It's winter in Iowa, and she has two casts, so it's a workout in itself to first of all find her cold weather gear that fits. So I dig out two sets of my ski gear and dress her in it well enough to take her outside.

Twenty five minutes later, we're both dressed, she's mounted on my back, and I'm making my way up onto the roof of our building. It's a perk of owning one of the top floor apartments, and the rooftop parties over the summer months are epic.

Sweat streams down my face as I get her outside. The wind whips around us and she clutches me tighter. I make my way over to the perimeter wall, holding her in place and letting her acclimate to being outside before I maneuver her to sitting with her back against my chest.

"Don't let go." Her voice is quiet in the tranquil night.

Tightening my arms around her waist I nuzzle close to her. "Never." I doubt she realizes just how fucking serious I am.

She inhales deeply, breathing in the crisp night air, her shoulders rising and falling with each breath and puffs of steam blowing out of her nose.

"I haven't been outside since I got home from the hospital."

"I know. That's my bad. I should have dragged you out kicking and screaming."

"I'd have tried to push you off this damn rooftop, Pollo." She giggles.

"I can take you." Resting my chin on her shoulder, I sigh. How have I missed this for so long? Standing here, her leaning against my chest, braced against me, my arms holding her to me, it feels so fucking right.

We stay in silence for a long time, watching the twinkling lights and the occasional car passing below in downtown Cedar Rapids.

"Thank you, Apollo."

Brushing my nose into her hair, I mumble, *"De nada, princesa."*

"I needed this."

"Lo se." And if I have to carry her to the roof every fucking day and night, I'll do it. "You know, Ares knows a doctor. He's treating Eloise's arm pain."

Edith squirms in my arms, half turning to look at me, demanding more information with her eyes.

My phone vibrates in my pocket. When I pull it out and we both see it's Papá, she jerks her chin to the phone. "You should take that."

I should. I've been dodging his calls more often than not lately, and I have some paperwork to sign and return to him that is a few days overdue. He wants me, us, to buy another business. He called it a merger, but from the plans he presented me with, it's a hostile takeover of a rival company, and I'm not sure how I feel about that. They have very public, ethical differences to my father and how he runs his business, so I'm pretty sure he will strip any good from them if he gets his hands on it.

It's just business, he says.

Doesn't feel that way, however.

Even if I wanted to talk to him, I wouldn't right now. I ignore the flashing screen, tuck my phone back into my pocket, and glide my fingers over Edith's cheek. "After Eloise's accident she started experiencing occasional arm pain. Doctors couldn't find anything wrong with her, and I guess her therapists said it was psychosomatic or something. But Ares found a doctor who believes that she's got this pain sometimes, and I think they found something."

I clear my throat. I'm overstepping, but I do it anyway. "I don't know all the details, that's not my point. My point is, I can take you to that doctor if that's what you need. Tell me what you need, *princesa*." Desperation claws at my chest as I cup her face, cradling her porcelain skin.

Her whisper is so quiet I barely hear when she speaks. "I need for you to kiss me again, Apollo."

So I do.

I'd move heaven and earth to help this woman recover, to find her strength, even if it costs me everything I have.

CHAPTER 14

Edith

A heavy arm bands across my waist, and a warm body presses against my back. Apollo's warm breath flutters my hair with each measured exhale. Everything hurts, a constant ache in the very core of my being. But for the first time since I got out of the hospital, I'm well rested. I slept. No nightmares, no night sweats, no bone-deep, skull-piercing agony, or emotional breakdowns.

When Apollo slipped me between the sheets, climbed in next to me, and pulled me to his chest, I passed out, hard. My arm throbs in my cast, my skin itching to feel the air sweep across the tiny hairs on the broken limb.

I shouldn't have flapping wings in my stomach as my best friend's thumb runs unhurried strokes back and forth on my arm, but I can't help it. He's warm, and strong, and solid. Oh... ohhhhhh. All of him is firm. *All* of him.

Holy shit. I don't need to shift my weight to check. That's most definitely his boner pressing against my ass.

This is weird. This is so epically fucking strange.

For most of our childhoods I was convinced Apollo had cooties. He'd pull my hair—I'd pull his right back—he'd chase me with worms, so I'd go find spiders. When he turned into a gangly teen, we made fun of each other, and for a while I thought I'd lost him to the gaggle of teenage boys he was friends with, and hockey.

Never once, in all the years we've been best friends, have I thought about Apollo de la Peña's boner. And now it's nestled against my ass.

I'm not sure when he filled out into this attractive... thing from that gangly thing he used to be, but I think I put it into the memory box right next to making mud cakes together when we were little. And watching him prank his siblings with his twin brother.

It's like I'm seeing him with fresh eyes, like I'm coming out of a weird friend-zone stupor and an Adonis is waiting for me.

"Don't make it weird, Edie."

I bite my lip to stop the groan aching to escape. His morning voice is gravelly, low, and right next to my ear. Don't make it weird, he says. Dude, your hard dick is against my ass, and I'm lying in your arms. In my world, it doesn't get much weirder.

It's as if last night was all a dream. He touched my clit. Actually, that's not true. He owned my clit. As soon as his fingers sank into my pussy, I belonged to the big spoon curled around me. His fingers sent me to places I've never been before, and I'm fighting really hard to find a reason why we can't be together.

I don't trust it. I'm not sure what's changed. Am I so blinded by a need for closeness and comfort that I'm ignoring warning signs that this isn't a good idea?

He's still here, right? That's something. He's literally seen me through the worst of times, and he's still here. In fact, he's more here than ever.

He hasn't moved against me. His stroking hasn't stopped,

and there's a throbbing between my thighs that's driving me closer to moving his hand where I need it to be.

That's what it is. Rational thought has left the building, and I'm running on vagina brain alone. The Lady Garden has taken control, and it wants a repeat performance of last night.

There isn't anything Apollo de la Peña puts his mind to that he doesn't conquer. He's a master of chess, he's a top scoring hockey player, and unless he does something to immensely fuck up his degree, he's going to graduate at the top of his class. No matter what he says.

His idea of a "passing grade" isn't the same as everyone else's. If he's "just" passing, he's failing.

He's an achiever. And last night I realized, he's an achiever in the bedroom too. A shiver rattles through me, followed by his low chuckle next to my ear.

"You're making it weird, *princesa*."

"I think weird is in the rearview, *príncipe de las tinieblas*." I wince at the car reference, grateful that my back is to him. I'm not sure how I'm ever going to get into a car again. I start PT in March, and it's not something I'm ready to think about. If I think about it, I'll have to accept that I'm not making my audition. And I'm not there yet. I'm not. "Your dick is hard, Pollo." Classic deflection.

I half expect him to move it away from me at my declaration, but instead, he pulls me to him even more tightly. "*Sí*. It is. But that doesn't mean things have to be uncomfortable between us."

It's on the tip of my tongue to make a crack about how uncomfortable such a raging hard on must be, but I swallow it down. Not sure I'm ready to make jokes about his peen.

"Do you want me to leave?"

I don't even need to think about it, I shake my head.

"What do you want, Edith?"

A loaded question if ever I heard one. But my foo foo is

flexing. She knows exactly what she wants. I don't want to use my best friend for sex—I love him too much to do that to him. But I'm stressed, in pain, and so confused and overwhelmed right now I don't have the emotional spoons to—

His hand moves.

I don't fight the groan this time, nor am I surprised when his fingers slide through my pussy with ease. It's difficult not to be wet when a gorgeous, strong man who dries your tears and helps pick you up off the mat has an erection for you.

"Don't overthink it."

Like his demand will make all the thoughts of how strange it is that the attractive, robust man has been my best friend since we were little.

His mouth finds the side of my neck, and he skims his lips across my skin. Who'd have thought that I'd be getting more action than I have in months after an almost life ending car accident? I'm not given much time to think about it, because Apollo removes his hand from my pajama pants, and slides down my back.

"Wh-what are you doing?"

He settles between my legs, tugging my pants off. "Having breakfast."

My rational brain says I should argue, should resist, should remind him we're best friends, and we need to inch back across that line for our own good. But that feral look in his eyes demands my silence while challenging me to protest.

"Do you have a problem with that?"

Definitely should. I should have many, many problems with that. But I can't think of a single one right now. The only thing consuming my entire being is the pulsing in my pussy.

Is he as skilled with his tongue as he is with his fingers? I should find out, right? For science?

He nips at the inside of my thigh, and I yelp. "No. No problem."

I push up onto my elbow, needing to watch with my own eyes that this is happening, but he presses a warm hand on my stomach. "Lie back, and let me enjoy you, *princesa*."

"You're so bossy."

"This isn't news." His tongue leaves a cool trail up the inside of my leg before he drapes it over his shoulder. Sucking in a deep breath, I wait. Part of me hopes he's terrible with his tongue. Because if he's not awful, I might not be able to stand up to the demands of the va-jay-jay.

When his mouth doesn't connect to my pussy, I blow out the breath in a huff.

"Patience, *princesa*."

"Easy for you to say. I'm the one—" My words choke on a gasp as his finger glides through my soaked lips.

"Shhhhhh."

"Are you just staring at my pussy?"

"Tal vez."

I try rolling my hips, but that makes him chuckle.

"You're such a tease, Pollo."

"I'm enjoying the view, Edie." He sinks his tongue into my pussy, making me moan. "I've never seen a prettier pussy, and I plan to enjoy it."

His tongue tickles my clit, soft and slow strokes. I'm already well on my way to my release. He takes his time, his velvety tongue gliding against me like he's done it a thousand times before and knows exactly how to give me what I need.

The fire builds low in my belly. "Apollo."

He hums against my pussy, sending vibrations through every nerve in my body. My fingers find their way into his hair, pinning his head in place as I ride his face with abandon. I don't want this to end. Ever. The bolts of pleasure zapping all over my body from the skilled lashes of his tongue against my clit consume me.

I don't make sweet gasps. I'm whimpering and moaning,

crying out, screaming and pleading with him not to stop. I barely cling to the edge for a few more blissful seconds before I ignite. My body trembles, his hot palm pressing on my stomach to hold me in place.

He doesn't stop as I crest the wave. He shifts my leg still over his shoulder and buries his face with a renewed vigor that both terrifies and excites me. This is how I die.

My throat is raw from screaming through my release, and he grunts as he drives me relentlessly closer to a second with rhythmic flicks of his tongue.

It's not easy to make me come, but he's making such light work of it that I wonder if any of my previous boyfriends ever knew what a clitoris even looked like. Apollo is a master of my pussy, and I'm a helpless passenger, going where he demands I go.

My muscles clench as shivers of ecstasy course through every inch of my body. "Apollo... fuck me."

"No." He growls against me, sending sparks through my pussy. "I won't fuck you until you're sure." He laps at me, slurping like he can't get enough. "The next time you ask me to fuck you, it'll be with a clear head, and a ready heart, *princesa*. I'll do anything else you want and need me to in the meantime, but I won't fuck you until you're truly mine."

I barely get a second to process his words when another orgasm hits me. My legs are jelly, my mind is calm, and my bed is soaked.

This thing between us is not clunky or awkward. We're still the same people we were before, but with way more nakedness. And... I dunno, I think I like it.

CHAPTER 15
Apollo
(JANUARY 15TH – DAY 19 POST OP)

Tonight the UCR Raccoons return to home ice at Trash Can and welcome the Cincinnati Vipers, after an eight game road trip stretching back to November.

In their last game before this weekend's double header against Cincinnati, the Raccoons had trouble burying pucks early, and fell behind 1-0 to the Sioux Falls Phoenix. But once things got rolling, it was hard to stop UCR.

Slater Goodwin and Apollo de la Peña each scored, twenty-eight seconds apart, late in the first period. Jackson Gilbert and Raffi Shaw tacked onto the lead from there, and the Raccoons were on their way.

Cedar Rapids is currently thirteen in the Pairwise, and a loss this weekend and some twists of fate could keep them out of the NCAAs.

The pressure is on for our beloved Raccoons to perform well against Cincinnati this weekend, or our championship run may very well be over before it starts.

Tabitha doesn't beat around the bush in this week's Trash

Can Tattle. But "the pressure's on" is a fucking understatement. I'm fucking exhausted.

My whole life I thought I wanted to play professional hockey, and one night, one crash, one near miss, one major setback in my life and now I'm questioning everything.

Do I love the game? Some days more than I love oxygen.

Do I think I can keep up with this grueling training and game schedule? I thought so, I truly did. But the longer I'm away from Edith, the more I wonder. Is this lifestyle really for me? I could suck it up and sink into the role my father wants me to take in the company, base myself here in Cedar Rapids, no traveling across the country, no early morning skates, no skills camps, no injuries, just me and my girl. She wants to travel for dance, but ultimately, she's always been an Iowa girl at heart. This is home.

I could play rec league hockey, find a local team to play with when the craving hits. I could still be happy if I don't reach my dream of playing professional league hockey, right? I'm almost sure.

She'd kill me at first, but she'd get over it, eventually. I think.

Before the accident I lived my life through tunnel vision. Everything was about the game and keeping Papá off my case. But since my life flashed before my eyes... I guess Edith's right in a way, it's given me a new perspective.

As much as I want to play hockey, as much as I want to score goals and help my team win championships, a life with Edith is worth far more to me than winning Lord Stanley. Without question.

This is the first game in my entire life where I'm apathetic in the dressing room. I can't shake this funk, this tug at the back of my head that I shouldn't be here. I should be with Edith, helping her through her challenges. But I'm here because if I was there, she'd sever my throat with my own skate.

Left shin pad, right shin pad, left skate, right skate. I dial in the motions, my mind wholly fixated elsewhere.

I'm the first player after Ares to step out into the rink. Every single game. And as soon as my blade hits the ice, the energy of the home crowd seeps into my bones. There's nothing like it.

Within the first three minutes of play, my teammate Raffi Shaw takes a hit so hard the whole arena holds its breath.

Shaw has barely hit the deck when McLeod, our trainer, is out on the ice faster than we can blink. We like to tease him that he's a distant relative of the old Calgary Flames trainer Bearcat Murray. He was known for how fast he could get to a fallen player, and McLeod comes a close second. He crouches over Raffi's motionless body on the ice, a scowl furrowing his forehead.

It's not long before Raffi is stretchered off the ice, and the tension in the barn reaches suffocating levels. It's never a good thing when a player goes down, but when it's one of your own it hits like an enforcer against the boards.

The Viper gets a penalty, play resumes, and we have our asses handed to us in a 3-0 loss. But none of that matters, because all I want to do is get back to my girl, hold her close, and forget all about how fucking fragile life can be.

CHAPTER 16

Edith

I hate this.

It's been two weeks since Apollo's face was buried in my pussy, and I'm aching for a do over. Stupid hockey and stupid school have kept us apart, and I. Hate. It.

He's so busy. All the freakin' time. The Raccoons have had back to back away weekends, first in Kansas City, then they played Notre Dame. If it's not at hockey training and games, it's papers and studying, and if it's none of those, he's working with his father. I can't even complain. I mean, I will, because it's all I fucking do these days. It's not like I have a packed schedule since I'm still laid up with this recovering fucking foot.

But before the accident, that was my life too. It's why our friendship worked so well together. We understood the demands of each other's lives. It sucks when I'm laid up with a broken leg and can't do the things that bring me joy.

If one good thing has come out of barely seeing him for the past two weeks it's that I haven't been distracted by his toned chest and chiseled jaw every day. And I've been able to do some low-key exercises without him giving me shit about it.

I'm lying on my living room floor, sweat trickling down my temples, staring at the ceiling, my core burning from all the crunches. Bacon snorts quietly at my ear.

"She's coming, piggy." I scratch behind his ear as he plops down beside me.

I have shared custody of the pig. He's litter box trained so he's not too much work. Who even knew that was a thing? I had no idea you could litter box train a freakin' pig!

Eloise is on her way to pick him up for the next few days before he comes back to visit me for a sleepover. I thought it was a ridiculous idea at the time, bringing a pig to visit to cheer me up, but Bacon has been the best therapy animal I could have asked for.

He listens to all my depressive soliloquies and doesn't judge me. At least not out loud. He's also the most high maintenance pet I've ever known. His wardrobe is more extensive than mine, and I'm a performer. Was.

"Knock, knock!" Eloise's voice rings out around the room. "Sorry. I did *actually* knock, knock, but I guess you didn't hear me."

This is what happens when I daydream about my best friend's washboard abs and grumpasaurus smolder. Eloise is with one of the other camera-winning-smile de la Peña brothers. I don't know how she ever leaves his orbit to live her life.

If Apollo wasn't the prince of darkness, and flashed his pearly whites at me more often, I'd be a quivering wreck of pure need. We didn't just open a window between the two of us, we kicked down the damn door and detonated the walls. He's not consuming my every thought, but it's getting close the more time I spend within this apartment.

"Hey, Eloise. How are you?" I push up from the floor with a grunt, pulling myself up to stand with the arm of the couch. It's not easy to do with two limbs in casts, but Apollo was right about one thing, my other arm and leg are stronger, so things aren't as hard as they could be. I try to remind myself of that, at least three times a day when things feel shitty. So, every day.

Eloise doesn't move to aid my movements. She learned that lesson the hard way last week when she stepped forward to help, and I snapped her face off. Understandably, she's been a little skittish with me ever since. Can't blame her. Even Pen feels like she's drifting. I tried to talk to her, apologize for yelling at her, but I'm not sure it stuck.

Eloise slides her backpack from her shoulder to the floor before crouching down to scratch Bacon's tummy. "I'm okay, thanks. How are you doing?" She pins me with a piercing stare. There's no sympathy in her gaze, but concern weighs heavily on her face.

Shrugging, I brush it off. "It depends on the day." With Apollo gone so much, my sleep pattern is fragmented. I never thought I'd be the girl who needs a snuggle buddy to sleep, but apparently I am. Not just any snuggle buddy either. When she was around, Penelope tried to spoon me a few times over the past couple weeks, and it didn't work. Like, at all.

Turns out, my best friend has magic, trauma fighting arms. My gaze drifts past Eloise to the half played chess game on the table behind her. If I was only craving sex, or the company of a warm body, I could probably booty call someone from one of those apps online. But I'm not. I'm yearning for one very specific person, and I'm still a little torn about that. Fine. A lot torn. What will things look like when I'm back to my own life and neither of us have time for the romancing?

"You don't have to talk to me about it, Edith. But it'd be a good idea for you to talk to someone professionally." Her fingers drift to the scars on her face. "Ares found me a really great trauma specialist to talk to. She's helping. If you want, I can—"

Holding up my hand, I shake my head. "Thanks, but I'm good." I'm not good. She knows it, and I know it. I have no idea why I'm lying to her face, but to her credit she doesn't outwardly react.

"Okay. Well, when you're ready."

I nod, and she stands, picking up her bag. "I brought you this month's book club book."

Raccoon's team captain, Justin Ashe, started a book club for the players a while ago. "Get Lit." It's a no girls allowed zone for the time being because Justin has been trying to develop a safe space for the players to talk about all things books and romance. And feelings.

It's been growing in number from month to month, and Savannah, Justin's girlfriend, has been telling Eloise, Penelope and me what the books are. The three of us have our own renegade version of Get Lit. We read the books every month and chat about them among ourselves. Considering I have a lot of free time on my hands, the books, and the company, are a welcome distraction.

"Thank you. I appreciate it." And I mean it. I gave up on my last read, having to mark it on my Goodreads account as another "DNF." I hate not finishing books, and the last three in a row I've started to read, I've stopped at various points. "What's this month's read?"

Her face lights up. "It's called *A Kiss of Iron* by Clare Sager. I'm sooooo excited for this one. The reviews say it's like *A Court of Mist and Fury*, Netflix *Bridgerton*, and *The Bridge Kingdom* had a glorious, perfect baby." She squeals. "These are a few of my favorite things," she sings.

Admittedly, my interest is piqued. Folding my arms, I narrow my eyes. "Tropes?"

"Morally gray hero, enemies to lovers, Fae, curvy heroine." She ticks them off on her fingers, her voice getting more excited with each one. "It's going to be so good."

"I love that Justin changes up the types of romance we're reading."

Nodding, Eloise hugs the beautiful hardback copy of *A Kiss of Iron* against her chest, and I quietly hope this copy is for me to keep. The dagger through the silver crown laden with rubies on the cover would fit in perfectly on my bookshelf.

"Me too. Paranormal, military, hockey, and now fantasy. It's a lot of fun."

I gesture for her to sit down on the couch. My leg is trembling from remaining standing for so long and sweat pools at my lower back. But I don't want to sit while she stands. It's rude. "Is Ares reading?"

She nods again. "He resisted the book club at first, but Justin has picked such great books that Ares gets sucked in and can't put them down. Most of the team read on the bus to games. What about Apollo? Is he reading?"

Something in her stare makes my cheeks heat. "I... uh... I'm not sure. I don't know if he's gone back to book club since the accident. He doesn't have much time for reading. He's so busy."

"It's always worth making time for the things we love." She tilts her head. "Maybe you could buddy read together. Ares and I have started reading them to each other." She fans herself. "It's been a revelation."

My face is on fire, and I can't meet her eyes. "I don't... I wouldn't... I..." What even are words?

She giggles but it's not unkind. "Just a suggestion." She levels me with the knowing in her eyes. "When you're ready to talk about *that*, I'll be here, too."

"About what?" My attempts at playing it cool are not working. Sweat beads in my hairline.

"Honey, I'm hooooome!" Penelope saves the day, bursting into the room with a flourish. She heard Apollo announce his arrival one day, and now they both do it to annoy me, trying to one-up each other getting louder and louder. Jerks. "I come bearing pie." She brandishes a cardboard box our direction and Bacon huffs at my feet. Her face falls. "What's wrong?"

"Nothing."

"I was about to quiz her on her feelings for her *neighbor*." Eloise grins at me.

So much for being saved from an uncomfortable conversation.

"And I was about to go for a nap. I also have no idea what you're talking about."

Pen guffaws. "Liar, liar, pants on fire," she accuses, plopping down on the recliner facing the sofa. "If I'd known we were going to talk feels, I'd have brought some liquor."

"We aren't." I fake a yawn, stretching my arms above my head for emphasis. "Nap, remember? And I can't drink on these meds."

"She's not ready to admit she's feeling *things* for Apollo, Penelope."

"De-nial is not just a river in Egypt, my friend." Pen cracks open the pie box and breaks off a piece of crust. "I'm not going to push the issue. However, at some point you're going to have to decide whether you're going to take a shit or get off the pot."

"Ew." Eloise scrunches up her face.

Pen shrugs. "I said what I said."

"Say fucking less, Pen." I hold out my hand for the pie. "I don't know what you're talking about."

She gets up from the seat and heads toward the kitchen. "And I don't believe you."

Eloise pats my thigh. "We're ready to listen when you're ready to face up to the fact you're crushing on Apollo."

Crushing is an understatement. Crushing was weeks ago. I'm in deep water without a float. If I'm not careful, I'm totally going to drown.

CHAPTER 17

Apollo

(FEBRUARY 14TH – DAY 49 POST OP)

"You're sure it's not overkill?"

Athena and I are in a local jewelers. I've picked out the perfect Valentine's Day gift for Edith, and my sister came along to "help."

In fairness, I'm not sure if she's is helping me or fucking with me right now, but I'm enjoying the one on one time all the same.

"It's definitely overkill, *hermanito*. But she's known you for long enough that I don't think she'll mind much. Has she mentioned Valentine's Day to you?"

Shaking my head, my stomach clenches. "We're not really... I mean..." I scratch the back of my neck with my hand. "She's not... We aren't..." I grunt. "*Mierda!*"

Athena laughs in earnest. "You've got it bad, Apollo."

There's no denying it, so I don't even bother.

"She's reluctant?"

I nod, afraid of what train wreck will come out of my mouth if I open it.

"She's afraid of losing your friendship?"

"And that I'm only interested in her like that because I saw the light at the end of the tunnel."

"Put the necklace down."

"But—"

"*Ahora, cabrón.* We need to dial it back." She pats my shoulder, and I bristle at the condescension. I know Edith and the kinds of things she likes. What does Athena really know about her?

"Don't give me that look." She wags a finger at me. "Going in hot like this will chase her away. She likes Valentine's Day, you know that for sure, *sí?*"

"It's her favorite. She's a hopeless romantic."

"But you haven't defined your relationship?"

Why does my sister always sound like she's making a transaction at the bank when talking about romance? And why does what we have need defining?

"Look." She sighs. "She's afraid she's going to lose you as her best friend by becoming your girlfriend. So be her best friend, *pendejo.*" She smacks me upside the head like it's obvious I'm a complete idiot.

But I still don't get it. Why can't I romance her while also being her best friend?

"Don't spook her, Apollo. She might be wealthy and not at all intimidated by your bank account, but she's also hurt. Recovering from the accident isn't easy for her. She needs stability. Changing gears between you both might result in being one adjustment too much for her right now. Play it safe. A diamond fucking necklace isn't playing it safe. Even if it is adorable. Don't be a *cabrón, hermanito. Confía en tu hermana mayor.*"

Trust her? I'll try. But who knew ordering three dozen pink roses, a bottle of Cristal, and a necklace was overkill? Okay, fine. It probably was, but I really wanted to make it special for Edith. "I'll send the flowers to Mamá from all of us."

Athena nods. "Good idea. What is Edith into other than dance?" She guides me out of the store, directing me to a bench right outside, then makes me sit.

"She loves crappy chick flick movies."

"So why don't you just watch movies with her?"

It's my turn to look at her like she's an idiot. "How is that different to every other night we've ever spent together?"

"Exactly."

I'm not sure I truly understand my sister's point, and I'm not sure why I'm trusting her since she's always single. But I can amend my plans and hope that my girl doesn't think it's shit that I didn't put any effort into her favorite holiday.

CHAPTER 18

Edith

When I hobble into the living room, Apollo is placing a second vase next to my "never empty" vase that's currently filled with orchids. The new container has baby pink roses in it.

"It's Valentine's Day." The words slip out of my mouth, more thought than intentional and he spins to face me.

He's wearing a hot pink T-shirt with a white circle on it, like the Dr. Seuss "Thing One" and "Thing Two" shirts, but instead of "Thing One," it says "Bitch one." He has pink-framed love-heart shaped shades on his face, black cat ears on his head and metallic pink beads dangling around his neck.

It's the most adorable thing I've seen. He's dressed as Francis, a character from my favorite Anna Kendrick film *Mr. Right.*

He holds up a finger before darting to a bag on the couch and pulling out a second shirt. He tugs it over my tank top, places matching shades on my face, completing the outfit with a red clown nose that he pops over my nose. Then he pulls two plastic fishbowl glasses out of the bag and bendy straws and stands facing me, a glass in each outstretched hand.

"What's the plan, Pollo?"

He shrugs, a blush creeping into his cheeks. "I figured it was obvious. Virgin cocktails and movies."

I cross my arms. "Which movies?"

He rolls his eyes. "Your choice, obviously. But I'm thinking *Mr. Right* since we're all dressed up."

"What about dinner?" I jerk my chin to the paper bag on the table.

"Vietnamese food. Summer rolls, pho, noodles..." Hope laces his tone. His gaze searches my face. "I can be your best friend *and* your boyfriend, Edie. It doesn't have to be one or the other."

Warmth spreads in my chest. And as we sit on the couch eating my favorite food from my favorite restaurant watching my favorite movie with my favorite person, I'm starting to hope he might be right.

CHAPTER 19

Apollo

(FEBRUARY 25TH – DAY 60 POST OP)

"You've been avoiding me."

It's true, but I won't be telling that to Papá. I've been dialing it in. Completing the bare minimum I need to for the company. Delegating where I can, playing fast and loose with my responsibilities.

I knew it would come back to bite me in the ass, and if I'm honest I got longer out of it than I expected. I don't regret my actions, but I also don't have the bandwidth for a confrontation with my father.

"No, Papá. I've been busy. I just arrived at the rink for the first of two games this weekend."

"If you weren't playing that stupid game you could dedicate more time to your role in the company."

This is true. But if I wasn't working at the company, I could dedicate more time to doing other things, with other people. I'd never say that out loud though. There's no way he'd understand.

"Have I missed something? I sent the Q3 budget forecasting to Lucy and picked the candidates for the short list for management in our plant in Atlanta."

"Leaving messages with my staff is not the same as doing your job, Apollo. You know I dislike chasing my employees."

Company before family. You'd think I'd be used to it by now, but it still stings. His aerospace business came before any of us, it was and always will be his first baby. He loves it more than all of us, Mamá included.

It's on the tip of my tongue to quit. To tell him I'm done with his job. I don't need it. I don't need him. My apartment and my car are mine outright, I have enough money of my own that I don't need him to bankroll me. Every time the thought crosses my mind, something stops me, and I fall in line.

Wouldn't it be nice not to have this anvil of responsibility hovering over my head all day every day?

"Apollo? Are you listening to me?"

"*Sí, Papá.*" Pushing through the doors of the rink, I sigh. This is the last place I want to be right now, talking to the last person in the world I want to talk to. I miss Edith. I'm worried about her. She's been pushing herself too hard, too fast, and I'm afraid she's going to hurt herself even further.

"Call Lucy and set up a meeting. There are some things we need to go through."

Bristling at his tone, I grind my teeth. The temptation to confront him, to tell him to shove his business, his legacy, up his ass is overwhelming. But I do as I always do, play the part of the dutiful, loyal son, working to take over his *pendejo* of a cheat and swindling father's business. Even if I'd rather chew glass.

The Minnesota Snow Pirates are out for blood. We're in the second period, my limbs are like lead, sweat pours down my face, and I don't remember a game where I've had to work this hard just to stay upright.

The ref missed a boarding call on Raffi, who took matters into his own hands, bagging himself a time out in the box. Less than a minute later, Scott took a slashing penalty, and landed us on a 5-on-3 penalty kill. It's fucking brutal.

Legs burning, it's as though I'm trudging through sand. Hockey has always come as easily to me as breathing, but since the accident, it's been... challenging. I don't know how to get my fire back, but I want to.

Artemis passes to Tate at the left point who gives it to me. I sail it toward the Minnesota net, and while their goalie Séb gets a piece of it, it makes it past him. The crowd erupts, my teammates rush me, and that familiar flicker of pride sparks in my chest.

"Get out of your fucking head, *hermano*." As though reading my mind, Artemis bumps my arm. "Be here, now. Enjoy the game." He says it as though it's that simple.

Nodding, I head to the bench for our high-five celebrations with the rest of the team before circling back for the next face off.

We win the face off, and Raffi, out of the penalty box, drop-passes it to me. I move the puck point to point to Jackson Gilbert who takes a couple of long strides, puts his head down, and lets it fly.

From Séb's point of view, the puck must look like a missile flying straight at him. It went off the outside of his left pad and under his stick.

The more we score, the angrier the Snow Pirates get. But I'll be damned if I let them beat us in our own fucking barn. If they want the "W," they're going to have to work harder than this.

Scott blocks a clearing pass, setting Myers up in the slot. The crowd screams at him to shoot, but he fakes Séb out of the crease, and passes it to me for the finish. He points at me with his glove when the lamp lights, and I shake my head.

"You could have scored that."

Tate shrugs like it's no big deal. "Maybe I thought you needed the win."

Warmth engulfs me at my team rallying around me. They've obviously noticed my head isn't where it's supposed to be lately. And instead of making me feel like shit about it, they're coaxing me back.

By the time the final buzzer sounds, the place is electric. Tomorrow night's game against the Snow Pirates is going to be interesting to say the least. No one likes having their asses handed to them but for now, we're relishing the win. It feels pretty fucking good, and there's only one person I want to share it with.

CHAPTER 20

Edith

(MARCH 1ST – DAY 64 POST OP)

My hands shake as I sit in the waiting room of my physical therapist. It's been a long and grueling seven weeks, but I'm ready to get evaluated and start my road to recovery. I only have a few weeks to get audition ready, which is why I'm here early.

My PT said twelve weeks post op is the usual timeline for starting physical therapy, but he reluctantly agreed to see me today. Must have been the three thousand calls I made. I'm nothing if not persistent. And I need to step out in front of that panel in a few weeks.

I've spent every day working on strengthening my body in whatever ways I've been able. My casts came off a few days ago, and while it's freeing, and a huge relief, my limbs are also fragile, shaky, and not at all like my own.

I hate it.

But I have one last shot to audition this year. It has to be my last year. I'm almost too old. The thought of having sixteen-year-olds dance circles around me at the next audition makes me want to vomit.

My motivation has never been higher. I've lost so much of

the progress I made at my last intensive, I've missed so much class, I need to get back. Like I keep reminding Apollo, training doesn't last if you don't maintain it.

He offered to come with me today, but I made him go to school instead. He's already made so many sacrifices for me over the past couple months that I'm not prepared to let anything else slide because of this stupid injury.

We're closing in on playoff time—his team needs him, and he needs to shine. He's fully match fit and isn't missing a single beat out on the ice. The news reports expect there's going to be the hockey equivalent of a bidding war for him, and I've never been prouder. But I'm also not going to let me, or us, or my recovery take his focus away from where it needs to be.

"Edith Fisher?"

I nod in the direction of the guy who called my name.

In the months I haven't been training, my turns would be off, my balance gone, my feet getting soft... I've lost the calluses on my feet.

It's a travesty across the board. I've let myself cry and wallow for two months. Now it's time to get my shit together, knuckle down, and get back on the stage.

Pushing myself to get back to class might not have been my best idea to date. I thought I was fine. I thought I knew my limits, that I was getting stronger, but something's going on in my ankle, and I'm definitely not fine.

I was allowed to take barre. No relevés, or balancing on demi pointe on one foot. But I was back. Sort of. I was in the studio at least, doing the bare minimum. I was chafing so bad to get my pointe shoes back on, I couldn't fight the lure. Once they slid onto my feet, something felt wrong.

I've fought the sinking dread in my stomach for a few days, but I'm sitting in my orthopedic surgeon's office waiting to get called for the results of my latest x-ray.

PT said it was too soon.

Ortho said it was too soon.

Apollo said it was too soon.

I really, *really* don't want x-rays to agree with all of them. Because while he'd never come right out and say it, "I told you so" would hang heavily between us.

I'm called back, follow my ortho to his office, and take a seat, my palms sweaty as I await my fate.

"It's not good, Edith."

Going back to dancing before an injury is healed and ending up reinjured is super common in my world, and from the grave lines on his forehead, and the sadness in his eyes, I've become a statistic.

"I know you wanted to get back to peak fitness by the end of the month for your audition, but..." He swallows, time hangs heavily, the weight of his tone suspended in the air between us. "I'm sorry, Edith. But we're going to need to take you in for another surgery."

My stomach plummets. My ears pop. I blink frantically trying to clear the debris from the bomb he's just dropped on me. His lips continue to move, but I only hear every few words, "floating tibial piece..." "not healing correctly..." "metal plates."

He can't be serious. He can't be telling me I need hardware in my ankle. So I pushed myself a little harder than I should have. A bad sprain, perhaps. But another whole surgery?

This has to be a sick joke, a twisted exaggeration of the truth to teach me a valuable lesson about letting my body rest and heal. Tears blur my vision as my whole body shakes. I'm not going to make my audition. I'm not going to get back to class any time soon.

As he goes through surgical options with me, my dancing career slips through my fingers like grains of sand. Being careless with my recovery has clearly come back to bite me in the ass.

If I've missed my chance at auditions this year, what are my options now? Do I try to find a college summer intensive for next year? Is there someone who does coaching online that I can hire? Maybe Progressing Ballet Technique, or a retired dancer from the long list I stalk on socials.

Could I teach? If I want to teach how do I get started?

Should I do a certification? ABT's Teacher Certification would be the obvious choice for me. Do I need to change majors? Take a leave of absence from school? What major would I even change to?

So many questions. And not many answers.

Fuck.

Have I really ruined any chance of getting back into a pair of pointe shoes?

CHAPTER 21
Apollo
(MARCH 20TH – DAY 83 POST OP)

Every goal is scored because someone makes a mistake. Not even our three-on-one breakaway was enough to even the game last night against the Cyclones.

Losses suck, and I miss my girl.

With our last four games at home, Edith and I have started to make some real progress. Playing chess and watching movies between away games, eating meals together, and simply hanging out and enjoying each other's company. On a foundational level, everything has changed between us, but I'm doing my level best to ensure that everything also stays the same. At least for now.

No sudden movements, like Athena said. Don't spook her. It seems to have been working.

But she's been distant over the past week or so. Avoiding me, even. While I thought it was because she's not going to make her audition deadline at the end of the month, I'm starting to wonder if it's because she's coming out the other side of her injury, and she's realizing she doesn't want me.

The curdling in my stomach is worse than when the final

buzzer sounded in the Kansas City Cyclones arena and their home crowd erupted at our defeat.

I need to talk to Edith.

Something isn't right from the minute I walk into her apartment.

There's an eerie quiet, a sterile smell that takes me back to when she was first brought home from the hospital. She's not on the couch watching TV, and the kitchen is empty, save for a small pile of dishes from the night before in the sink. It's early, but she's always been a frustratingly chipper morning person.

I peek into Edith's room. She's lying on the bed out cold. Movement in my periphery draws my attention to Penelope sitting in a chair next to Edith, quietly turning the pages of her book.

Edith's leg is propped up on pillows, and it's then the details hit me. Fresh cast. Fresh hospital band around her wrist. Fuck. All signs point to something I can't process.

Penelope sees me lingering in the doorway and leaps from her seat, coming out to meet me in the hallway. "It's not what you think." Her whispered tones contrast the bubbling anger searing my veins.

I'm shaking. My chest is tight, my breath thin and ragged. "Did my girlfriend have another surgery behind my back?"

Penelope goes bright red. "Okay, it's exactly what you think. But she had her reasons."

Her fucking reasons are bullshit. She didn't want me to leave my team, to stay by her side and hold her hand because of my responsibility to my teammates, and my fucking future in the NHL.

Spearing my hair with my fingers, I pace back and forth like a caged animal in front of Pen. She's pale, watching me with caution as I mutter to myself, trying to rationalize Edith's behavior.

She doesn't want me to fuck up my career, I get it. But keeping this from me. This... this is big. I can't believe she didn't give me the choice to be by her side when she needed me.

She needed me. Fuck. I can't make this all about me, no matter how tempting it might be. She's had another surgery, which means her foot didn't heal right the first time. Spinning to face Pen, sympathy flickers across her face as she gives me a sad nod.

"They put pins in her foot. It's... not good Apollo." She shakes her head. "She's going to have to learn to walk again. Dancing... I don't know. It was a stretch before. Now..." She reaches out and pats my bicep. "She thought about telling you, made me promise not to though. She knew you'd skip the game if you knew she was going back in again."

Damn fucking straight.

"She didn't want you to get in trouble with your team." She winces. "Or with your dad. She's day two post op."

"I don't need her to be a fucking martyr. I need her to let me love her."

Penelope nods again. "I know. I tried to tell her you needed to be here for her as much as she needed you to be here, but she wouldn't hear of it." She smiles. "Downside of being in love with a fellow athlete I guess. She understands what it takes to excel at what you do."

"Maybe I don't want to fucking excel. Maybe I wanted to be by her goddamn side."

"Don't be so dramatic, Pollo." Edith's sleepy voice washes over me, calming some of the ache. "And you can't be mad at me. I'm broken and in pain." She grunts.

Penelope and I go back into Edith's room, she's trying to sit up. Rushing to help her, I almost trip over a duffle bag on the floor. Penelope leaves me to get Edith sitting upright, and when she returns a few minutes later with a granola bar, meds, and some water, we're still sitting in silence, staring at each other.

"You need to eat more than that."

"I'm nauseous."

"That's only going to get worse when you take meds on an empty stomach." My words are ground out through clenched teeth. I'm trying hard not to be angry, but I'm being accosted by strong emotions making it hard to be rational right now.

"Should I stay, or...?" Penelope hooks a thumb over her shoulder.

"I'll be okay, thanks, Pen." Edith gives a reassuring smile to her friend, but Pen nails me with a hard stare.

"I'm good." I'm not at all good, but I need to be, for Edith.

When Penelope leaves, Edith gives me a playful slap. "You need to calm down, Pollo."

"If I'd gone and had surgery behind your back, you'd be pretty damn pissed off, too, Edie. What the fuck were you thinking?"

She grimaces as she reaches for the bottle of water on the bedside table. "I was thinking that you needed to keep your head in the game. We both don't need to be taken out by this stupid injury of mine. You have goals, and dreams, and I'm not letting you set them aside because of some goddamn broken bones that aren't even your broken bones."

She can't open the bottle of water, so I take it from her and twist open the top. A growl rumbles in my chest. "Princesa—"

"No, Apollo! Don't." Tears stream down her face as she shakes her head. "Your dreams matter, even if mine are in tatters."

I don't tell her that nothing matters, not hockey, not my father's company, not the world outside this building.

"It's okay. I've got you, Edie. It's all going to be okay." I put the water back down and pull her against me, holding her while she cries.

I fix her some real food, sitting with her while she eats, and about thirty minutes after she takes her meds she passes out on my chest.

My phone vibrates in my pocket.

Athena: 911. We're on our way.

Fucking perfect.

~

"We need to talk."

I want to talk, just not to my siblings. But Athena called a family meeting. We don't run from a 911 regardless of who sounds the alarm. It's not "someone died" level of importance, that's a code black, but it means drop what you're doing and assemble.

Considering I did almost die, if this isn't life-or-death important, we should rethink our system a little.

Since we were kids, it hasn't been something we can shirk out of. So Ares, Athena, Artemis and I are sitting around my dining room table while Edith sleeps across the hall, snuggled up to Bacon who Ares brought back for another visit.

"The words 'we need to talk' chill men to the bone, Hen. I'm glad we're not dating." My muscles ache, I'm exhausted, and the only person I want to see right now is Edith. Creepy as it sounds, I want to watch her sleep, to be there, a silent strength lending her whatever energy I can while she heals.

I'm going to be away a lot over the next couple weeks. But she refuses to let me take time off from the team, and insists I need to keep up my obligations. It's hard when all I want to do is hold her until she's better.

Being in love with your best friend is exhausting. Especially when they refuse to accept that they love you back. I think she's finally come around to the fact that I love her as more than a brother-slash-best friend, but she's still fighting an inner battle I can't help her with.

No one around the table laughs at the joke I almost forgot I made. In fact, no one even cracks a smile. Somber faces stare back at me as I survey my siblings.

"What is it?" I don't have the energy for any more drama, but from the pained expressions on my siblings' faces, I'm about to get handed a shit storm.

Ares doesn't meet my eyes. He's picking at invisible lint on his pants. Artemis picks up one of the four glasses anything iced water in the middle of the table and moves it so it's in front of him. "There's something we need to tell you."

"Okay?" Is someone sick? Is it Mamá or Papá? It's the only thing I can think of that might bring them all around the table with such a heavy air hanging over them. "Is Abuelita okay?" I've always believed she'd outlive all of us, but maybe—

"Papá cheated on Mamá." Athena shifts in her seat.

It's like she punched me in the stomach. All the oxygen in my body dissipates at once, leaving a tight pain in my chest. My head snaps between my brothers and sister, searching for the punchline, or any sign of humor. But there is none.

"What?"

She reaches across the table and takes my hand. "We have at least three half-brothers, *hermano*."

"*Mierda*." It's as though someone has blasted a horn in my ear. I can hear what she's saying but she sounds so far away, her voice is quiet and hard to hear.

"Our Papá cheated on Mamá. And we have half-brothers." I'm parroting her words back more for myself than anything else. No one else at the table is outwardly surprised, which tells me they've all known for a while.

"You knew?" My question is directed at Artemis. We're twins and tell each other damn near everything. Everything, that is, except for this. "How long?"

"Don't be pissy with him. We decided it was best not to tell you because of the accident and Edith." Ares finally lifts his head and his eyes are red-rimmed.

They have no idea she had another surgery. They thought they were being kind waiting to drop this on me, but their timing is almost comical. My chest is being sucked into a vacuum, pressure building up inside my body. My brain is racing, frantically trying to come up with something, anything to refute their claims. But my heart knows they aren't lying. It's not some cruel joke.

"At the hospital." I turn to Athena. "You said I didn't need to know something then, right?"

That whole night is a little fuzzy, but I recall the heavy looks Ares and Athena shared. She nods. "We'd planned to tell you, but you really didn't need to hear all of this that night."

"You had enough on your plate, and we didn't want to add to it. Now that Edith is out the other side and well on her way to recovery, well, you have a right to know." Ares's anger is thinly veiled. His muscles are tight, and his fists are clenched on his thighs. He looks more like Mamá every passing day.

My stomach sinks. Mamá. "Did you talk to Mamá?"

Three heads shake.

"We didn't do anything. We haven't reached out to the boys, we haven't spoken to our parents. Nothing. We wanted you to know before we did anything." Athena sounds like she's deciding what to have for lunch, not telling me our father is a cheating *cabrón*. But I appreciate they didn't act without bringing me in first.

"At least three half-brothers?"

She nods. "A guy called Mathias found me a while back, we've been in touch a little for a few months. Thiago found Ares on campus one day. I hired a PI to do some digging, and that's how we found Alejandro."

My stomach churns so hard I might puke on my dining room table. What the fuck am I supposed to do with this information? I lean forward, forcing air into my body with a deep inhale. Raking my hands through my hair trying to make sense of what I'm hearing.

Cold, heart-stopping dread crashes into me and my body snaps upright. "Did he force himself on those women?" It's out of left field but for some reason it's where my mind goes. Papá is a lothario, sure, but a rapist? Just because I can't see it, doesn't mean it's not possible.

Ares bolts up as though the thought hadn't occurred to him.

Athena moves her chair closer to me, placing her hand on my shoulder. "We don't know. I want to believe it was consensual, but we have no information, *hermano*."

My gut is so heavy, I'm afraid it's going to fall out of my body. For a beat I think she's trembling, until I realize it's me.

Does he talk to them? Or see them regularly? Or does he act as though they don't exist? Acid scratches the back of my throat. If he raped those women... *Puta madre*. I slam my fist on the table, making the water in the barely touched glasses slosh over the rims.

Athena pulls me to her, closing her arms around me as I fall apart. I may not have wanted to take over the family business, but the man was kind of my fucking hero. The only one I had. I was proud to work for his thriving empire, for our family name, to be a well-respected family above reproach. He has marred all of us by his actions.

It's like the stitching holding me together has come loose.

Between this escalation in family drama and the unexpected second surgery my girlfriend went through alone, Athena's grasp is the only thing keeping me from being completely undone.

I don't know how long we sit there, my brothers silent, Athena holding me, and I wish I could say I feel better when I finally pull back from my sister's embrace.

"Edith had another surgery while we were gone." My voice is raw, thick grief. Athena gasps while Artemis groans.

"No. *Carajo*! Is she okay?" Athena grips both my shoulders, forcing me to look at her.

Shaking my head I fight the sob building in my chest. "She's not. They put metal in her foot. I don't think she's going to dance again, Hen. I really, really don't. And she won't let me take time out from playing hockey."

"All that's left is the Frozen Four. A couple more weeks and you can spend the summer helping her rehab." Artemis, ever the voice of reason.

I nod. Rationally speaking I know this. But the first two weeks post-surgery were the hardest for her last time and our next three games are all away. I don't want to leave her. I don't want to fucking leave her.

As if she can read my mind, Athena speaks up. "I'll sit with her. Whatever you need. We're all here for you. Fuck. I'm sorry we dropped this on you. We thought she was home and dry."

"So did I. I went to see her this morning, and she's starting over, ground zero. New surgery, new cast, new timeline. Fuck! I could have been with her."

Ares shakes his head. "She knew you'd get into shit if you missed all our extra training sessions this week, *cabrón*. She was protecting you."

I don't need lessons on Edith from my kid brother, but I don't have it in me to retaliate. I'm spent.

"What about Papá?" Artemis's hard stare makes me shift in my seat.

"He called. He's pissed that I've been absent. I almost quit."

Athena strokes my back. "If that's what you need to do, he'll get over it." Gotta give it to her, she's almost convincing. "We need to come up with a plan for how to deal with his indiscretions, and what we're going to do about our half siblings. But that can wait, right now our priority is getting you through the Frozen Four and get Edith back on her feet. Okay?"

"Okay."

My phone vibrates on the table. Papá's name lights up the screen. *El Diablo* himself.

How the hell am I supposed to talk to him, to work with him, knowing what I know? I let the call go to voicemail before playing Papá's message for everyone.

He's pissed as fuck. He somehow found out I've been using his plane to travel back and forth to see Edith. Misusing business resources. Head not in the office, nor on the ice since the accident—no mention of my studies. No leeway, no understanding, "in our life this is what we do," no time for superficial injuries, no time for distractions, pull your shit together, or else.

Today couldn't get much worse. I'm ready for a fucking nap.

"Apollo?" Edith's tired voice carries across the hallway. I left both doors open so I could hear if she needed me. She calls my name again.

It's time to get my game face on and go comfort my girl.

CHAPTER 22

Edith

Something's wrong with Apollo, and I have no idea what it is. He's keeping something from me, but I've known him for long enough to know that things aren't right. Even when I'm high on pain meds.

He's grunting at a stack of paperwork on my dining room table, periodically running his hand through his glossy dark hair, and muttering strings of swear words under his breath. Stress emanates from him in uncomfortable waves, leaving an almost acerbic taste in the air.

Is he keeping it from me because he thinks I can't handle whatever he's going through? Or am I the thing that's stressing him out so much he looks like he hasn't slept in a week?

"Pollo?"

His tongue snakes out the corner of his mouth, his brow furrowed in deep concentration. He doesn't react to my voice. That in itself is unusual. He's been tuned into my every pained breath, grunt, wince and gasp since I got home from the hospital. Whatever is going on with him, I don't think it's me.

At least I hope not.

"Apollo?"

His head snaps up, eyes glassy and tired. *"Sí, princesa?"*

Patting the couch next to me, I wave for him to join me. His hesitation wouldn't be noticed by many, but I don't miss the extra fraction of a beat before he puts down his pen. When his body drops onto the couch next to me, I try to move to him, but everything hurts. Looping his arms around me as though I weigh nothing, he pulls me to him, holding me against him.

"Estás bien?"

"I'm okay." I search his face. "But I don't think you are."

He sighs. A loud cheer erupts from his apartment, and he rolls his eyes.

"Is your family over there?"

He nods. "They came over earlier for a family meeting."

"And they're staying until you're done with me?"

He shrugs. I'm not sure how I feel about that. It's nice they're waiting around for him to be free. I love that he's working next to me while I read my book, but we could really all be doing something together.

"What is it, Apollo? Talk to me."

"You have enough on your plate right now, Edie. I don't want to burden you." He's taken to calling me Edie a lot more since the accident. It's become one of my favorite things. So full of affection.

But this time when he says it, I don't know whether to slap him, punch him, or pinch him, but I'm tempted to do all three. "We're best friends. Helping each other with overloaded plates is our superpower. Keeping shit from each other because we have a lot going on isn't what we do, Pollo. And what's more, you know that."

His face softens. "I'm processing." His words take the

fight out of me. Not being ready to share is way different than keeping something from me.

I cup his face, turning him toward me before planting a quick kiss on his lips. His shoulders sag, as though a little of his tension has melted away.

"Artemis!" I yell his brother's name so loudly that everyone in the building probably heard me.

Apollo jams his finger in his ear as though I deafened him, and he's checking that his ears still work. Over his shoulder, Artemis and Ares burst into the apartment, eyes wide, half confused, half amused.

"What's wrong?" Artemis addresses Apollo, but I cover Pollo's head with a throw pillow from the couch.

"What are you guys playing over there?"

Ares's eyes light up as Athena joins them in the doorway. "You want to play something?"

I nod, as Apollo shrugs off the cushion still pressed against his head.

"He's grumpy and overworked." I gesture to the stack of papers on the table. "And I'm so freakin' bored and sick of hearing myself complain."

I hate being needy and pathetic, so my face burns as I silently implore Athena not to laugh or reject me. Artemis disappears for a moment, returning with a chair, Athena collects Apollo's work from the table, pausing to look over the pages he'd been staring at in distress. "I can help you with this, *hermanito*. No stress."

Apollo nods but remains quiet. Artemis tucks the extra chair around my table, but it occurs to me we now have more chairs than people.

"What's that for?" I gesture to the seat.

He points at my leg. "You can't play anything if your leg isn't elevated, Edith."

I almost laugh at how much like Apollo he can be. "You're not the boss of me." I wag my finger with a grin.

"We need something low energy. What games do you have?"

Apollo stands up, indicating where my game stash lives. "She has Five Crowns in that drawer. That'll work. We all know how to play, it takes about an hour for a full game, it doesn't need any physical energy, and Ares can't cheat."

The sibling in question covers his heart. "I would never." He winks at me before picking a chair and sitting. Then bounding to his feet like he forgot something.

Apollo hauls me off the couch, then carries me to a seat at the table. When I move to put my leg on the seat beside me, he stops me. He sits down, then guides my leg onto his lap instead, stroking the skin between my cast and my shorts.

Mortification prickles over my flesh. "Stop." His thumb stops moving, and everyone's attention lands heavily on me.

"I haven't shaved." My words are quietly squeezed out between gritted teeth.

His hand moves again. "I don't give a shit where you've got hair."

My face burns even hotter. Oh my god.

Ares points at Apollo. "You know he waxes his back right? He's like fucking King Kong when he misses a waxing. And Art doesn't even bother with the wax." He tugs down the neck of Artemis's t-shirt as though he's trying to show me his brother's hairy back.

I'm still giggling when Athena returns to the table with the card game and takes her seat. "I get it, Edith. I'd be the same. But considering all you've been through lately, a little leg hair isn't going to deter my brother from showing you affection. He's a goner for you."

Apollo covers his forehead with his palm, but doesn't say

anything. The pink tinge to his cheeks is adorable, though. I've always enjoyed spending time with his siblings. None of this playful banter is new to me. The fact that my fledgling relationship with their brother is the subject of their humor is new.

It's clear he's told them about his feelings for me. None of them are visibly surprised that he's touching me, no one batted an eye that I was in his arms on the couch when they walked in. No one is ribbing him for having a crush on his best friend, or making 'oooooooohhhhoooo' noises or singing about us kissing in a tree.

That warms something inside me, but it also sparks a seed of anxiety in my chest. Would they still talk to me if everything between Apollo and me were to fall apart?

I bat away that thought, and take in his family. Artemis has gotten us all drinks from the kitchen. Ares has opened a giant bag of Lays and retrieved a couple of jars of dip from Apollo's fridge. Athena wrote our names down on a notebook and is shuffling cards.

This is so fucking nice. Getting together with all of his siblings at once is not something we do often, but I'm hoping that will change. There's a coziness here. Apollo has relaxed enough that his shoulders have stopped hugging his ears. His family is so important to him, but it's clear from how they are settling into my space right now that they know I am important to him, too.

As his best friend they knew I was significant, but as his girlfriend... I don't know. It feels like I might be becoming important to them, too.

Athena hands me the first card of the deal. "You should probably know that our dad is a cheating fucker, and we've recently discovered that we have half-siblings."

No one breathes, no one moves, the air grows so thick and

stifling I can't breathe. Apollo's hand stops moving on my hairy leg, and his face falls like he might break at her words.

My beautiful prince of darkness has been here for me for months. And from the pain etched on his face, it's he who needs me now.

CHAPTER 23

Apollo

My siblings won't go the fuck away and leave me the fuck alone. They've decided to crash for the night at my place across the hall. They seem to think news of my father's indiscretions might drive me to, I dunno, drive over and punch him or something.

I can't deny that it's tempting.

Ironically, I'm not even the hot-head of the group, nor the enforcer. When I get into fights on the ice people think it's hilarious. I generally leave life's throw-downs to my brothers. How Ares can even move with those big pads strapped to his legs, let alone fight... anyway, it's not my jam. As much as I can be a petty fucker, I'm a lover, not a fighter.

There's a nagging tug in my chest to confront Papá, though. But that would mean actually talking to him. For all his bullshit about *family first*... my stomach lurches. Just how big is his fucking family, anyway?

The wheels in my head spin so fast I can barely keep up. His betrayal of Mamá sours in my gut. Does she know? Has she met the other women? The other children?

Fuck. Raking my hands through my hair, I shudder. What

am I supposed to do with this information? How am I supposed to reconcile the father we know, with this... this... *pendejo*?

A feather-light touch glides up my jaw, bringing me back to sitting on the couch with my girl. Her face is scrunched up as she regards me, head tilted, lips downturned, grey eyes swimming with concern.

Golden strands from her ponytail have fallen loose, framing her face, in the light, the smattering of freckles across her nose and cheeks are more pronounced. They're one of my favorite things about her.

"Penny for your thoughts?" Her voice is soft, like she's been watching me in silence for a while.

I can't let her into my head right now. No matter what she says about sharing my burden, she has enough on her plate. And if turnabout is fair play, then she's kept some things of her own to protect me lately. What would I even say? My father is a *cabrón*? From working with him, I knew he was an asshole in business. And even growing up, he wasn't the warmest of fathers to any of us—except Athena—but he's dickish to her in other ways.

I had no idea how good an actor he was, until my siblings told me the truth about his secret life of getting multiple women knocked up. He looks at Mamá like she hung the fucking moon. Does he look at those other women the same way?

My brothers and I are no saints, but we've never cheated. If Ares had ever been in a committed relationship before Eloise, he'd have cheated, but monogamy has always been important to us. It doesn't take a therapist to deduce that was because of the strong marriage between our parents.

Except it wasn't strong, was it? How can anything be strong if the foundations are rotten?

"Pollo?"

I'm back in my thoughts. Lost in the cycle of cheating and betrayal. "I'm sorry, *princesa*." I cup her face, drawing a sigh from her as her eyes flicker closed for a beat.

"What can I do?" Her voice is so pained it almost shatters my heart. "Tell me how I can help."

"Nothing, *mi amor*. You can't. I need to process it all and figure out a way through." I just hope that I can.

CHAPTER 24

Edith

I don't accept that.

When Apollo tells me there's nothing I can do, sure, my stomach swoops like it's going to hit the deck, but I. Don't. Accept. That. There's always something that can be done. Always.

He's been my rock, not only for the past few months since the crash, but since forever. I refuse to let his asshole father shit on everything Apollo is working so hard to build. I refuse to let him be torn down by some douche nozzle who doesn't deserve his time.

If I wasn't all casted up, I'd throw my leg over him and grind on him until he forgot not only his family woes, but damn near everything else, too. It's tempting, but that vase on the coffee table in front of us would absolutely be a victim if I tried to swing my leg anywhere. This sucker is heavier than it looks, even though they claimed at the hospital that it was lightweight. I can't fucking wait to get my boot in a few weeks.

Despite my physical limitations, maybe I can still bring him some pleasure, without the pelvic bump and grind. My arm might be weak now that the cast is off, but that doesn't mean I can't give him a hand job.

He's in low riding grey sweatpants. That's invitation by itself. Am I salivating? I'm definitely salivating.

Waves of tension and discomfort radiate from him as he tips his head back against the couch. He's stressed about his father, about work, about the playoffs, about me. If he goes onto the ice with so much crap in his head tomorrow he's going to make mistakes, and then he'll sink even lower.

I've seen him depressed a couple times over the years, watched him battle with his innermost demons. It's gotten dark once or twice. One time I had to physically shove his ass in the shower to get the funk off, while I tidied his filthy apartment and made him some food.

He generally rebounds, but as someone who likes to be in control of just about everything in his life, this is working on him in all the wrong ways.

Leaning over, I cup his cock through his sweats, enjoying the low hiss he lets out at my touch. If my panties weren't already damp, they would be now. Covering my hand with his, he shakes his head, opening his eyes. "You don't have to do that, Edie."

That makes me smile. In all our years of friendship, he has never made me do anything I didn't want to. And right now, I want to make him feel good, the way he makes me feel good with such ease it's as though he was born to take care of me. I want to take away some of his stress, even for a few short minutes.

Sliding my hand under the band of his pants, I curl my fingers around his already hardening dick and free it from beneath the fabric. "I want to. Please?" My hand is already moving, gliding from the base to the tip and back down.

He grunts, head dropping back again, chest rising and falling faster with each breath he sucks in. There's a powerful rush surging through my veins that my prince of darkness is submitting to me and letting me touch him.

I've loved this man since I was little, know everything about him. He has a soggy food phobia that means he keeps anything wet or potentially invasive on his plate separated. He broke his arm once when he was little, trying to build a tree-house for his big sister. He stood up for me against Billy Taylor once when he picked on me for my freckles and button nose. No one ever picked on me again.

In all our years of friendship, I never thought I'd know what his dick felt like, but it's in my hand, and the weirdness I expect to feel from crossing this line again, doesn't come.

I'm not sure what I expected to find in his pants, but he has a regular dick. It's a little long, but not particularly thick. No piercings, no weird dick tattoos, no excessive curvature, no herculean monster dick that won't fit in any orifice without careful planning and extreme preparation. Apollo de la Peña's peen is actually kind of... nice. As far as dicks can be nice anyway. And hard. So fucking hard.

Another lazy pump pulls a groan from him. His shoulders are still knotted tight against his ears, his thighs are tense, and stress lines cover his beautiful pale face. My thumb sweeps across the bead of precum glistening on the tip. Tightening my grip, I drag my hand along his length twice more, a little quicker.

He mutters something in Spanish, too quick for me to catch, but remains unmoving. With each movement of my hand, he starts to unwind. His hands move from being balled up fists by his thighs to stretched out across the back of the couch, giving me more space to work.

He no longer looks like he might want to commit murder. His features soften, his face serene, and his jaw no longer flexes from being clenched.

Another tiny bead of precum appears at the tip of his dick,

and I can't help myself. Shifting so I can give him head hurts like fuck, but I'm not letting this fucking cast, or this goddamn broken leg stop me from tasting him.

Then I lose my balance and face-plant into his crotch. A smile flits across his mouth before he rolls his lips between his teeth.

"Don't. Say. Anything."

He shrugs. "Didn't see a thing. But if I had, I'd comment on the fact that no one has ever taken a nosedive onto my cock before. You shoulda made airplane noises."

If I wasn't already sweating at the exertion of trying to sprawl myself out across the sofa so I could suck his dick, I'd smack him. But I'm in a good position, and I'm not risking that.

When my tongue finally meets the tip, a shiver rolls through his muscles. His breathing picks up again as I lap up the salty bead of liquid with a hum of satisfaction.

"Edith." My name is a strained word, but he still doesn't move.

"Just enjoy it, Apollo." As I skim my other hand up his chest to settle him, a flicker of heat laps low in my belly. Man, this guy is ripped. His muscles have muscles. The ridges and planes of his body are already familiar under my fingers, but I'm exploring them in a new light. Though I want to take my time to investigate every single ab and inch of skin under his t-shirt, his need for release is almost tangible in the air.

Sucking him all the way to the back of my throat, I hum again. He's slightly too long to fit, and I'm not prepared to get messy deep-throating him on our first try. I wanna suck his cock like a princess. Clamping my hand around his base, I start with a slow bob, dragging my tongue along his shaft as I explore his length.

When I swirl around his tip then flick the head before taking him to the back of my throat again, he growls. It's the most primal, terrifying, and erotic thing I've ever heard. It's a low rumble that travels through my whole body.

Hollowing out my cheeks, I suck hard, picking up the pace. Is he a ball-squeezing kind of guy? Guess we'll find out. I cradle his balls in my palm and gently squeeze.

Fingers tease their way into my hair as his hand travels to the back of my head. I guess he's reached the end of his allotted window for someone else to take control, and he's ready to steer the ship.

It's tempting to push back, to enforce restraint, to snatch control from him and make him wait. But he needs this. He needs the release, the endorphins. His body is taut as he fucks my mouth, grunting with each jut of his hips.

As I grip his balls again, his thrusts stutter, his rhythm stumbling over another growl. Huh. My prince of darkness likes having his balls played with after all.

Things I never thought I'd learn about my best friend.

Tears prick behind my flickering eyelids as his cock hits the back of my throat over and over at speed.

"Edith?" The question comes out on a grunt. "Are you okay?"

The fact that he has the mental capacity to ask me that question means I'm not doing a good enough job at taking his mind off things. I want him to be so gone he can't form words, so out of it that his legs tremble and his hands shake.

I flex my hand around his sac again, and suck harder, faster, deeper, determined to make him lose his fucking mind.

I might not be his first blow job, but I'm sure as hell going to make it the best he's ever had.

Humming around his cock seems to shift gears, and his hips buck sporadically instead of in a rhythmic pattern. He curls his fingers into my hair, he wraps it around his hand, the bite of pain making me moan around him.

"Fuck, Edith."

My put together hockey player is losing control, and it's so fucking enthralling that I want to push him even further, see how much I can make him fall apart.

"Edith, I'm going to come."

I cover his half-open mouth with my hand, signaling him to shut the fuck up and enjoy the ride.

It's a matter of seconds before warm jets of salty cum spray into my mouth as he roars through his release.

I did that.

My guy is a feral animal consumed by lust and need, and I made him fall apart with my mouth and hand. Feels pretty good.

His entire body softens as the last trickle of cum meets my tongue. Swallowing every drop, I stroke the inside of his thigh to reassure him I'm okay while he settles. I rest my head on his lap, and his fingers trace the side of my face as we both catch our breath.

Part of me still waits for the ick to set in. The guilt of stepping over that line with my best friend. But the rest of me preens and purrs like a fucking cat knowing that this soft and sated Apollo is because of me. I can't wait to do it all over again, to get rid of this fucking cast, to claim him as mine.

Mine.

The more I look back over our time together, the furtive touches, the tenderness and care, the easygoing nature of our friendship, it's becoming more and more apparent we've been in a relationship this whole time, just without the romance and sexy times.

Now we've cracked that door open, things feel complete, right, and the lump of emotion in my throat reminds me that I've spent the past few years searching for the perfect partner only to realize he's been here all along.

CHAPTER 25

Apollo

It's the Frozen Four quarter finals against Massachusetts. If we win tonight, we play Penn State in the semis in two days, and for the first time in a long time, we might actually have a chance at beating those fuckers.

My fire is back.

Maybe it's 'cause my girl sucked every ounce of negative energy from my dick like it was a fucking straw last night. If we win, she and I may need to discuss pre-game blow jobs going forward. Like, forevermore. Somehow I think she'd be down for that. My fierce little flame definitely enjoyed making my eyes roll back in my head.

She didn't push for me to talk, she didn't guilt me into sharing, she accepted that I wasn't ready... and then gave the best head I've ever had in my whole fucking life.

I'm not admitting to the rest of the guys that my girl's tongue is the reason I've plucked my head out of my ass, but she definitely gave me a beat of clarity, repose, then subjected me to murder documentaries. She's spending too much time with Eloise. Or Penelope. Or both. But she's happier and that's all I care about.

I'm reluctant to acknowledge it in case I jinx it, but we're halfway through the second period of this game and everything feels *right*. The crowd is in full voice. Playoff hockey is my favorite kind of hockey. There's something about the balance between speed and gritty, hard-hitting plays, and the crackle of excited anticipation in the stands.

Scott passes the puck through to center ice, Justin taps it to the outside where I pick it up and take the quick shot. Raffi's rebound attempt is wide of the target. Massachusetts defense collectively jabs a little poke check, but they don't get a shot away.

Another shot from Raffi, another rebound, off the back of the net. I thought it was in, so did the fans, so did Raffi and Justin, but their goalie got enough of it to stop it. *Puta*.

My legs burn, sweat's trickling down my temples and into my ass crack, and all I can think of is scoring for *mi princesa*.

She's watching at home, not ready to venture into the crowds with her cast, and it's driving her up the walls. She's been to damn near every hockey game since I learned to skate. Wearing my number and cheering my name.

Fuck.

She wears my number.

In a split second that takes on a whole new meaning, and I'm suddenly fighting a boner the whole way to the bench.

It might not be every hockey player's fantasy to fuck a woman in their jersey, but it sure as hell is mine. It's not something I've done before, but I make a mental note to tell her that at some point, I'm fucking her senseless with my name across her shoulders.

There's under two minutes left in the second. We know what's on the line right now. Everyone sitting in this barn knows what's on the line.

Tate Myers picks up the puck off a smooth as shit pass from Gilbert and absolutely fires it past Massachusetts goalie.

It's 2-0 Raccoons, and I'm not the only one out on the ice who wants to drive up the score and utterly annihilate this team.

By my last shift of the third period, I still haven't scored. We're 3-1 up. But it's not enough. I skate across the blue line into the offensive zone. Should definitely have been an offside call, but the on-ice officials miss it, and we're going to capitalize on that.

As Raffi skates deeper into the zone with me, one of the Massachusetts forwards gets back to help out with some defensive play. Getting the bodies in front of us. Running interference between us and the target. It's not enough, though. I want a fucking goal. For Edith.

Good positioning by their goalie, and smart play by the defensemen, keeping the pressure on the forecheck, means I have to work harder, and smarter. Big save from a shot from the point by Raffi. They're closing ranks.

I could coast through the last sixty seconds of the game, but I don't fucking want to. Spying a space in Boston's defense, I smack the ice for the puck. Sometimes too much defensive traffic in front of the goalie can be used to your advantage, and I plan to do just that.

Justin sails it to me without hesitation in a move we've practiced no less than a million times in practice before I tap it into the glove side of the net.

At fucking last.

It wasn't the first goal of the game, it wasn't even the go ahead or game winning goal, but it was the sweetest goal I've had in a while. And my girl's at home cheering for me at her laptop in bed. She might even have my name across her shoulders.

"Food?" Artemis skates up to me as the buzzer sounds and the crowd erupts. He pulls me into a tight hug. "Way to get out of your fucking head, *hermano*." He grins like he knows exactly what helped me quiet the noise in my brain. "She's good for you."

I don't deny it. Even if he couldn't read me like a damn book, they definitely heard my roar last night when I came. The people who live below Edith's apartment hit the ceiling with something, probably a broom, yelling at us to keep it down.

Challenge accepted. I can't fucking wait to see how loud I can make my girl scream, and how often we're going to get hollered at.

"Food?" Ares joins us out in open ice.

"I just asked him." Artemis tips his head my direction as he pulls off his helmet and shakes his hair out like he's in a damned shampoo commercial. I think I hear the collective swoon of every vagina in the place, and some dicks too. He's so fucking extra.

"I'm good." I unclip the strap under my chin.

"Oh. I bet you are, lover boy." Ares gives me an exaggerated wink. "I want to rib you, *hermano*. I truly do. But I get it. If Ellie wasn't with her dad tonight... well. You'd be dining alone, Artemis."

Artemis gives a frustrated grunt. "Abandoned by my own brothers for pussy."

Ares wags his glove at him. "Wait until you find her, man. You'd set the world on fire for her, just to watch it burn. Maybe you should start looking closer to home. Turns out Apollo's woman has been here all along. Who knew?"

The look they share makes it clear that they both did. And now that I do too, I gotta get my ass the hell off this ice, showered, and home to her, so I can snuggle up with my girl, my brother's pig, and eat pizza in bed before I have her for dessert.

CHAPTER 26

Edith

(MARCH 27TH – DAY 10 POST OP)

Why have I never before realized how hot a hockey player stretching his groin is?

Yes, I'm aware it's the semifinals for the Raccoons and if they win this they go up against Alabama State in the finals next week. But... the stretching.

My temperature has risen by at least five degrees as Apollo humps at the ice, opening out his hips. He moves into pigeon, folding himself forward with such grace. How have I never recruited him into pas de stick?

If I wasn't spread out on the bed snuggling with Bacon, the snoring pig, next to me, I'd break out the battery operated boyfriend to take the edge off during warmups. Who knew hockey was so fucking erotic?

The first period passes by in a blur of pain meds and penalties. It's hard to keep up. After a trip to the bathroom, a Milky Way candy bar that Apollo left next to my bed before he left helps me perk up a bit for the second.

When I turn the volume up to pay closer attention to the commentary, Bacon grunts in his sleep. Scratching behind his ear, I shush him. He's like a giant toddler.

Out of nowhere, Gilbert shoots and scores. Jackson Gilbert is taking a lot of flak this season about not finding the back of the net, but what a beautiful finish that was. His thirteenth of the season.

Gilly *has* been on the receiving end of a lot of shit. It's largely a mental block more than a physical one, and the fact he was dropped back to the third line can't be helping his confidence either. Maybe I should talk to Apollo about helping him get out of his own way for next season. If anyone's in a good place to help someone with performance anxiety, it's the man who is helping nurse me back to health.

The line changes, and from the second Apollo's skates hit the ice, he commands every inch of the space.

De la Peña passes back to Raine who tries to feed it back to Apollo de la Peña but Penn State's defensemen intercepts. We all know what Apollo can do. De la Peña helps it off the pads and into the corner. Despite personal circumstances, he's been brilliant all season. He barely missed a beat after the car crash that could easily have ended not only his season, but his career.

Bitterness surges through me. Trying to swallow it down doesn't help. Yes, Apollo was lucky, but he almost threw the friggin' season away just because he didn't want to keep going. Idiot.

The flames of hope that had been fierce in my chest since the accident have started to wane. I've left the group chat for my dance class—it was too hard reading about people who were achieving every single thing I can't. Acknowledging that I might never be able to reach my dreams has been the most soul-crushing, painful realization of my life so far. Not knowing what's next is terrifying, and the welling panic gripping at my throat tightens.

Fuck.

With a shaky hand, I manage to sip some water. Eyes closed, I take a steadying breath, focusing on the analyst's excitable tone and rhythmic commentary.

There's a two on one developing on the left side. The Raccoons are looking to feed it through. Great pass from Captain Justin Ashe, into the circle, de la Peña with the shot, he scores, and finishes that off for his fortieth goal of the season. If you're looking for an early goal from the University of Cedar Rapids, it all comes from moving Ashe to get a lovely pass forward to de la Peña.

With Apollo de la Peña aside the goal like that it's almost always going to hit the back of the net. That's his... eighty-seventh point of the season.

I'd bet that my guy is going to go for ninety, overachiever that he is.

Shot from distance there by Penn State, saved by de la Peña halfway through a UCR penalty. The young rookie goalie is pulling out all the stops tonight. He's had a spectacular first season with the Raccoons. I have to admit, I wasn't sure how he'd blend with the team. Having seen him play in high school and knowing his reputation for ego... well, let's just say I'm glad he's managed to shelve it in the name of teamwork.

Penn State still looking for a chance here. Savage lines up, and, gah, he gets it in the back of the net on the power play. That was such a drive into the net on the left hand side. Making it 2-1 with 13.26 left in the second.

Penelope bursts into the room with a bag from Taco Bell in one hand, and a gallon of ice cream in the other.

"What? You think I'd let you freak out through the whole game all by yourself?" She climbs onto the bed, passing me the bag of burritos and quesadillas, before ripping off the lid of the ice cream and wasting no time stabbing at it with a spoon.

"Sorry I'm late." She hasn't even swallowed, so the words are mumbled around a huge mouthful of rocky road.

She scoots closer on the bed, and I appreciate her presence more than I'm willing to admit. My thoughts were starting to take me onto a destructive path. The Raccoons are charging down the ice toward Penn State's net. My stomach clenches, burrito paused halfway to my mouth. Pen grabs my arm as she shovels another heaped spoon of ice cream into her wide-open mouth.

Back to the point again, Slater Goodwin wrists one, just wide of the post. Lawson picks the rebound up, a little wide, Goodwin picks up the second rebound and it's in! Thirty two seconds into the period and the raccoons have extended their lead, restoring the two goal lead again. We're up to 3-1 for the Raccoons.

"Yesssssssssssssss!" We high-five, fist pump, and tears spring into my eyes.

The Raccoons win the face off and suddenly eating Taco Bell feels like it was a bad idea. A really bad idea. I'm starving, but the anxiety and anticipation brewing in my veins have left my stomach sloshing.

The puck bounces off the top of his stick, good speed, sends it through, there's a chance here for Penn State to break the numbers. Down the right side, plenty of space, what a save from de la Peña, back to the Penn State rookie, backdoor shot with a deflection out front. Another shot, a lot of traffic in front of de la Peña's crease, he's definitely getting chippy with his stick. And Penn State makes it 3-2.

Shit. Shit. Fuck. Mother fucking crap.

The next few minutes pass with hard hits and choppy fights for possession in the corners. Both teams are digging deep, and with how fast the puck is being turned over, it truly could be anyone's game.

But it needs to be ours. The Raccoons have fought so damn hard this season. If there are scouts in the crowd, any number of the twenty-two man team could be picked up based on this Frozen Four run alone. They've all upped their game inordinately. I'm so fucking proud of them.

De la Peña back on the forecheck. Passes the puck back to his brother on the blue line who gives it to Ashe, Ashe gives it to Shaw.

If I was sitting on a seat, I'd be clinging to the edge of it. This game is shredding the fuck out of my nerves.

Great play behind the net from Ashe and Shaw, he puts it onto a plate for Apollo de la Peña who taps it into the back of the net.

When you give de la Peña the puck in that position, there's only one place that puck is going... in the back of the net.

Eight seconds remaining in the game. Penn State won the faceoff, and coming in with the shot high, bounced over the top of the net. Rebound attempt, picked up by Justin. It takes a fraction of a second to score, and the final seconds tick down on the screen in front of us in painfully slow motion. Penn State have got one last chance to tie the game. They shoot, it travels toward Ares with precision, but he saves it with ease right as the final buzzer sounds.

I scream, burst into tears, and almost pee myself. We're going to the motherfucking finals!

CHAPTER 27

Apollo

(MARCH 30TH – DAY 13 POST OP)

"So here's what I'm thinking."

It's been a few days since the semifinals of the Frozen Four and my muscles are finally starting to think about working again. Between hockey practices and classes, Edith and I have spent damn near every second curled up in bed, or on the couch watching old horror movies, icing my tender limbs, and making out.

It's been fucking amazing. Low-key, just us, tactile touches and tender kisses.

She's gotten a little better on her feet since her last surgery. I'm not sure how much of that is sheer grit and determination, versus actually feeling any better, but she seems to be more mobile two weeks post-surgery number two, than she was after her first surgery.

"Did it hurt?"

"Huh?"

She's staring at me with a lopsided grin on her face. "You said you'd been thinking. I know how hard that is for you, and I was going to offer my support as your girlfriend during this difficult time."

I'm not sure what I love more, the warmth flapping in my chest any time she calls herself my girlfriend, or the fact that glimpses of my snarky best friend are starting to reappear through the doom and gloom.

Seeing her so down for such a prolonged period of time has been hard. I'm not stupid enough to believe she's magically through it, though. I made that mistake once before. Then found her sitting on the kitchen floor covered in melted ice cream, and angry cry-screaming about how much everything sucked.

We're taking it day by day here on recovery road, and good days don't mean that things are good. It means that in that moment, she's feeling a little less bad about all the shit she's swimming through.

"What's that look on your face?"

She shifts her weight on the couch and her calves move in my lap. I press my thumb into the arch of her foot and shrug.

Jerking her bare leg to pull my attention back to her face, she snorts. "Nice try, Pollo. I've known you long enough to know that face means something. Spill."

Oh, I must have really done it now because her beautiful freckled face is crinkled by a frown and arms are folded across her new "My Heart Belongs to a Snow Pirate" t-shirt she ordered online to fuck with me.

"Can you not wear that, please? It has to be bad luck or something leading up to the playoff finals, right?" The words are barely out of my mouth before I realize my mistake.

Gripping the hem of the shirt, she pulls it over her head and throws it at my face. When I finally wrestle the grey and powder blue material from my face, her bare tits are just... right there.

I groan, as my dick springs to life. I try to tell it that it wasn't *for* us. To stand down. That it was to *torment* us, but he doesn't get the memo, and suddenly my sweats are bulging.

"You were saying."

My eyes stay firmly planted on her pert little rosy nipples. They're hard, probably because of the chill in the air, but I want to think it's because she feels my cock getting hard for her under her legs, and she's soaking wet for me.

"I was... what?"

She snorts again. "My eyes are up here." She gestures to her face, but I can't break boob contact. They're not even moving, but I'm hypnotized and want those buds between my fingers and teeth so I can make her moan.

"I know where your eyes are, *princesa*. I'm having some quality time with your titties right now."

"And they say romance is dead."

"Your titties?"

She arches a brow.

"You can't expect me to have a rational conversation when you're half naked and your nipples are whispering to me."

She cracks up at that, and her boobs jiggle. Not helping my now painful hard on.

She presses them together, and the only thing that would make the image more perfect would be if my dick was wedged between them. "They're not whispering, they're yelling at you to tell me what the fuck you were going to say."

Brushing her leg against my cock, she hums. "I see you like talking titties. I always knew you were a deviant."

It's tempting to shut up her sass by sticking my deviant cock in her face and telling her to suck on it, but someone knocks at the door, and the two of us scramble to reach her discarded shirt.

When she tugs it over her head, she nods. "Okay, I'm ready. But for the record, we're not done with this conversation. Summoning someone to my door because you don't want to talk about whatever you were thinking about won't get you out of the discussion."

I'm still chuckling when I tug the door open, but it's short-lived, as my father—who doesn't wait for an invitation, charges through the door, striding at me with his finger outstretched.

"Papá?"

"Don't you Papá me, you little shit. You're avoiding me." He sends a glare at Edith on the couch and every primal, regressive instinct zings to life as I angle my body so it's between him and my girl. "What the fuck are you playing at?"

Walking me backward, he launches into a diatribe in Spanish, questioning my loyalty, my capabilities, and scolding me for having the sheer audacity to force him to have to leave his golden palace to slum it on my side of town.

This pompous fucker doesn't know when to quit. It's on the tip of my tongue to launch every missile in my proverbial armory right back at him. But the air, and the words, are punched from my body when my father shoves me against the wall.

Edith gasps. "Mr. de la Peña, this isn't appropriate." Nails scrape against fabric. She's trying to stand up, and while I'm *almost* sure that he won't harm her in any way, I'm not *completely* sure.

"Stay out of this, Edith." His snarl is unkind, and I want to rip his face off for disrespecting my woman.

Squaring off to my dad wasn't on my bingo card for the day, but these things happen, right? I straighten my spine, channeling every lesson in negotiation and conflict resolution he and his team have ever taught me.

If there's one upside to having been the chosen one from a young age, it's that my training began early. "Papá. You need to leave, and you need to leave right now."

"I'll leave when I'm good and ready to leave."

"If you don't calm the fuck down, I'll make you leave." My throat tightens as the words tumble from my lips. I have never disrespected Papá like this before. Not once. The words are foreign in my mouth. They taste bitter, and my stomach rolls and rolls as it waits for his reaction.

He laughs before patting me on the chest. "Is that what you've been doing with your free time, *mijo*? Stand-up comedy?"

There's no smell of alcohol on his breath, so he mustn't be drunk. It's early in the day, but I doubt that'd stop him. Alonso de la Peña makes up his own rules as he goes. But I don't know what's pushed him to this level of losing his shit at me. It's not like him.

"Papá, you need to leave." My voice is stronger when I repeat it, though the tension in my muscles is verging on painful.

"You're avoiding me." He takes a step back, and I dare to risk a breath.

"I'm handing all of my work in on time, I communicate with your personal assistants, and to my knowledge none of my work has been erroneous."

He points at me again. "You're avoiding me."

Schooling my face, I shake my head. "I'm busy. Between work, school, and the playoffs, I have a few things on my plate."

His hand flinches, like he's fighting the urge to slap my face. "I know *exactly* what you've been busy with."

Edith huffs as though she knows he's hinting at my relationship her. "Mr. de la Peña, you're out of line, and I need for you to leave my home, now. Before I call the police."

He spins to face her, finger stabbing the air in her direction. "I'm going to assume that accident broke your brain and you forget who you're dealing with right now, little lady."

She shakes her head, golden strands swishing across her cheeks. "No sir. I know *precisely* who I'm *dealing with* right now, and if you don't leave, I'll call the police." As if she's calling his bluff, she picks up her cell phone from the coffee table.

His gaze lands on the cell for a beat before flitting back to me. "You belong to me, kid. I made you, and I can easily unmake you. Be in the office next week, on the 7th at 11A.M. There are some business associates flying in that you need to meet with. We're moving forward with the merger."

"B-but that's playoff day. I'll be in Alabama for the finals."

He waves his hand like he's shooing away a mosquito and turns on his heel.

I bet he did it on purpose. He probably messaged them and told them to come to town on the one fucking day he knew I couldn't do.

His eyes narrow, challenging me to pick a fight, but I'm scrambling for solid ground. He leaves as quickly as he arrived, taking all the oxygen in the room with him before slamming the door so hard I'm amazed it's still on its hinges.

I sag against the wall, not sure what to think, feel, and almost too scared to breathe. I've never seen Papá so angry. I'm trembling, fear seeping through my layers of skin and muscle, settling deep in my bones. Playoff final on the same day as a business meeting I can't miss. Responsibility tugs at my dreams, threatening to pull them apart at the seams.

Puta!

What the fuck am I supposed to do?

CHAPTER 28

Edith

"Where is he?" Artemis cautiously makes his way around the door, giving me time and space to shuffle out of the way. Crutches aren't my favorite things, but they sure as hell beat trying to haul my ass around in a wheelchair. Despite being a graceful dancer, I am *not* in any way coordinated enough to drive that thing. If there was a test to pass, I'd never get a license.

I hook a thumb over my shoulder to where Apollo is sitting on the floor, hugging his knees to his chest. "I didn't know what else to do." I called Artemis the second Alonso barged into my home and started yelling at Apollo.

I wasn't afraid for my own safety by any means, but watching my beautiful prince revert to a scared little boy in front of me was crippling. Definitely called for reinforcements.

Artemis pats my arm, then crosses the room, before hauling Apollo to his feet. He wraps him in an embrace that even I can feel from where I stand. "You want to talk about it?" Artemis's words are mumbled against Apollo's shoulder.

Apollo shakes his head, clinging to his brother. This is definitely going to need further reinforcements.

Pulling out my phone, I text Penelope, asking if that pie place we all love is on a delivery app or if she knows someone locally who'd pick up a pie for me. Hint, hint. This situation needs pie. If for no other reason than I need to feed my feelings buttery, flaky pastry, and sweet, tender filling.

I'm helpless in this moment, but pie would certainly help. Pressing down the fat shaming voice at the back of my head reminding me that I need to be careful what I eat while I'm not dancing, I swallow.

Pen: How much pie do you need? Like a slice? Two?

Edith: We might need two pies. Possibly three.

Pen: Whole pies?

Edith: Whole pies.

Pen: Daaaaaaaaaaaaaaaaaaaaaaaaaaaayum. What the fuck happened?

Edith: Apollo's dad showed up and yelled at him pretty good. He's a fucking mess.

Pen: Oh, the poor little rich boy got spanked by his big rich daddy.

Oof. She's definitely got some unresolved issues about men with money, but that's a step too far, even in the moment.

Pen: Sorry. That was inappropriate. Struggling to make ends meet right now. Doesn't give me the right to belittle someone else's problems. I know this.

Pen: I'll bring apology pie. And regular pie.

Half an hour later, the boys have moved to the dining table, sitting next to each other in silence. Apollo still hasn't said anything, and I can't tell if Artemis has endless patience, or if they're having some kind of telepathic discussion.

My phone chimes with another message from Penelope.

Pen: Pies are at the door. Brian charged them to the DLP account. Did you know the DLP have a line of credit with Brian the pie guy?

Pen: Have you met the pie guy? He's a tall, dark, mountain of a man. I could totally climb him like a tree.

Pen: And he has an accent. I love accents.

Pen: I totally need to get laid.

Pen: Do you think Brian the pie guy's dick tastes like cinnamon sugar?

Pen: Grab the pies while they're warm, idiot.

She must be waiting for the elevator to take her back to the ground floor.

Edith: You want to join us?

Pen: Thanks for the invite, but I don't think your boy would appreciate me landing at the doorstep. Even if I did bring the best pies in town.

Pen: You need anything else, boo?

Edith: You really are the best, you know.

Pen: I know. I know. I'm amazing.

Pen: When you're back on both feet and ready to reenter the student scene, you're going to be making it up with me when I'm on the prowl. Mama needs a good seeing to.

Pen: Speaking of the sexy times...

Edith: Still no.

Pen: Okay, but why? If a DLP twin was into me, I'd let him be, y'know *in* me.

Edith: Stop talking.

Pen: In fact, if they *both* wanted to be into me...

Pen: Shit. Spank bank. Cha-chiiiiing. DP from the DLP. So fucking hot.

Pen: Enjoy the pie. I'm going home to fantasize about your boyfriend and his brother going to pound town on me at the same time.

Shaking my head, I open the door and bend down to pick up the bag of pie. It takes me an age to make my way back through the apartment to the kitchen. Sweat pools at the bottom of my back, and the neck of my shirt is damp.

When am I going to be past this part? I'm so tired of breaking a sweat from just... existing. I used to be fucking strong. A warrior. I could withstand hours of relentless practice. Repeating petit allegro, fouettés, and bourres until my legs burned and my toes bled.

Tears prick my eyes as I unpack the Get the Fork Out boxes. Pen did great with the on-the-fly pie selection. She picked up a savory pie which will do nicely for lunch. It's a curried chicken, potato, and spinach pie, and for dessert she brought cherry pie, and lemon meringue pie.

If there wasn't a golf-ball sized lump lodged in my throat, I'd be drooling.

The curry pie is hot, so I grab three plates, pull out the Tupperware container of prepared salad magically ready for me in my fridge, and serve. There's no way I can carry three plates, plus myself on these damn death sticks.

"Artemis?"

Apollo appears by my side in seconds. "Are you okay?" His pale face is marred with worry, and my heart swells, threatening to break through my ribcage.

Rolling my lips between my teeth so I don't cry, I nod. "I need help with getting lunch to the table."

He ushers me out of the room, following behind me with plates. Artemis grabs silverware, napkins, and drinks, and we eat in an almost contented silence. Apparently I didn't give the boys nearly enough pie, and with promises that they'll replenish it, they polish off the entire damn thing save for the slice I had.

Just when I think I might finally be able to tell when Apollo has had enough to eat, they break out the cherry pie. Animals. They don't even bother to cut it. Or get clean forks.

They dive right in and plow through the pie like they'd never been fed.

"So, what are you going to do?" Artemis's enunciation around a mouthful of pie is pretty impressive.

Apollo shrugs, shoveling a heaped forkful of oozing cherry pie into his mouth. Some of the sticky, bright red filling sticks to his lip, and so help me the temptation to lick it off of him is overwhelming.

"Don't you fucking dare." Artemis levels me with a heavy glare. "If you lick him, I leave."

Apollo perks up at the word lick. "What did I miss?"

Artemis points to his mouth. "You've got shit on your face and Edith looks about ready to mount the table and lick it off."

My face is on fire. Apollo's grin is nothing short of wolfish. "That so?" He spins toward me in his seat. Without breaking eye contact, he drags his thumb along his pink bottom lip, catching the pie filling on the pad of his digit. Instead of sucking it off like I expect him to, he holds it out to me.

Artemis groans, and I'm pretty sure that noise is the sound of his stomach lurching. Dude's gonna puke his pie.

That's definitely a him problem though, not a me problem, because right now I'm caught in the unrelenting hold of my prince of darkness's heated chocolate stare. When I open my mouth, he doesn't hesitate to slide his thumb between my lips. The tiny taste of tart, sweet cherry filling explodes on my tongue with two contented groans—his and mine—and a groan of dismay from his brother.

"I don't know what I'm going to do, *hermano*. Thankfully, I have a few days to think about it."

I share a look with Artemis across the table. We both know what Apollo is going to do. It's what he always does, bends, folds, twisting himself into a human pretzel to appease his father.

Hundred bucks says this dumb fuck is going to quit the team.

CHAPTER 29

Apollo

(APRIL 4TH – DAY 18 POST OP)

My girl deserves better.

I've been like a sad fucking donkey for the past few days, and it's time to stop being a giant *pendejo* and cheer her up. She's been every bit as miserable as I have. She missed her audition last week. We knew she couldn't dance for it, but I guess, seeing the date on the calendar when she was supposed to get her "last chance" really hit her hard.

Try as she might to avoid what now feels like her previous life... her friends posted a pre-audition selfie, and videos on the socials that, if she hadn't already been upset, would have upset her. But considering she was already cut up about it... well, there has been a dark cloud over both of us over the past couple days.

"How was practice?" Edith's on the couch playing a *Pokémon* game on the TV. I don't remember the last time she's been outside this apartment. That's going to have to change.

"Exhausting."

She tosses a bottle of water at me, then pauses a second before tearing her eyes off the screen. Her nose wrinkles in the way I love, but the disgust on her face makes me chuckle.

"I need a shower."

She wafts the air around her face. "No shit, Sherlock. You stink."

"So, I've been thinking."

"Me too." She turns her attention back to the game. "I've decided you're going to be my sugar daddy so I can spend all day playing video games. Then I won't have to decide what the fuck to do with my life now that my dancing dreams are like tattered tulle around my feet."

I roll my eyes. "Okay, drama llama. But if you call me Daddy in the bedroom, we're going to have issues. That is not my kink." I shudder. "At. All."

She's laughing so hard she almost drops the controller. "What were you thinking about?" She glances at the door. "Last time you had a thought, well, Alonso burst through my door."

"Don't remind me. So my thinking today is the same thinking from that day. We never circled back."

"Before I forget, did you spray down your pads? If that stench is strong enough to cross this room, you know that kit bag is going to fester."

Grinning, I nod. I love that there are no lines with her. "They're airing out over at my place."

She creases her face up again, and a tremor rattles her whole body. "You have sixty seconds to talk, then you need to wash. Because, ew."

This woman. I fucking love her. I haven't said the words out loud to her yet because I'm convinced she has one foot out the goddamn door. I also don't want her to think I'm saying it because *life* is happening around us and kicking us both in the crotch.

Stripping off my shirt, I chuckle, then threaten to throw it at her.

"Pollo, I swear to all that's holy. If you chuck that thing at me, I'll stab you."

I believe her. Shrinking away from the offensive fabric, I nod. "That's fair. So, I was thinking. You, me, a real date. I'll pick you up, flowers, dinner and a movie, ice cream. I'll get strawberry, and you'll get that gross butterscotch crap you like. We can sit with our frozen treats while you fall low-key in love with me, watching the cars go by and talking about life. Perhaps a kiss good night... on your clit."

Shrugging, I try to hide my racing heart behind a wall of nonchalance. I've never asked my best friend out on a real date before. But I want her to know that I don't expect us to fall into routine and comfortable silences simply because we've known each other for our whole lives. And I'm worried about her. She barely leaves the house, she's becoming more and more reclusive, and I hate that for her.

She gives me the softest smile. I should have waited until I was less smelly before having this discussion. I've realized the error of my ways because I have an overwhelming urge to kiss her fucking freckly face right now.

"You'll bring me more flowers?" She points at the vase on the coffee table with her controller. "But you only brought those yesterday."

Shrugging again, I'm failing to play it cool. "You like flowers."

"This is true." Her cheeks are pinking, and it's the most adorable fucking thing I've ever seen.

"One thing, though?"

I jerk my chin at her to continue.

"I can't low-key fall in love with you."

My heart sinks, my stomach plummets, and a chill consumes my entire body.

She stands up, drops her controller onto the couch, and hobbles over to where I'm standing. "I can't low-key fall in love with you." She cups my face, her grey eyes piercing into me. "Because I'm already high-key in love with you, Apollo. Total-key, head over heels in love with you." Her voice drops to a whisper. "I'm still scared. But once I set aside the fear. It's always been you, *príncipe de las tinieblas. Siempre has sido tú.* How did we never notice?"

Tears well in her eyes as she plants a chaste kiss on my lips before dipping her forehead to rest on my chin with a giggle. "You smell so fucking bad, Pollo."

Tipping her head back, I meet her eyes again with an intense stare of my own. "You know I love you, right? Like shave your legs for you, give you the last piece of pie, and wear his-and-hers matching outfits kind of love, right? The real shit, not that fake Hollywood, swoony eyed bullshit. The lasting kind."

She nods. "I know."

"And not because of the crash, or because my dad's a *cabrón*, but because I'm head-over-heels in love with you, Edie."

She bites her lip, and something inside me cracks as her eyes fill with tears again. "I know, Apollo. The big, scary kind of love."

The weight on my chest lifts. Her eyes tell me that she gets it. Not only does she understand and feel my love for her, she feels it too. Fuck. My girl loves me.

She smacks my arm. "Take your goofy ass to the shower and scrub that stink off so we can... y'know..."

Gasping, I fan myself. "Edith Fisher. Do you mean..." I drop my voice. "Sex?"

Shoving both my shoulders, she sways on her feet. "Go, before I change my mind and make you do all the other stuff you listed before I let you take me to bed." She turns and squints at the vase of flowers. "Now I think about it, I could maybe use some fresh flowers."

My shoulders relax when I hold my hands up. "Gimme fifteen."

"You have ten. Then I'm getting my vibrator."

My dick likes that idea, but there's no way she's using a machine to get off tonight.

"I've seen your STD screening report from your last physical, too. If you're down for it…" She sees all of my reports, all of my mail, we have no lines, and for the most part no secrets. Her face is red, and her voice shakes, but my dick has already made the connection and is rising like a flag on a fucking flagpole.

"Bareback?"

She nods.

"I fucking love you." I grab her for another quick kiss, but she presses her hands against my chest.

"Shower. Now."

As I back away from her, I throw her some finger guns, because what else can a man whose best friend just told him she loves him do?

CHAPTER 30

Edith

The anticipation of waiting for Apollo to get out of the shower burns me from the inside. Nervous energy courses through my whole body. My legs and lady bits haven't been shaved, my stomach is squishier than it's ever been, and I'm sporting a pretty hefty monobrow. Safe to say personal grooming has gone by the wayside since we almost died. He doesn't care, but I'm tempted to do a panicked sesh in the bathroom to take care of business.

And all things being equal, I probably would. But I'm saving my strength for the boy-bonking. I don't want to try to shave my legs, throw a stitch in my ribs, and be a sweaty, out-of-breath mess *before* we get jiggy with it. Or worse, be too exhausted from fixing myself up for sex, to have sex.

Pen: Fucked him yet?

Edith: Still no.

Pen: Dream Apollo is *chef's kiss* in the bedroom. Can confirm.

Edith: You don't think it's at all fucked up that you're dreaming about your best friend's boyfriend in the sack?

Pen: You know I'd never act on it. And I've done some dream analysis.

Edith: I'm listening.

Pen: Turns out dreaming about getting DP'd by hockey playing twins is a perfectly normal dream. Super common. It's in all the books.

I can't help but laugh. She's a dork.

Edith: And what do the books say this super specific, verging on creepy and inappropriate dream might mean?

Pen: I need to get laid.

Edith: I know that, but what does the dream mean? ;-)

Apollo steps into the living room completely bare-assed naked, brushing a towel over his hair. I drop my phone. I'm not sure whether my brain or my lady brain short circuits, maybe they both do, but I was not prepared. At all.

Water trickles down his chest, and if both my legs worked fine, I'd vault over the back of this couch and lick every drop.

Naked Apollo de la Peña is... breathtaking. If we were in a romance novel this would be about the time where I'd let go of a breath I didn't realize I was holding. Because holy fucking shit, I forget how to human while he strides toward me, dick dangling in the wind.

"Why are you still sitting there, Edie?" He points at his cock. "It's not going to fuck itself."

My jaw drops open, but I grope at the seat next to me for a cushion to throw at him. "Maybe it *should* fuck itself."

He snorts. "I'm trying too hard to make sure it's not weird, aren't I?"

I hold my finger and thumb a little bit apart in response.

"And making it weird?"

Nodding is the only thing I can do, I'm still focused on all... that. He could crack a coconut between those thighs, if that's something he felt like doing.

"You've gone from wining and dining, low-key falling in love and kissing my clit goodnight, straight to hop on board the peen train. Choo-fucking-choo, Pollo."

He pumps his now hard dick twice in response. Fucker. I can't help but laugh, which is absolutely his desired effect. Licking his lips, he closes the remaining space between us and holds out his free hand to help me to my feet.

Once I'm standing, his knees soften and he hauls me over his shoulder. Within seconds, I'm naked and spread eagle on my bed. Apollo stands over me, as if committing every single inch of my bare skin to memory.

"You're so fucking beautiful, Edie."

A voice screams at the back of my mind. Yelling all the negative things our innermost demons holler on the regular. But instead of letting the voice get louder, I shut it down. Apollo is looking at me like I'm a fucking goddess, his cock is hard, precum glistening under my bedroom light.

Opening my legs further apart, I point at my pussy. "What are you waiting for? It's not going to fuck itself, Apollo."

The grin he flashes is savage, and I know I should pray to every god there is because he's about to destroy me. Apollo de la Peña is going to brand me from the inside, stake his claim, and ruin me forever. And I can't fucking wait.

Closing my eyes, I sink into the bed. His fingers skim along the outsides of my calves with a feather-light touch as his weight lands on the mattress and he maneuvers into position between my legs. His eyes darken. "You sure, *princesa*?"

Nodding, I sigh. So sure.

"If it gets too weird, or... whatever... let me know, okay? You can say no at any point, and it won't change a damn thing between us, okay?"

"Fuck." If I wasn't already soaking wet and ready for this man, that would have done me in. "Consent is so fucking sexy."

He licks his lips, picking up my not-casted leg by my ankle. "Does that mean I can make you come now?"

The shiver that rolls through my entire body is as delightful as the bite of pain as he nips the inside of my calf. "Use your words, Edie. I want to hear your filthy little mouth tell me all the dirty things you want me to do to you."

I'd answer, but his fingers have found the puddle of need between my thighs. My hips buck to meet his hand as his digits glide through my wetness with wholly unladylike squelching noises that are so far from romantic and sexy, I want to cry.

The appreciative hum Apollo makes as his fingers explore my soaked pussy vibrates through the bed. "So wet for me, *princesa*." He dots a kiss on the inside of my knee, then leaves a cool trail to my pussy with his tongue along the inside of my thigh.

My body is frozen in place. I'm his instrument to play however the fuck he wants, and I trust him implicitly to make me sing.

He drags the full, flat part of his tongue through my folds, leaving my leg hanging loosely over his shoulder. "Mmm-mmm. My girl likes dirty talk, does she? *Princesa sucia... Princesa mojada...*"

His fingers tease at my entrance, circling, flexing, tempting, while the tip of his tongue flicks at my clit with a relaxed... almost laziness I'm not feeling. Frustration pools between my thighs as I fist the sheets at my side, arching my back. Sweat's already prickling at my temples and the nape of my neck.

Like a pot of water ready to boil over, my body bubbles and jerks, pure need consuming every cell. When I lift my head off the pillow, his eyes meet mine and he grins against my crotch.

"*¿Que lo que, princesa?*"

With a pained groan, I roll my hips. "Your cock. I'm pretty sure your cock is up, Apollo."

He slurps my juices like he's trying a five-star soup or sipping on the most expensive wine in the world. "You're not wrong. But this isn't about me. You need to be ready."

What fucking planet is he on that he thinks I need to be readier... readied... more ready...? Slamming my fists on the bed, my hips twitch when his fingers slide a little further inside me. Fuck, I've never been so needy, so primed, so damned hungry for another person's touch than I am in this moment.

"Apollo, plea—" My words are replaced by a squeal as he buries his face between my legs and sucks at my clit with a fierceness that draws the oxygen from my lungs at the same time.

The passion inside this man is life altering. My limbs tremble, my body no longer under my own control. My aching legs spasm and quiver as he slips his fingers deep inside, finding my g-spot without hesitation. When he presses, sucking at my clit, I squirt all over his face.

My thighs clench, the temptation to close my legs to save me from further embarrassment a heady, demanding feeling. But he shoves my legs further apart and growls against my pussy. The friction of the roughness of his tongue coupled with the prickles of his facial hair shunt me over the edge and into a freefall before I even know what's happening.

My arms and legs jolt and move as though I'm a fucking marionette doll, but instead of a handle above my head, my clit and g-spot hold the key to making me move on command.

The wave of ecstasy that collides with my body is so intense my mind goes blank, and even though my eyes are still closed, I see stars.

He's not slowing, the quick pace of his tongue makes indelicate slurping noises in the soaking mess that is my pussy. My body is Jell-O, boneless, yet heavy, weighted to the mattress with a delicious blissful buzz settling into my muscles.

But he's not quitting.

My second orgasm smashes into me with even less notice than the first, and I buck upright on the bed with a scream. Threading my fingers into his dark mane, I brace him against me so he doesn't stop. Jerky thrusts against his face help me ride out my release.

He grips my hips, pressing his face against me. I've never known a man to enjoy going down on women like this one. He's possessed. Every squelch, squirt, and squeal drives him to go harder, faster, and shove me closer to bliss.

When the wave crests, I flop back onto the bed with a thump. "Fuck." My throat is dry, voice croaky, and a sheen of sweat covers my whole body.

Apollo gets to his knees between my thighs, and licks his lips. "I want to taste your pussy every damn day for the rest of our lives, Edie."

He must be pussy drunk. That's an awfully long time, and an awful lot of oral. He strokes his dick as he inches himself closer to me. When he doesn't stop at the apex of my thighs, I wonder what the hell he's doing.

Straddling my chest, he grins down at me before placing his dick between my tits. "I've wanted to do this since your titties talked to me."

I can't help the laugh that bursts out of me, enjoying how real and fun things still are between us. I squeeze my boobs so his cock is nestled between them, and he starts to move.

He looks like something inhuman, something other-worldly, like how authors describe the Fae as being so breath-takingly beautiful and bewitching. A dark wave of hair slips down over his forehead, as intensity burns into me through those delicious eyes of his.

Has he always looked at me like this? Has he always regarded me as something precious? Treasured? Adored? Fuck. I could get used to this euphoria.

He picks up speed as he fucks my tits, and I curve my neck, sneaking my tongue out to brush his tip. He taps my nose like he's scolding a puppy. "I'll blow my load all over your sweet face, *princesa*."

"So?" I grin at him.

He slides himself down my body, the hard ridges of his muscles pressing me further into the bed. When his tip grazes my pussy, my higher brain function stops dead on a gasp. "Apollo, please."

Brushing his nose against mine, he breathes me in. "I said I'd never make you beg again, Edith. But there's no sound more fucking enjoyable than hearing you whimper my name, than knowing there's something you need that you only want from me."

He inches inside me, just the tiniest bit, and my body starts to quiver.

"Apollo."

His name is a choked gasp.

"Please, please make love to me." I barely finish my sentence before he's sliding inside me, and finally, I can breathe.

CHAPTER 31
Apollo

It's fucking embarrassing how quickly I shot my load into my girl on our first time. My dick felt her tight, velvety walls and lost his shit. We're giving him a hot minute to recover before we go again. But damn, I need to up my game.

Edith is like putty in my hands, supple, relaxed, with a blissful, hazy smile on her face. What did I do to deserve this woman?

Her back is to my chest, head tipped back, my cock nestled against her perfect peach-shaped ass as I trail my fingers down the length of her arm, dotting kisses on her shoulder.

She moves ever so slightly, the faint smell of strawberries meeting my nose from her hair, or her lotion, or... somewhere. I'm not sure where, but it makes me want to cover her in strawberries and eat them off her one at a time.

I've never had an oral fixation before Edith. I mean, I've given my fair share of lip service. But Edie is different. Her salty-sweet taste, her uninhibited mewls and pants while I suck her essence from her body. It's so fucking hot.

She gets so wet we might need to put down mattress covers

going forward. The sheets beneath us are soaking, there's no way it didn't seep into the mattress, and I'm totally fucking here for it. I love how messy my girl gets for me.

She moves my hand from her arm to her chest where the nipple I can reach is hard. Giving it a little twist, I smile against her creamy skin as she whimpers my name.

It doesn't take long before I'm hard again, and my princess clearly knows, because she's wriggling her ass against me, squirming like she's trying to send messages without saying a word. But I don't do subtext.

"Can I help you with something, *princesa*?"

"I need you, Pollo."

I nip at her skin with my teeth, enjoying the little shivers and clenches her muscles do in response. "What do you need?"

I'm already hooking her thigh over my forearm, and lining my cock up against her pussy. I've never taken someone on their side like this before, but it feels like a perfect fit, so it's worth a try.

"I need you inside me."

Not letting her say please, or beg, I thrust inside her in one push, enjoying the resistance her tight little pussy gives me as I enter.

Okay. I totally lied.

I thought the second time would be easier for me to give her the seeing to that she needs. But from the minute I bury myself in her, it's a fallacy. Maybe I'm doomed to short shoot my way through life with this woman. Her pussy grips me like it's owned me forever, firm, demanding, and squeezes with each movement of my hips.

My lips skim the salty-slick skin where her neck meets her shoulder, and she softens in front of me. My girl doesn't seem to be the type to come with g-spot stimulation at all, though if she was, I wouldn't know yet, since I can't keep my shit together long enough to pound the fuck out of her and find out.

My fingers find her swollen clit, sending another shiver through her body against mine. "Close." She pants. If nothing else, it seems as though I'm not the only one struggling to pace myself. I can't imagine she'll be this easy to drive to climax forever, but I'll take the wins wherever I find them.

She arches her back, and the thigh draped over me tenses as her hips buck. She's so fucking perfect. The scream that rips from her body is loud enough for everyone in a two block radius to hear, and it only serves to spur me harder.

When her walls clench tightly around my cock, the tingle brewing at the base of my spine explodes like a firework. No edging, no holding myself back, no breathing through it. Its impact is hard and fast, punching the air out of my lungs in less than a second as I fill her with my cum one more time. I'm pretty sure I black out.

When we both recover a little, and our gasped rasping breaths return to some semblance of normal, she shifts her leg off me and I move my hand back to her pussy.

"What are you doing?" Her hoarse voice is sexy as sin, and if I hadn't come twice, I'd be ready to take her all over again.

My cum is trickling out of her, so I catch the dribbling liquid with my thumb and push it back inside her. Pressing a soft kiss to the top of her shoulder, I do it again. "Owning you."

(April 5th – Day 19 post op)

Getting up for morning skate when entangled in the arms of the stunning, naked woman pressed against my body is literally the worst. She's curled into me, warm and snuggly. She's adorable. Not even her flyaway hair sticking to my face is making me want to move.

If I could stay here forever, I would. It's perfect. The stillness of the early morning, her body heat, the steady rise and fall of her chest. She's truly at peace. For a while after the crash, I wasn't sure we'd ever find our way through the darkness to this place. But her bad nights are getting further apart, and she's working through her trauma like the badass queen she is.

"Don't leave," she mumbles, pressing her face against my chest and curling her arm around my waist.

Kissing her temple, I brush her hair back. "I'll come back soon." I kiss her forehead. "Coach will kick me off the team if I don't show up. Two days to finals."

"Does that mean you've made a decision?" Her words whisper across my skin.

It has to mean that, right? Because what kind of asshole

would abandon his fucking team two days before the Frozen Four finals?

The thought of calling Papá, or worse, not showing up and letting him realize I'm not coming all by himself, is pretty sickening. The pull between what I want to do, and what I should do gets stronger by the day.

Edith's warm palm glides along my cheek. "You have time to decide. Trust your gut, Apollo. It's never led you wrong before."

She's already asleep before I get out of bed, but as I slide my clothes on, getting ready for training, I can't help but wonder if she's right. My gut and my heart both scream hockey. But for so long I've listened to my brain, my father's voice inside my head telling me I was born for greatness.

Maybe I was. But what if that greatness is hockey and not aviation?

CHAPTER 32

Apollo

(APRIL 6TH – DAY 20 POST OP)

I'm going to hurl.

All over my fancy, Italian leather shoes.

Right here on the street.

Standing outside my father's office in downtown Cedar Rapids, everything inside my body hurts. I hadn't realized how much stress and heavy anxiety I was carrying until Papá threw down an ultimatum. Everything is dialed up to eleven.

My phone buzzes in the pocket of my dress pants—can't show up to de la Peña headquarters wearing jeans or they won't let you through the door—and I damn near jump out of my skin.

Artemis: Gone in yet?

Ares: Of course he hasn't. Fifty says he's standing on the street staring at the glass fucking doors.

Athena: You've got this, hermanito. Let me know if you need back up.

Hen sends an emoji of a fist, and I crack up laughing. I love my siblings. They're the ultimate definition of ride-or-die.

Artemis: Just come home, Po. It's better to ask for forgiveness than permission.

Ares: Can confirm. I've done it for most of my life.

Athena: They're right, Apollo. If you can get your mind to settle, play the game tomorrow, then deal with the fallout.

Athena: Whatever happens, we've got you.

The idea of going up against Papá in any manner is beyond distasteful. It's terrifying. It's not something I'd have ever considered before the accident, either. That damned crash changed everything. And while I'm scared down to the very marrow in my bones, the fallout from the car accident hasn't led me wrong yet.

Things with Edith are going better than I ever could have hoped. Perhaps there's something to that whole, *seeing your life flash before your eyes* thing.

If my gut was right about my relationship with Edith, maybe my gut is right about hockey, too. I can't keep living straddling the line. I can't keep one foot in each space, hockey and the family business. I need to pick a path, and my gut says it's not aviation.

I want to play hockey.

I've always wanted to play hockey, but I've pressed it down, hidden it, squashed my dreams into some tiny box in the closet and ignored it for years because of what I *should* do.

Edith's right. It's time to say "Fuck *should*" and stop half-assing my life.

Fear tugs at my chest, threatening to collapse my lungs and steal all my oxygen, but it's not taking up as much space in my body as it was a few minutes ago. It's as though making the decision to follow my heart, to chase my dreams with both skates has settled something inside of me.

Papá won't be happy. But he doesn't need to be.

Edith's right again. It's my life, and my father doesn't have to live it. I don't know if she's always been this smart, or if breaking her leg and spending months on end in her apartment snuggling with a pig—and Bacon—has made her philosophical in her new hermit life. But either way, Papá doesn't have to like my choices. He doesn't even need to respect them.

As I spin on my heel and walk back to my SUV, it occurs to me that I don't *need* anything from him. I don't need his money, his teaching, his contacts. I don't need to learn anything from him that I can't learn anywhere else.

As I start the car and point it toward home, it hits me that what I've been doing this whole time, what I've been chasing, is my father's love and approval. When what I should have been chasing, is my own.

By the time I pull into the parking lot of our apartment building, an odd peace has settled over me. Worse comes to worst, Papá cuts me off, strikes me from his will, and I lose my inheritance.

I can't think of a world in which that would impact me as much as I've been afraid it would for years. The apartment is paid off and in my name, same for both my cars. I have a trust fund that no one but me can touch, and my bank account is healthy from the occasional dabble with crypto.

Not to mention, if I play my ass off on the ice and get picked up by the NHL... even if something *did* happen to financially topple my ass. Well, the NHL pays pretty well from what I see on TV.

The only thing I can think of is that he'd exert some influence over Mamá. Losing her would destroy me. It would break me on a level I'm not sure I could recover from.

My siblings have my back. And if I need to, I could tell Mamá that Papá is actually a cheating scumbag and she could do better.

The family restaurant downtown, Guac 'n Roll, is in her and Abuelita's names. There was no prenup when they got married. I guess at some point, he really did love the server from his favorite taco place in town.

My steps are lighter as I ride the elevator to our floor. I walk through the door to Edith's place. With a clearer head, I finally have some perspective. It's time for us to combine our resources and move in together. We could take my apartment, she could rent hers out—after extensive screening of candidates—and she could use that money for whatever the hell she wanted. Savings, college fund for our future kids, blowing on booze and hookers, I don't give a shit. But it might give her enough security to breathe a little.

She's in a tailspin about what to do with her life, how to make a living, how to thrive when she's lost the power to do what she loves. Maybe what she needs is some financial reassurance, some stability, some security, and the knowledge that even if she wants to sit and play video games every day for the rest of our lives, I'm okay with that.

Whatever it takes to make her happy.

Fuck.

She was right again.

"Why don't you ever do whatever it takes to make yourself happy, prince of darkness?" She'd asked me that question weeks ago, and I didn't have the answer, so I didn't give it a second thought until right this minute.

My heart soars as I walk into the kitchen and find her, hands on hips, scowling into an open fridge.

She spins toward me, pointing at the door. "We need to go out."

My pulse skips faster. I don't remember the last time she volunteered to go out of the house without it being for therapy, doctors and surgical appointments, or surgeries themselves.

"Did I forget to put a doctor's appointment on my calendar?"

She shakes her head. "Worse." She reaches into the fridge and grabs the carton of orange juice. "Ares brought extra pulp orange juice." She hurls the carton into the sink. "What kind of fucking masochistic monster is he that he thought to assault me with not only pulp, but *extra* pulp? And without warning!" Her hands flap up into the air with such drama that Bacon lifts his head to see what all the fuss is about.

"I'll bring you groceries, Edith." She waves a hand. "Got you OJ, Edith." She waves the hand again. "Who the fuck doesn't tell someone they brought pulpy fucking orange juice?"

I dunno. But her righteous anger at the pulp situation is something I'm going to rib her about forever. Her crinkled nose, the way the freckles on her face stand out against her red cheeks, her popped hip, foot tapping. I've never seen someone fired up so much about fucking orange juice before and it's epically glorious.

"Okay then, let's go get some orange juice. Then we can go kick the crap out of Ares and teach him a lesson."

Can't have my girl upset about pulp now, can I?

CHAPTER 33

Edith

(APRIL 7TH – DAY 21 POST OP)

Frozen Four final –vs– Alabama State

Nervous energy courses through me as we enter the arena. I've barely been out of my apartment for months. Some of that has been due to my physical struggles, but if I'm honest with myself, it's mostly mental.

Being out today, after having been out yesterday, feels weird. Getting special treatment at the arena so I don't have to walk forever or climb a bazillion steps, that feels gross. But by the time we settle into our seats at the plexi glass in the front row, I'm grateful for the wheelchair assist by the hospitality staff. Clunking down all those stairs with my cast and a crutch or with the help of my friends would have ended in absolute disaster. I don't need a third fucking surgery on this damn leg.

Sometimes it's nice to know the badass brunette with perfectly manicured nails and six inch stilettos at a hockey game.

"You good?" Athena takes her seat next to me as I nod.

We even managed to convince a reluctant Tori—Savannah's hockey hating best friend—to come along to the finals, so she's on my right side, and Savannah and Eloise sit to the left of Athena. I couldn't convince Penelope to come.

Unsurprisingly, most of us are wearing de la Peña shirts.

Before Apollo left for morning skate, I confiscated his phone. His father has been blowing it up all day. Every single voice message he leaves and text he sends, I delete.

My prince of darkness doesn't need that negativity.

The overhead clock counts down the seconds to warm up. Apollo has no fucking clue that I'm here and that feels sneaky. And fun. I've missed fun. And I've never been more grateful for my friends' patience during the past few months.

Most people would have given up waiting for me to turn the corner and left me in their rearview.

Some of them did. I still haven't heard from anyone in my dance classes. Dance worlds are so insular, and when someone leaves it's like they cease to exist. But this family, my hockey family, my boyfriend's siblings, they stayed the course.

Apollo's phone vibrates on my thigh. Alonso again. No doubt attempting to call to derail him before the game. Athena reaches for the offending device, but I block her hand, clearing my throat.

"Mr. de la Peña, it's Edith. What can I do for you?"

Grumbles and grunts stall out the conversation on the other side of the line. "Where's Apollo? Why do you have his phone?"

"I have his phone, sir, because it's the Frozen Four finals and Apollo doesn't need any distractions today. Is there something I can help you with? Can I give him a message when he's off the ice? If you're calling to wish him good luck I can have someone bring him the phone."

Athena snorts next to me, her shoulders bouncing with silent laughter.

"I mean, it's a pretty big game. One might say it's a potential turning point for his career. I'm sure that has to be why you're calling, right, Alonso? I'm sure any parent would want to support their child on such a momentous occasion."

I've never called him by his first name before, but I no longer care about showing him any respect.

The line goes dead without another word. I turn off the phone and tuck it into the bag at my feet. When I sit upright again, Athena holds out her fist for me to bump.

"You're a fucking badass you know."

Coming from her, that means the world to me. I've never looked up to anyone as much as I have to Apollo's big sister. She's always been my idol, and to be sitting with her, hanging out with her, whether that's playing cards in our apartment, or watching her brothers play a hockey game, well, in truth, it's surreal.

Little girl Edith is pissing her pants with excitement right now.

Athena de la Peña is everything I strive to be. Strong, composed, smart, talented, and a leader. She's also stunning. If I wasn't in love with her brother, I'd at least be bi-curious for that woman.

Tori hands me my cup of pop, and I take a slurp before thanking her, then burping, because I'm a fucking lady.

"Do you need help finding a tenant for your apartment?" Athena chews on a Red Vine. I don't know that they sell them here, but she's got an entire packet on her lap, and I'd love to see someone try to wrestle them from her.

"Actually, we're going to stay in my apartment and rent out Apollo's. Mine has a better view, and is ever so slightly bigger."

"So my brother saw how much shit you have and thought it'd be easier to move his shit into yours instead of vice versa."

That's exactly what happened. I laugh. "Yup. He's having paperwork drawn up to put both our names on the deed to his place. I don't know what's gotten into him since the crash, but he's been fiercely protective. He's nesting like a pregnant woman."

Athena nails me with that x-ray vision stare she uses on her brothers. On them, it's highly amusing watching as they scramble to figure out what they did to deserve it. On me... I'm glad I have a strong bladder.

"Girl." She nudges my knee with hers. "He's been fiercely protective of you his whole damned life. If that car accident didn't knock your heads together, I was going to have to do it myself." She holds out her hand to inspect her nails. "And you know how I love getting my hands dirty."

I fucking love this woman.

"Do you remember that little fucker who used to trip you up at recess in kindergarten?"

Barney fucking Keith. The little asshole with two first names who made my life hell for weeks before he magically stopped.

I nod.

"Apollo."

My eyes widen.

"And the girl who talked smack about you in middle school?"

Mute. I nod again.

"Also Apollo. And when Fletcher Fowler broke your heart in high school?"

My stomach drops, knowing where this is going. "Uh huh?"

"His broken arm was no accident." She smiles at me like it's completely obvious that Apollo has been mine since we met. How blind have I been?

"H-he broke Fletcher's arm? For... me?"

"*Amiga*, he'd burn the fucking world for you."

Tori leans into our conversation fanning herself. "It's so fucking hot."

I am such a goddamn idiot. "You've known this whole time?"

"We all have." Athena pats my leg. "We've all been waiting to see how long it would take you both to figure it out. I was starting to think it might be too late."

My face, my whole body warms. "I had no idea."

She laughs out loud at that. "I know. And I have no clue how. He's been a goner for you since day one, Edith."

Her words curl around me like a warm blanket on a cold day, or, as is more accurate right now, inside a cold rink. The door to the tunnel opens and Ares steps out onto the ice. My guy is always the first out behind the goalie, always, and when his skates hit the ice, Athena slides her hand into my left hand, and Tori takes my right.

It's game time.

CHAPTER 34

Apollo

"Hey, Apollo." It's rare for Ares to call to me directly from his crease during warmup. He's always focused. All focus, all the time. It's a goalie thing.

I watched a video of him playing pee wee where he stood in the crease, mic'd up, telling himself to focus over and over and over. *If you don't focus, you'll let everyone down and you'll lose, Ares. Don't lose your focus.*

Of course, he was so busy focusing on staying focused, he had his ass handed to him. Talk about a lot of pressure to put on yourself at nine years old. But there's a reason the NHL will court him soon. He's pushed himself to be the best. And as his big brother, I'm proud to say he is.

Fuck.

I have no time to get emotional or reminisce about old times. It's me who needs to fucking focus.

Artemis skates up beside me and taps me on the ass with his twig. "Eleven o'clock, at the glass."

I want to punch him. He knows I have no time for bunnies, I'm with Edi—

Oh my god, she's here. Like, right there, in the stands,

staring back at me. She's sitting at the plexi. Her long, golden hair is pulled into a high ponytail on top of her head, and she has giant satin black and green hair ties holding it up.

She has face paint on her cheeks, a brilliant smile on her face, and my last season's game worn Raccoon's jersey on her back.

She stands up, sways a little as the blood rushes to her still-casted leg, and holds up a sign that says, *#17 you give me that end of the third, tied game, powerplay hattrick kind of feeling.*

I almost fall over from laughing. My funny, sassy girl is right there at the plexi, watching me chase my dreams while her own are murky and uncertain.

I'm a strong-ass man, but that almost undoes me on the spot. Fuck. I swallow, trying to clear the lump in my throat.

Artemis nudges me again. "Go see your girl, *hermano*."

I skate around the edge of the ice until I come to a stop in front of her. She drops her sign and covers her heart with both palms. "I'm so proud of you, Pollo," she calls over the glass before blowing me a kiss.

If I were never to play hockey again for the rest of my life, I've peaked. This moment of support and solidarity, this moment of love, and encouragement with my girl has me so in my feels that it takes everything I have not to cry right here on the ice.

"Te amo, princesa."

"Yo también te amo, príncipe de las tinieblas."

I love when my girl brings the Spanish. And the hockey. I've gone from ball of weepy emotions, to wanting to rail her against the plexi in under thirty seconds.

She jerks her head to the warmups behind me. "Go get 'em."

I salute, glove to forehead and as I head back to where my team is preparing for battle, I'm ready.

CHAPTER 35

Edith

When Apollo hits the ice for the game, he looks more relaxed than I've seen him in, well, I guess forever. He skates my direction, cracking his stick off the plexi right in front of us. I blow him another kiss, toss back some pain meds with a slug of pop, and I'm ready to watch our boys win the championship.

Except Alabama wins the face off.

Assholes.

It's fine. It's totally okay. It's the first puck drop, not the final one of the game with only seconds to go.

"Easy, tiger." Athena pats me like that'll magically wash away all the stress in my muscles. My leg throbs inside my cast, but other than the anthem, I've sat on my ass with my leg slung over Tori's knees the whole time.

I'm really past this whole thing. Looking forward to the dumb boot, and then physical therapy in a few weeks. That's my light at the end of the tunnel.

For a couple months after the accident, the light at the end of the tunnel was dancing again. I've had to rethink my entire life, not simply lower my expectations.

Oh! Justin gives a little tap in front of Alabama's net that leads to confusion. Everyone's battling for it, and when they pull themselves together, the away team's goaltender comes up with a couple of good saves.

By the end of the first, the Raccoons are up by two. I've never seen any of the de la Peña brothers play so well. Never.

Ares is standing on his head, Artemis is crushing every-thing that moves, and my prince of darkness? He got his stick to both of those goals for two assists and counting. He's lighter on his skates, too. Like a weight has been taken off his shoulders.

He's picked his head up and is skating like the ice is an extension of his body, like he was born to play, and it's about fucking time, too. Because he was.

Athena bounces in her seat during the period break but claims she doesn't need to pee. "You know, I stopped coming to games for so long. It's only really since Ares got together with Eloise that I've started to come back more than a game here and there."

The temptation to lean into her and sniff her hair is over-whelming. But that's weird, right?

She sees me staring and lifts her hand to her hair. "What? Did I get something in my hair?"

I giggle, shaking my head. "You've been my hero since we were kids. Part of me can't believe we're sitting here, side by side watching your brothers play."

She arches a perfectly manicured eyebrow. "And the other part?"

"Really wants to smell your hair."

Tori and Savannah burst out laughing. Eloise stands to go to the bathroom. And by the time the second period starts we all have refills and fresh snacks.

That doesn't last long, because within the first ten seconds of the second period, Raffi gets his stick to a messy rebound and bags a bar down goal. Athena launches herself out of her seat, screaming, and proceeds to knock her large tub of popcorn everywhere and kick over two cups of soda at the same time.

For someone so epically put together, you really can't take her anywhere. I can't help but laugh.

When play restarts, Alabama dumps the puck. Scott Raine picks up the puck to the blueline. He blasts it through for Apollo who takes a right-handed shot on the left side, trying to catch the netminder off the post, but the over-sized netminder is somehow quick to get back.

Apollo is pissed. I've seen it so many times over the years. Once he goes to the effort of bringing the biscuit to the basket and misses a great scoring opportunity, he does what he can to make it right.

He doesn't owe this game anything. He's already collecting points like Mario collects gold coins, but the hunger on his face is clear, from the way he smacks the stick on the ice calling for the pass, to how he carries himself on his skates. Apollo is here to win.

And it's so fucking hot.

The line has barely changed when Apollo mounts the boards on the bench, pleading to go back on the ice. He's poised like a lion, ready to strike when Coach gives him the nod.

My stomach clenches as the shift changes. If he gets called for too many men, he's gonna lose his shit. But my anxiety is unnecessary as he handles the changeover seamlessly.

My muscles don't relax though. Justin hammers the puck off the cuff of the Alabama goalie's glove. He has no business making that save, but he totally robs our captain of what would have been a beaut.

I can't breathe.

By the end of the second, we're up by three. While

Alabama didn't score during that last twenty minutes, they also didn't let one in either. It feels like damage control, but I'm not naive enough to think the game is over.

Hockey games can turn on a dime.

Athena grabs my hand with freakish strength. "I need more snacks."

Hopefully this time she won't launch them all over the fucking stands. "Athena?"

"Sí amiga?"

"I already broke my arm once this year. Could you... you know...?" As tempting as it is to let Athena break my arm for fun, I really am done with fucking casts. I hope to every god I can think of that they'll let me get this cast off my leg soon. Surely a boot would be better than this thing... right?

Athena gasps, then strokes my hand. *"Lo siento,"* she coos.

It's not long before the game restarts. A couple minutes in, there's a little bit of back and forth in the Raccoons offensive zone that finishes up in their defensive zone.

"They tried to get it in deep there."

I'm not sure Tori realized what she said, but the rest of us are choking on our drinks and snacks as we fall apart into a mess of laughter.

Savannah raises her hand. "Not gonna lie, I like it when Justin gets it in d—"

Eloise claps her hand over Savannah's still moving mouth. "It's a family show, and there are kids behind us." Her face is bright pink. For someone who dates our team's resident bad boy, she sure is shy and unassuming.

It's hard to picture that the woman currently embarrassed about dick-talk was the same woman Ares reportedly banged over his goal last week.

Yup. The idea of being fucked on the ice makes my vagina freeze. It's not even the least bit enticing to me, and I have no idea how Ares didn't slip, or Eloise didn't crack her face open on the crossbar. But rumor has it, he nailed her pretty good, and since it resulted in a win for the team...

Goalie code demanded he do it again tonight before the game. It's why we were here so damned early.

A shiver jolts through me, making me jump. "Still thinking about my brother banging Eloise on the ice?"

Eloise elbows Athena. "Would you keep your voice down, please?" She drops her head, but we can hear her as she grumbles. "We all have to do our part for the team."

We've barely caught our breath when Alabama scores. It's been brewing for a while, but the Raccoons are pissed. None more so than Ares in goal.

When Alabama scores again less than ninety seconds later. Ares paces his crease like a feral animal before he smashes his stick off his post.

I smother a giggle. I've known him since he was a snot-nosed kid. So when he throws a tantrum, all I can see is the gangly little boy wanting to play with his older brothers.

It's a 3-2 game.

Alabama has the momentum, but there's no rage like de la Peña rage. If it's possible, Artemis and Scott pick up the hits on the top line defense. I've never been one for fighting, but a clean hockey check does things to my nether regions. If Apollo was on the blue line, I'd have already come in my seat by now.

An across ice pass comes from Apollo to the Raccoon's captain. Justin tries to get on target, and it's in. Holy fuck. The whole arena erupts a beat or two later. None of us thought it would go in. Not even Justin.

Alabama meets us goal for goal, and within another few minutes it's a 4-3 game. Ares rolls his neck and squares his shoulders. That's his sign for "no fucking more."

We're into the last five minutes of play, and we just need to hang on to the one-goal lead. But that doesn't seem to be enough for Apollo. He comes through the slot, and oh my holy fucking wow, he pokes one home. It's 5-3.

After his team are done hugging him, he turns directly to me and points. My heart flutters as I point right back at him.

The tension holding my muscles hostage feels like we're on game seven of the Stanley Cup finals. Athena hasn't breathed in at least four minutes. Tori is leaning so far forward I fear she's going to topple out of her seat. Savannah's puking in the bathroom, and Eloise looks like she could join her at any time.

We definitely need to work on our constitution and tolerance for high stress hockey situations.

With a little over two minutes to go, Artemis gets sent to the box for a questionable holding call. It's not the most ideal situation. Alabama hasn't given up. Their heads haven't dropped, and they're still fighting for possession at every turn. This could all go terribly wrong.

But it won't. I shake my head. This is our time.

Cooper Duke joins Scott on the top line while his d-buddy is in time out. Where are they drawing the energy from to finish this game? Our first line has logged more ice time tonight than any game I've seen them play. And I think they've asked for it. I'm exhausted and all I'm doing is watching.

The team finds enough reserve energy to throw down some hits as they race the clock. Kade checks an Alabama player and takes the pass. A fancy little wrist shot that Athena takes a moment to appreciate.

"Nice."

I'm not sure she even knows she's doing it, but her muttered commentary on the game tells me she never took a time out. I imagine she's spent whatever time she said she's "hated hockey" secretly following the game like an obsessive fan, just like the rest of us. It's hard not to when her brothers are so fucking good.

Sixty seconds left in the game.

Lincoln Scott snaps the shot up the ice. It's knocked out of the air by Apollo, but his stick isn't too high. I shift to the end of my seat, hands locked on my lap as temptation to press myself against the plexi to get a better view takes over. The puck lands in the back of the net and the crowd goes wild.

Nothing beats a short-handed goal in a championship game.

Nothing, that is, except the delight on my boy's face when the final buzzer sounds and his team takes the win.

CHAPTER 36

Apollo

We fucking won.

I'd love to say that the final buzzer of tonight's game was my favorite part of the evening. But it wasn't. It wasn't the goals, the points, or even watching Ares have a tantrum on the ice like a threenager.

It was Edith.

I've seen her at games my whole life. She's been at almost all of them. Every game, she wears my number on her back and arms, my name across her shoulders, and she cheers for me with an almost demonic possession.

She's not a dainty hockey fan. She's aggressive, knowledge-able, and damn near an extension of the game. She can give a play-by-play better than some of the sports commentators I've listened to, can call a penalty before the refs, and her team spirit is unrivaled.

I'll be surprised if she still has a voice after that game. Every single time I looked at her—which was admittedly a lot—she was like a woman possessed. And I fucking loved it.

Watching her scream, pound the plexi, and cheer for me,

for the team, it was an entirely new experience with her as my girl. I've been fighting a hard on in my pads all fucking night.

I messaged Athena from Artemis's phone as soon as I hit the dressing room doors, telling her to bring Edith down to the locker room. She's going to be pissed as hell at the wheelchair I had the arena team bring to her, but she needs it. Her leg needs to heal, not take fifty thousand steps at a hockey game. She was on her feet enough during the game.

I sure as shit hope she kept on top of her meds, because if not, her leg is going to hurt like hell tomorrow.

My shower is cold in an attempt to deflate my cock, but it's not working. My balls ache with heaviness, and I'm light on my feet with the championship winning energy thrumming through me. I'm absolutely not making it back to the house before I fuck her.

Toweling off, I pull on boxers and dress pants in the dressing room, but leave my chest exposed. Even if there are press, or family members in the locker room, I'm decent enough.

I guess I took forever in the shower. Or perhaps most of the guys wanted a quick turnaround so they could get to the celebrating part of the evening. I don't blame them.

Athena, Eloise, Edith, and Savannah stand around the room with Ares, Artemis, Justin, Scott, and Raffi. I don't know where Victoria is—she spent the whole game sitting next to Edith. For women who claim to not like the game, Athena, Eloise, and Tori sure can fake it.

Edith's in the wheelchair, her casted leg raised. Her face paint is a little smudged on one side, and her high ponytail has fallen to the side like she's from a 90s workout video. When she spots me, she blinds the whole room with her smile, shrieks, and takes-off out of the chair in my direction.

The urge to hug her, pick her up and spin her around is overwhelming. But the need to fuck her wins. I soften my knees, and right at the last minute, her eyes widen in understanding as I scoop her over my shoulder, hold up five fingers to our family, and turn back toward the dressing room.

I don't give a fuck if someone's in the showers, or if any straggler is getting changed, or if our friends hear me drilling my girl through the walls. This feral need to be inside her, to celebrate with her, it's consuming.

She's a wiggler. Swinging her legs and giggling. "Put me down, you fucking cave man."

"No." I smack her ass. "You were on your feet way too much tonight, so you're staying off the ground." My fingers find the band of her leggings under her jersey, and I somehow manage to jerk them halfway down her legs before swinging her carefully onto a bench.

I kneel in front of her. "Here's what's about to happen." I tug off her sneakers. "I'm going to fuck you senseless, then we're going to eat something, then we're going to have a drink with our friends and family, and then I'm going to fuck you some more. Okay?" I undo my pants zipper and free my cock.

The flush across her cheeks is adorable, but the hunger in her eyes is the money shot. She nods. "Can I consent to all of that right now? Like, frontloaded consent?"

She's barely finished her sentence before she's dangling over my shoulder again. As I walk her back toward the wall, my fingers slip between her thighs. The squelching echoes around the room.

"Neanderthal kink, eh, princesa?"

She's breathless as I slide her down the wall, bracing her with my hips to take the weight. "I've been soaked since warm ups."

"When I blew you a kiss?"

She shakes her head and flicks her eyes from mine. "Groin stretches."

I can't help laughing. "You've seen me do those for well over a decade."

"It hits differently when you're fucking the guy humping the ice."

Speaking of fucking, my cock twitches. I lower her with one arm, as my other hand guides me inside her. Hissing out a slow breath, I grit my teeth. This isn't going to take long. She's soft and smooth, and so fucking hot and tight, that I'm going to blow my load in seconds.

Dropping my forehead to hers, I sigh. This. This is what I've been looking forward to for the last few hours. When her eyes meet mine, they're so full of love. She plants the tiniest of kisses on my nose.

"Fuck me, champion."

I pull out before spearing back into her with one deep and brutal thrust. Her nails dig into my bare shoulders as her head lolls back against the wall with a groan she attempts to silence.

"You want to be quiet?"

She nods, color deepening on her cheeks. Her eyes sparkle when I cover her mouth, giving into the fierce need to fuck her without mercy.

As I pound into her over and over, her scent from my fingers covering her mouth makes me salivate. "Slight detour, princesa," I growl beside her ear.

Dropping to my knees, I somehow manage to keep her against the wall without dropping her. Planting her pussy on my face, I go to town, bracing her ass cheeks with my palms. She's going to buck. She's going to wiggle and move, shift her weight, but I'm stable and strong, and so fucking determined.

Her legs dangle down my back, the cast bumping against my body every time she squirms. Her slick salty-sweet taste explodes on my tongue as I eat her with fervor. She's perfect. I get her right to the edge. Her legs clench around my head, squeezing me tightly as she approaches her orgasm. Her muscles ripple around me, and her juices drip onto me from above.

I've never had locker room fantasies, but this is so fucking hot it's going to be repeated for sure.

When she detonates on my face it takes us both by surprise and she smacks her hands over her face to drown out her frenzy. I hold her, lapping at her delicious pussy until the last aftershock rakes her body.

Shoving her up like I'm bench pressing at the gym, the transition from eating her out to having her back on my cock is smoother than I expected.

She's frantically kissing me, fingers caressing my face before spearing into my hair and scraping my scalp. When she tips her head back, I cover her mouth again with my hand and nibble my way down her neck.

With each grunt and thrust, I charge closer to my release. Body tense, balls heavy. She moans behind my palm, her eyes are heavy, filled with bliss and lust. This woman does me in.

The door to the dressing room opens and Myer's calls to someone that he'll only be two minutes. Edith freezes, but I keep my hand over her mouth and drill into her without missing a beat.

Myers isn't going to ruin this for me. I couldn't give a fuck if he walks past us right now, and I need to communicate that to Edith. I don't know how she reads it, or whether my assault on her g-spot with my steel-stiff cock is what distracts her from caring, but her body softens.

The edges of my vision blur reality and ecstasy as I burst apart inside my girl. I thrust every last drop inside her, needing to mark her as mine from the inside.

A few minutes later, chests still heaving and my cum still dripping into her panties, I piggy back carry her out into the locker room. Our friends are now drinking sparkling apple cider from champagne glasses, wearing championship t-shirts and hoodies.

"Who the fuck got these done? Talk about tempting fate." I place Edith back into her wheelchair and put her casted leg up on the rest.

"Feel better?" Scott holds out a glass to me with a grin.

No point in even trying to deny it. "Much."

Myers hands a glass to my girl. "If it helps, all I could see was his naked back."

If I had something to throw at him, I would. But the resulting flush spreading down Edith's neck is delectable.

"Nicely done." He offers me a fist bump, and when my fist connects with his, Edith groans and hangs her head in her hands.

"I hate you all."

"Payback is a wench." Eloise's voice is small, but no one misses it and we all crack up.

"How did you not get frost bite?" Savannah's eyes widen. "What if your peen dropped off because it got so cold?" Her questions are directed to Ares, but her eyes remain on Eloise. "So fucking badass."

"You know." Raffi takes a sip of his drink. "It's not super easy to do it around these parts without getting caught. Unless getting caught is your jam." He winks at Ares who tips his glass to him. "But in case anyone should need to know, the tables in the training room are the perfect height." He drinks again. "Or so I'm told."

The conversation buzzes around us, but I can't take my eyes off my princess. One thing's for certain—no way in fucking hell I'm making it through dinner without banging her again.

CHAPTER 37

Edith

My boyfriend is fucking feral.

I've never had someone's tongue near my ass before, but holy crap, it feels kind of nice. I've seen his tongue, I've sucked his tongue, I've had his tongue inside me, but right now, as my ass is in the air and my face planted into the sheets on our bed, I've decided he has *two* tongues.

He's somehow everywhere, all at once. Licking, sucking, biting, I can barely keep track of what he's doing. My clit throbs, skipping along with the rhythm of my racing pulse, my pussy is drenched, slick and squelching as he drags his tongue and digits through my lips.

His finger circles my ass, and while I've never been even so much as curious about having something in my butt, color me officially butt-stuff-curious.

I should be embarrassed at the state of myself right now. I'm grinding my pussy on his face, fisting the sheets with my hands, while making animalistic noises that definitely couldn't be mistaken as human.

As I press back against him harder, he chuckles, sending tiny vibrations through my pussy. Slipping two fingers inside me, he curls his fingers against my walls, and I fall apart. My body jerks, juddering, shaking, vibrating with pulse after pulse of pure euphoria rippling through every inch of me.

I don't scream, I roar. Like a wild animal in the jungle, squirting cum all over my boyfriend's face. But he's not done.

He slides underneath me, between my legs, and pulls my hips down, planting my pussy on his face. "Ride my tongue, Edie."

So fucking bossy. "I don't think I can come again, Apollo."

I feel his grin against my pussy. The wide curve of his lips tickling my labia. "Challenge accepted." His words are garbled, like he's under water. And considering how squirty and squelchy I've been, well, that tracks.

Gripping me against his face, he goes to work. I've quickly become addicted to his oral obsession, and within seconds I'm gripping the edge of my headboard and bucking against the flat of his tongue like a bitch in heat.

I'm chasing an orgasm I'm not sure I'll reach. But he's determined. And the more he flicks his tongue the more it feels tangible, achievable. My prince of darkness is unrelenting in his hold.

He hums against my swollen clit, and my muscles clench, flickering with anticipation around his mouth. Jesus Christ. It's no wonder I never stayed with my exes for very long. This is what I had been searching for without knowing.

He sweeps his fingers past my asshole, and I'm almost disappointed. But when the pads of his digits press against my g-spot, driving me across the finish line, I'm too busy chanting his name and mumbling incoherent gibberish to care.

The release doesn't stop. It keeps thundering into me,

wave after glorious wave of bliss as I empty my soul onto Apollo's face.

He swallows, audibly. How much of me has he drunk? He doesn't quit though, holding me against his hungry face, lapping at me, slurping me in until every last ripple, aftershock, and muscle twitch passes through my body.

I don't know how I'm still upright. My leg is throbbing. Being on my knees was a good idea at first, but now it's aching. As if he can sense my thoughts, he tugs me, flips me, then cages me in on the bed with his whole body.

His mouth is soaked, my arousal literally dripping from his chin as he grins at me. "I'm going for the hat trick."

Somehow I manage to shake my head. "I can't come again, Apollo. I can't." I can't move my arms to point to my crotch. "It's broken. You broke me."

He grins again. "Maybe I fixed you. Can I try again?"

I nod. "As long as you're not offended if I can't come again."

He guffaws like it's not even an option, then kisses a wet trail down my body, pausing to bite at my nipples. I'm well aware that my soul is about to leave my body. If nothing else, at least I'll die happily. And my killer is unaliving me in the best possible way. With his skillful tongue, while drowning in my cum.

"You ready?" Excited chocolate eyes stare up at me from between my thighs, his hand pressed on my abdomen.

"Aren't you tired? Don't you want a turn?"

His grin is devilish, almost sinister, but filled with promise and mischief. "This *is* my turn." He buries his face into my pussy like he hasn't tasted me in weeks, making me scream as his teeth nibble at my swollen joy-button.

I swear to all that's holy if he breaks my fun controller or bites it off I'll kill him.

He tickles the nub with the tip of his tongue, fluttering so gently like the kiss of butterfly wings before sucking it into his mouth with a chuckle.

This asshole really is trying to kill me.

CHAPTER 38

Apollo

(APRIL 8TH – DAY 22 POST OP)

I've been waiting in the lobby of my father's office for ninety minutes and counting. My letter of resignation burns a hole in my pocket as I pick invisible lint from my pant leg. His secretary sends me sympathetic glances every few minutes, tipping her head with that "you know how he can be" look pasted across her soft features.

"He shouldn't be much longer."

Another glance at my watch tells me it's been closer to two hours than an hour and a half, and something inside me finally snaps.

I'm done.

I'm done being his business clone.

I'm done being punished for playing hockey instead of going to his client meeting.

I'm done waiting around to be yelled at because of my life choices.

I'm done spending one single more second trying to do right by a man who hasn't done right by any of us, especially Mamá.

Tugging down my pant legs as I stand, I slide the envelope

from my jacket pocket and place it on the secretary's desk. "Can you make sure he gets this, please, Janet?"

"Oh, I'm sure he won't be much longer, Mr. de la Peña. He said—"

Raising my hand silences her as I shake my head. "I'm no longer interested in what he has to say, Janet. Please ensure he gets this, and since I've always liked you, I'll give you a heads up. You might want to start pulling employee files to search for my replacement."

She pales, stuttering and stammering half sentences as she shakes her head, pushing the envelope back across the counter toward me.

"It's done, Janet. Waiting two hours for a face-to-face to deliver the letter sealed the deal. This isn't the place for me."

"B-b-but, Mr. de la Peña..."

I'm already halfway out the door, feeling lighter than I have in years. If my father wants to discuss further business with me, *he* will have to make an appointment with *me*. And should that time ever come, maybe I'll make him wait for two hours to make a point.

"How'd it go?"

When I step into Edith's apartment—*our* apartment—there are bodies everywhere. I was only expecting to find Edie on the couch, but she's got Bacon across her lap staring up at her lovingly like she created celery.

Ares, Artemis, and Scott are at the dining table playing Monopoly, and Athena is on the loveseat with her back to me, scrolling on her phone. The sight of my people gathered to support me—at least I hope that's why they're all in my space —brings a lump to my throat.

"*Sí, hermanito.* How did it go?" Hen tucks her phone in

her pocket and looks at me expectantly over her shoulder. Her eyes swim with concern. If I didn't know her better, I'd say she wants to launch herself over the back of the loveseat and throw her arms around me.

But it's Athena, and she doesn't do that kind of thing. At least not very often. She's more than met her quota for the year.

Except, she's standing, turning, and coming at me pretty fast. By the time her arms lock around my body, squeezing the air from my lungs, I'm convinced she's been abducted by aliens.

"I'm so proud of you." Her mumbled words against my body make my brothers' heads snap up around the table.

Ares mouths, "What the fuck?" to me, and I can't even shrug in reply because our sister has me in a death grip.

"Athena? Are you okay?" I try to keep my voice low and even so no one else hears, but Edith's confused eyes meet mine, and she confirms with a single glance that I'm not over-reacting. Athena hugging and being all smushy is just plain fucking weird.

Athena nods against my shoulder. "Do you want to talk about it?"

I step back from her. "I didn't see him. *Pendejo* kept me waiting for damned near two hours. So, I handed my letter of resignation to his secretary and left." I wait a beat for the fear, the guilt, the regret... but none of those things hit. In fact, relief unfurls the tense muscles in my neck and shoulders, just a little bit more.

"Did you call Mamá?" Artemis asks from the table, moving his top hat a few spaces around the board. He's picked the top hat ever since we learned to play the game. I don't think even he knows why at this point. But he'd definitely fight for it if someone else dared to take it at the start of the game.

"No." I rake my hand through my hair. "I wouldn't know what to say. I wanted to figure out what we're going to do first before I called her. Just in case I fucked up, you know?"

Rolling the dice, Ares snorts from the table. *"Hola, Mamá. ¿Cómo estás?* Did you know your *cabrón* husband is collecting bastard offspring like fucking Pokémon? You could work that into conversation pretty easily, *hermano."*

Scott picks up the dice, he's basically part of the family, he knows all our dirty secrets. "How do you feel?"

Checking in with myself one more time, I pause before answering his question. Sucking in a deep breath, I let it fill every inch of space in my chest. "Free."

CHAPTER 39
Edith
(APRIL 12TH – DAY 26 POST OP)

I'm so fucking sick and tired of these crutches. According to my doctors, it's too soon for a boot. But this cast-and-crutches combo is ruining my life. Okay, so that's a smidge dramatic, but it's most definitely ruining the lines of my outfit.

I wanted to go ax throwing. I've *always* wanted to go ax throwing but it's not really an acceptable activity in the hyper-feminized ballet world. I couldn't get any of my friends to go with me, and I felt a tiny seed of guilt for even wanting to try it.

But *apparently* ax throwing isn't a good idea when you've got a broken leg, so we settled on a middle-of-the-day movie.

It's unfair just how handsome Apollo looks when he's not even trying. He's wearing a pair of dark wash jeans, and a dark green sweater that complements his brown eyes to perfection. I want to peel his clothes off him and drag my tongue all over his body. But he says we need to go on a date before too long passes, and we never get around to it.

I tried to tell him that we've done all kinds of date-like things over the years, but he's determined to have a real first date. A *proper* one, whatever the fuck that means. Do people even put effort into first dates these days? Isn't it all just dick pics and booty calls?

Who knew Apollo de la Peña was such a traditionalist?

The theater is almost empty. We're sitting far from the screen, near the back, and once he's done piggy backing me up the stairs to our seats, he disappears to the concession stand for snacks. Because no movie is complete without appropriate snackage.

I can't remember the last time I saw a movie in the theater. Always dancing, working out, meal-prepping... the little things like spending two and a half hours watching a movie fell by the wayside in lieu of something more important.

Unlocking my phone, I scroll through the socials, deliberately hunting out my old dance friends, watching and re-watching their short videos from the end of season auditions. It still cuts into my chest almost every bit as much as it did four months ago when we crashed.

Four months.

When I woke up in December all busted up and sore from head to toe, I was convinced that by March I'd be back en pointe. Instead, I'm still hobbling around like an old woman, unable to put my foot on the ground at all, and I have no idea how the bones are knitting together under my new hardware.

Will I need more surgery?

Assuming all goes well with my cast removal, I have six weeks until my first PT session. Maybe that will instill some hope into my aching soul. I've tried to spend some time thinking about life—long term—and how that would look if I truly can't dance again.

The crippling, consuming panic at the thought tickles at the base of my spine. Blinking back tears, I shake my head. I can't accept that part of my life might be gone forever. I just can't.

Maybe by the time PT starts I'll be in a better place emotionally to hear—again—that my life-long dream is gone forever. But today is not that day.

"What's wrong?" Apollo places the giant soda in the armrest to my left before handing me an equally giant bag of popcorn.

"Butter?"

He arches a brow. "This might be our first date, Edith. But I'm not new to how you like your snacks."

Rolling my lips between my teeth to fight a smile, I nod.

"Are you going to tell me what's wrong?"

Shoving my phone away with a sigh, I pop some popcorn in my mouth, groaning at the delicious buttery taste that explodes on my tongue. Drenched in butter, exactly how I like it. "Getting in my feels about dance again." The sadness devouring me is a constant companion, clawing at my chest. I've tried to press it down as best I can when I'm around Apollo and Penelope. They're probably so sick of my misery, and I can't blame them. I'm fed up with it all, too.

He cups my face, turning me to him. "We will face whatever comes, together. *Sí?*"

My internal monologue is stuck on repeat. Until I know how my leg is healing, and what my recovery looks like, I can't know for certain if I'm going to dance again, or if I need to find something new to do with my life. And that ambiguity seems to be engulfing me in the meantime.

At some point during the movie, Apollo hauls me into his lap. I guess sitting next to him was too far away. Pinned against his muscular chest, my head resting on his shoulder as his fingers skim my thigh, the anxiety loosens its hold for long enough to enjoy the film.

But it'll be back.

It always comes back.

"Lo siento, princesa." Apollo helps me into the car with ease. Helping me has become as much of a part of our routine as working out or cooking together was before the accident. I've given up fighting him—it's much easier for both of us if I accept defeat, and his help.

"What are you sorry for?"

He rolls his eyes before closing the car door, circling the hood, and hopping in the driver's side. "That wasn't the most creative date in the world."

I fell asleep during the movie, waking up having drooled all down the front of his soft sweater. After the movie, we went to see Brian-the-pie-guy for food, and I'm now stuffed and fit to burst.

"I keep telling you, we've been dating for years. We just had no idea." The idea is ridiculous, but paying attention to the time we spend together, the subconscious touches, the ease with which we exist in each other's space. It's hard to deny.

He starts the engine, and my stomach plummets. You'd think after four months it would get easier. My new therapist says it might never get easier. I'm as willing to accept that as I am to accept I'll never dance again.

My gut churns as he eases the car out of the parking lot. His fingers find mine, intertwining our digits, and he gives a gentle squeeze. "Keep breathing, princesa."

Nodding, I pinch my lips between my teeth to strangle the panic creeping up in my throat. It's not always this bad. Sometimes I can get into a car with barely a flicker of fear, but other times it's as though a heavy block has settled on my chest, preventing oxygen from getting into my body.

Apollo's phone lights up in the center console, and I'm right back to that night, on that road. The coppery tang of blood in the air, the bone-deep cold, the crunching of the glass as the emergency service people approached the car.

A shiver cracks up my spine, making me squeak.

"Rough one?" His hand tightens around mine as I nod, picking up his phone.

"It's Athena." A groan slips out between my lips, and he chuckles.

"What is it?"

"She wants to know if we can head to your parents."

His head snaps to me, then back to focus on the road ahead. "When? Now?"

The sweet apple pie in my stomach threatens to come back up. Neither of us want to face his father. But perhaps we need to get it the hell out of the way so we can move forward?

"Yeah." My voice is barely a whisper. "She said your mom sent out the bat signal."

He falls quiet for a moment, pausing at the lights at the intersection of Edgewood Road and Blairs Ferry. "Do you want me to drop you at home first?"

My heart flickers. His consideration, the desire to protect me from his family drama is touching. But I'm not letting him face this alone. "Can I come?"

He doesn't even blink before he's heading toward I-380.

This is going to be fun.

CHAPTER 40

Apollo

Watching Mamá throw her arms around my girl as she balances awkwardly on her crutches thaws something inside my chest.

"Edith, *querida*, how are you? It's so wonderful to see you." Her smile is warm and genuine, suggesting she's either not at all surprised I brought her, or she's not bothered. It might even be both. "How's your leg healing?"

Edith winces but smooths her delicate features as quickly as her next breath comes. "I'm okay, Gabi, thank you. It's a long road. It's going slowly."

Mamá nods, her lips turning down in sympathy. "And painful."

Edith shrugs like it's no big deal, but Mamá knows better. She's seen her hockey-playing kids recover from any number of injuries over the years. She knows there's no greater pain than being kept from doing something you love while watching your peers continue to thrive at something you're good at.

Abuelita hugs Edith next. She's always liked her, always

said she loved watching Edith take my bullshit, unwrap the pretty bow, and shove it up my—

Mamá grabs me in a bone-crunching hug before rubbing at my forehead with her thumb. "All that scowling will give you stress lines, *mijo*." She plants a loud kiss on my cheek before standing me back at arm's length. "Let me look at you."

Edith grins at me from behind Mamá.

"You look good."

Abuelita snorts next to Edith. "Good! He looks skinny." She cups my face with both palms. "You're working out too much, *Pico*."

She's called me "beak" since Edith started calling me "chicken." I hate them both.

From the cars on the driveway, everyone else is here. We probably should have carpooled, or coordinated so that four vehicles didn't all make the trip, but here we are. I try to distract Abuelita from the fact I have "no meat on my bones," and coax everyone into the house from the porch.

My siblings are already around the dining table, a variety of drinks in front of them as they chat. There's no sign of Papá, but the thudding in my chest reminds me of the fear he instills in me. Probably in all of us.

Artemis grabs Edith's crutches and tucks them out of the way while I help her sit in one of the high-backed dining chairs. When she's seated, I grab a footstool from the living room and slip it under the table so she can rest her foot.

Abuelita pats my cheek as she passes. "It's about time you two finally got together." She rolls her eyes. "This one needs someone who won't put up with his shit, Edith."

Edith's cheeks are the color of Mamá's claret tablecloth. "I'm not about to start letting his crap slide now, Abuelita."

Abuelita nods like she approves of the fact Edith is going to continue giving me crap now that she's my girlfriend. She disappears into the kitchen, and without a single word uttered

I know she's going to return with food. She keeps frowning at me across the table as though my bodyweight offends her.

"Where's Papá?" Athena draws her fingertip around the rim of her glass. "Isn't he joining us for this family meeting?"

"If it was truly a family meeting, *hija*, it would have remained between members of our actual family." Papá enters the room with a glass in hand, half full of golden liquid. He sits down on the chair at the head of the table, sending a barbed stare in Edith's direction.

I clear my throat. Edith takes my bullshit because she loves me, but she doesn't have to take his, and she's too damned polite to fight him in front of the rest of my family. "Actually, Edith has been family since we were children. Isn't that what you tell her father every time you see each other? How *close* we are as families?"

Papá grimaces but doesn't speak.

What I don't say out loud is that since I plan to make Edith my wife as soon as she's willing, his argument holds no merit. I don't want to make Edie any more uncomfortable than she is. I barely got her to be my girlfriend. I can't spook her by admitting I've already envisioned our future, our family, and our forever together.

From the smirk on Abuelita's face as she places silver platters of food on the table, she already knows. She taps the side of her nose with a sly wink that Mamá doesn't miss.

Papá hands a piece of paper to me. From the way it's creased, I can take an educated guess that it's the letter I handed to his secretary. *"¿Qué es esto?"*

The urge to smart mouth him is damn near overwhelming. "My letter of resignation, Papá. I thought it was self-explanatory." I've already had pie. In fact, I already had two kinds of pie, but I grab at the foil-wrapped burritos to give my hands something to do, and my mouth a chance not to snap at my father.

"Is this a joke?" He waves the letter my direction again.

"No, sir." I harden my face, clenching my jaw, and look him dead in the eyes. "I'm done working for you and the company. Thank you for the opportunities you've given me, but my path is taking a different direction."

The impact of his fist against the table causes the crystal glasses and silverware on the table to rattle. Edith tenses at my side before sliding her hand into mine. The gesture is small, probably subconscious, but it's more necessary than I realized. Knowing she has my back, no matter the outcome of this so-called-meeting, means so much to me.

"I could ruin you, Apollo. You might want to think twice before I decide to accept it." He glares at me over the edges of the thick, cream paper.

Mamá sits silently, watching me with a curious expression on her face. And as though my face betrays I need some additional support, Abuelita gives me a single, sharp nod across the table.

"I have my own money, my own apartment, my own car. I don't need your money. I have my own direction in life, Papá, my own dreams. I don't need to chase yours anymore."

Ares sucks in a breath. Athena's gripping the stem of her glass so hard, her knuckles are white. And I can almost feel Artemis's quiet support from across the table.

"You don't get to quit this family, Apollo." Papá slams his hand onto the table again. "You have responsibilities."

Edith taps my hand. "Actually, Alonso, with all due respect, Apollo isn't quitting the family, he's quitting the business. And his responsibilities are to himself. If he's not happy, it's up to him to make whatever changes he deems necessary to make himself happy. That is all. He doesn't owe you anything simply because you are related."

Papá's ears go red, and his nostrils flare. "You'd do well to stay out of this, Edith. Meddling girl, just like your mother, aren't you?"

Edith's spine straightens, and Mamá opens her mouth, I hope to come to her defense, but Edie doesn't seem to need it.

"And you'd do well to keep my mother and threats against me out of your mouth, Alonso. You might be business partners with my father, but in my house 'family first' carries a different meaning."

Papá grunts, muttering something under his breath. "And what the fuck is that supposed to mean?"

Edith doesn't blink, she doesn't look away. I've never loved her more than I do in this moment. My family collectively holds their breath. Athena's staring at Edith like she's seeing her for the first time, and Abuelita is grinning like the cat who got the fucking cream.

"It means one phone call to daddy about how much of a *cabrón* you're being to me, and who knows what that might mean for your business agreements? How do you think he'd react if I told him you made me cry?" She sniffs theatrically, and I swear to fucking God tears well in her eyes.

Papá's face is turning purple. "Who do you think you are, Edith? Coming into my house, disrespecting me? *Threatening* me?"

The corner of her lip twitches. "I am my father's daughter, Alonso. And if you got your head out of your ass for more than a hot minute you'd see that Apollo is his father's son. As such, he needs to find his own way. Just. Like. You. Did. He needs to blaze a trail of his own, in the sunshine, not follow along in his father's shadow."

My chest cracks in two. The ballet world thrives on conformity, on gaslighting girls and women into doing what they're told. Edith has a famous quote from Balanchine pinned on her mirror that says, *"Don't think, dear, just do."*

Her words are such a contrast with the fuckery of the

ballet world mentality, and I couldn't be prouder. Mamá looks like she's fighting hard to fan her cheeks as her eyes shine with unshed tears.

I've known for years that Edith has had issues with Papá, but I guess because I wasn't ready to step into my own power, to find my own path, she kept her ire tapped down. My lioness is roaring. And it's so fucking hot.

"We aren't done with this." He stands, waving the page at me again.

"*Sí, Papá.* We *are* done with this. I quit. I'm pursuing a career in professional hockey, and I won't have time to work with you anymore."

Edie squeezes my hand under the table.

"Was this the reason for the meeting? To try to scold me in front of my siblings? In front of Mamá and Abuelita? To have them *talk sense* into me? To make me see the error of my ways? To manipulate me into staying in a role that makes me unhappy? That causes me stress?"

Papá rolls his eyes. "What the fuck do you know about stress? You're a boy." He sneers at me. "And what do you plan to do when you get too old to play hockey?" He purses his lips like he thinks he's thrown the winning hand onto the table.

Edith pipes up again. "By then I'll probably have taken over from daddy, Alonso. I think we'll be fine."

Papá pales as the realization of the fact that Edith will inherit her father's half of the business in the future. She's never expressed an interest in taking the reins of the family business before, but it wouldn't surprise me if she does it now, out of sheer spite.

From the sparkle of glee in Ares's eyes, he's totally on board with her choosing violence. And without looking at her, I know Athena is as well. She's queen of choosing violence.

"You'll hand back your shares."

I snort. "I'll do no such thing."

"I'll buy them from you," he counters.

"I'm not selling."

Abuelita's head bounces side to side like she's watching a ping pong game, except instead of a ball, Papá and I are batting words back and forth.

He glances at Edith, as if to say *reason with this idiot*, except she grins at me. "Maybe I'll gift you my shares for your birthday."

It's the straw that breaks the camel's back. Ares bursts into peals of laughter, Abuelita doubles over, giggles shaking her entire body, and Papá bounds to his feet, mumbling to himself in Spanish.

None of us have ever stood up to him before. I bet he has no fucking clue what to do with it, or how to react, either. He looks to Mamá, but the only thing on her face is disappointment. "Are you going to let him disrespect me like this?"

She nods her head. "Even if I considered Apollo to be disrespecting you, I would. Yes, Alonso. Because he is right. It isn't for us to tell our children how to live their dreams. As their parents, we just have to support them where we can and hope they reach them." She turns to me. "You've always been so talented on the ice, *mijo*. Your siblings never stop talking about how amazing you are, they are so proud of you. And your statistics speak for themselves."

I thought she'd stopped watching our games when we went to college. I don't quite know what to do with that information, but she isn't stopping for long enough to let me process what she said.

"I was starting to worry that you wouldn't listen to the call of your heart." She leans across the table and takes the hand Edith isn't holding in her own before patting my cheek. "Clearly it took someone with a solid foot to kick you in the rear. And I can't wait to see you fly, *mijo*."

By the time Edith and I get back into my car and are

waving to Mamá and Abuelita standing on the porch, my muscles are relaxed, my heart is happy. And with the support of my girl, and my family, I'm renewed in my determination to make it to the NHL. Now I have to bust my ass to make it happen.

CHAPTER 41

Edith

(MAY 13TH – DAY 37 POST OP)

"How does it feel?" Tori sits across the sofa from me, my feet in her lap. They cut my cast off less than an hour ago, and everything feels kind of weird. I wiggle my toes, scrunching up my face.

"Like I need a fucking pedicure."

She giggles. "I won't argue there. You've got some seriously ugly feet right now, boo. Maybe we'll stop by that place Ares and Eloise use. They love going for mani-pedis."

I don't think I could ever convince Apollo to come get his toes done with me. I'd say it's because he has gnarly, gross feet, but even his little fucking piggies are fucking perfect. I bet even his butt hole is fucking perfect. Ugh.

"Sounds like a plan."

"What time are people arriving?"

"Any time now." We're hosting Get Lit, the Raccoons monthly book club. It's early this week as we're on the long stretch into finals before the summer. Or everyone else is, I'm still figuring things out.

Apollo and the guys agreed that Eloise, Tori, Savannah and I could hang around as long as we didn't make fun of the boys as they talk about their feelings on the book. Not that we would. I'm looking forward to getting a glimpse into what they actually talk about at these things.

A folding table is set up against the far wall in the living room. It has a stack of paper plates, napkins, and paper cups next to a slow cooker of some form of chicken with green salsa for tacos.

Cooper Duke arrives first with pies from Get the Fork Out. My stomach flips in glee. He not only pours himself a drink, but he gets one for Victoria and me. Then he plumps one of the couch cushions and puts it under my foot on her thigh.

Nothing makes me go ga-ga more than a giant hulk of an angry-looking man being warm and squishy. Cooper is a beautiful man. On the ice a single glare has some of the biggest men in the league quaking in their skates, but off-ice he is the sweetest man I've probably ever met.

He does door duty, letting everyone else in. Before long, the girls are in the living room, and Apollo, Artemis, Ares, Scott, Justin, Cooper, Slater, Tyler, and Jackson are all crammed around the dining room table with paperback copies of Lucy Score's chart-smashing hit *Things We Hide From the Light* in hand.

The food table bows under the weight of the aromatic dishes everyone brought with them. Everything from sandwiches to French toast casserole. Abuelita sent an entire pan of patatas bravas with spicy sauce with Ares from Guac 'n Roll.

There is even a stack of Tupperware containers next to the spread for everyone to bring some food home with them. Because there's no way Apollo and I can get through all of this by ourselves.

This isn't simply a book club, it's a bougie book club. I should have expected *extra* from these fancy pants players. They've got it all covered. Paperback copies for everyone—including extras in case anyone new shows up, enough food to sink a ship, and from the fact everyone took their shoes off at the door, I'd wager no one is going anywhere fast. It might be my new favorite thing.

Listening to Apollo as he deep-dives into the male psyche while flicking through his highlighted and tabbed copy of *Things We Hide From the Light* is more arousing than I expected it to be. I squirm every time he speaks, turns the pages, or glances my direction.

It's as though he can read my mind. He pulls off his sweater, revealing his tanned and toned forearms. Drool pools in my mouth. The only thing hotter than a delicious man turning pages, is when you can see the slight ripple in his muscular arms as he does it.

I'm so fucking hot for him right now. And I have two functional feet. Could I convince him to bend me over the bookcase and have his way with me?

He licks his lower lip, hooded eyes darkening like the hero his friends are talking about in the book. Something about how I'm staring at him has the corner of his lips tugging up in a knowing smirk. It's as though he heard my inner monologue screaming for his tongue to plant itself on my clit and lap like it's an Olympic sport.

"Stop eye-fucking my brother." A Cheeto bounces off my forehead and lands in Victoria's glass of wine. *Wine.* These college hockey players are so extra.

Eloise doubles over, laughing so hard tears stream down her cheeks.

Savannah points to me. "Do that again, Hen. I want to see if it was a fluke."

I dust off any orange powder from my forehead. "Thanks, but I don't consent. I have no doubt Athena could get it in ten times over if she wanted."

One of the boys hollers, "That's what she said," and Athena hurls a Cheeto at him too.

Eloise finally composes herself as Tori smacks my thigh. "Athena isn't wrong, E. There is some serious eye-fucking going on between you and her brother. The temperature has climbed four degrees since book club started. When they called it Get Lit, I don't think they meant it quite so literally."

"What are you girls whispering about?" Apollo knows exactly what the topic of conversation is, he's just being a dick. My face is on fire as half a dozen hockey players turn their attention from Nash and Lina in their books, to me.

Savannah opens her mouth to answer him, but I cut her off with a pointed finger and a snarl. "Don't you fucking dare."

Raffi chuckles. "They're talking about all your eye-fucking."

Tori tenses under my legs, but when I catch her eye she gives me that "Don't say a word" glare she's perfected. If she thinks I've forgotten that she owes us an explanation for all things Raffi, she's wrong. Some people might forget a woman dumping a drink all over a guy's head in a bar, but we aren't those women. She's not talking, though. So whatever it is, it must be bad.

If nothing else, they're sitting in the same room and she hasn't dumped anything over his head or smashed his face into something.

But I suppose the night is still young.

How long is an acceptable length of time to let your friends hang around your apartment to discuss a book when there's a low, heavy, and demanding ache between your legs? Asking for a friend.

The longer this night takes to wrap up, the more uncontrollable I feel.

Apollo barely gets the door closed behind our last visitor

when I launch myself at him, vaulting into his arms. He staggers backward against the door, cupping my ass, squeezing my cheeks with hungry palms.

"I've... wanted... agh. All fucking night." I pant out the words between kisses, and his answer is that rumbling chuckle that warms me all the way to my toes.

He flips us, so my back is against the door and grinds against me, pressure building between my thighs. He's refusing to kiss my mouth, and only letting me kiss his jaw, or cheek, playfully turning his head away from me any time I try to strike.

Fucker has provoked me all night. Maybe it's time to tease him a little back. Canting my head, I make a "hm" sound.

He pulls back. "*¿Que hm?*"

"I was just thinking. I'm not sure your dick is going to be enough for me tonight."

He bristles so hard I slip a little in his arms. "Is that so?" His voice is low with a gravely undercurrent.

I nod, barely containing a shuddering giggle. "I hear you and Artemis... you know..." I lick my lips. "Share sometimes."

His body slams against me with such force my head bumps the door. "No."

"No, you don't share women with your brother sometimes?"

The animalistic growl that comes out of my man is enough to make my toes curl. "No, I don't share *you* with my brother."

"But—"

His lips are on mine with ferocious intensity. His teeth tear at my lips as his fingers find the band of my pants and start working them down my thighs.

"No."

"But—"

He slides me to my feet before curling his hand around my

throat, bracing me against the door. I soaked my panties. This is going way better than I could have anticipated.

My nipples are cutting through my bra, my pussy tingles with anticipation... How far I can push him before he all-out snaps?

He puts his lips close to my ear as he flexes his fingers around my throat. "*Princesa*, if you want to be fucked by more than one guy at a time, we'll talk about it. We'll find someone together, but it will not, and I can't emphasize this enough, it will *not* be my brother. *Sí*?"

The heat in his eyes is enough to melt my clothes off. His chest is heaving, he's panting with physical restraint.

I can't help but grin at him, and that's what makes him snap. Before I can blink, he's crouching at my feet, pulling off my pants and panties. When he stands, he lifts me over his shoulder and carries me to the couch. I'm barely back on my feet when he shoves my panties in my mouth, grinning at me.

He folds me over the back of the couch and runs his already bare cock through my wetness. "I thought we were clear on who you belonged to, *princesa*."

Wiggling my hips, I moan into the fabric, desperate for him to give me what I need. If I flail much more I could hit the coffee table and send yet another vase of brightly colored fresh flowers sailing onto the floor.

"Ah, ah, ah. No dick until you tell me who this pussy belongs to."

When I don't spit out my panties, and instead choose to stay silent, he shunts me further over the back of the couch, ass in the air, and spreads my legs. "Tell me, Edie. Tell me who this perfectly pink little cunt belongs to or there will be consequences."

I remain quiet, a crackle of anticipation snaps the air around us, and I'm not sure if I'm anxious about where this is going, or so fucking excited I could die.

"Answer me, Edith." His commanding voice booms around the room. "Or I'll spank this pussy until you are in no doubt about who owns it."

Trying to swallow around the fabric, I refuse to answer. He gives me less than a second before his hand meets my soaking wet and swollen lips sending a sharp bite of pain through my body.

Kneading my ass cheeks, he hums. "Like a little impact play do you *princesa*?"

Moaning is the only answer I've got for him. Even if I could speak, my brain checked out the moment his hand cracked against my pussy.

"Like some pain with your play?"

I've never tried it before, never had the inclination until today, right this very second, with this man I trust more than anyone in the entire world.

He palms at my ass cheeks. I'm so wet we might need a new couch. There's no way my arousal isn't coating the top of this cushion.

"You want a spanking, *princesa*?"

The combination of his pet name, the pulsing desperation between my thighs, and the anticipation of his next slap has turned me into a mindless sex fiend. I nod, but no slap comes.

"Spit out your panties, Edie. If I'm going to slap you I want you to be able to tell me when you need me to stop, okay?"

I nod. I've watched *Fifty Shades*. It's the only kind of kink I've ever been exposed to. But from the authority in Apollo's voice right now, this isn't his first rodeo, and that makes me want it even more.

"Green is fine. Yellow is approaching tolerance. And red is stop altogether. Are we clear?"

I nod again, but apparently that's not enough.

"Verbal confirmation, Edith."

Christ, what is it about his demands that are getting me wetter and wetter? He's never been hotter.

"Y-yes." I swallow, my throat dry.

"Repeat it back to me."

"Red is stop. Yellow is warning. Green is fine."

As soon as the word fine leaves my lips, his hand is on the soft part of my ass with a loud smack. The flickering flames in my abdomen flare brighter as my whole body wiggles in satisfaction, aftershocks coursing through my limbs.

"I never thought your ass could look any finer, Edith. But having my bright red handprint on it..." He groans and a swishing sound follows. Is he fisting his cock?

When the head of his cock slips through my pussy, an inhuman noise falls from my mouth. "Tell me who this belongs to, and I'll give you what you need."

Shaking my head, I grip the throw pillow on the couch in front of me. This is going to sting. The clap of the strike meets my ears before the hot sting radiates through the cheek he didn't smack last time. An untamed scream rips out of my throat.

"Color?"

"G-g-green." I'm close to orgasm. I have no idea how. He has barely touched me yet. My body trembles with need, my skin tingles from the impact, and my stomach clenches. I need more.

"Are you ready to tell me who this pussy belongs to?"

Shaking my head, I'm really not. Maybe after another slap I'll give in and tell him what he needs, but for now, this... this... consuming need to have him smack me again takes over. I'm no longer in control of my body. He is. And despite the fact he wants the answer from me, he's also not ready for me to give it. His excitement sizzles almost as much as my ass.

"I'll give you to the count of three, Edith. Three."

A fresh rush of heat pools between my legs.

"Two."

My thighs clench in mouthwatering anticipation.

The smack happens right on "One" and the burst of liquid that comes out of me on contact has embarrassment crawling under my skin. He drags the tip of his cock through my slick folds. "Color?"

"Green"

"Still not ready to tell me who this belongs to, Edith?"

I need him inside me. I'm torn between giving into the answer tickling the tip of my tongue, and biting it down so I get more smacks. It's already going to hurt to sit down tomorrow, what's one more smack likely to change?

He pauses his dick at my entrance, making my hips buck against the couch. "*Dime*, princesa."

"You, Apollo. My pussy belongs to you."

When he thrusts his cock inside me in one hard, smooth motion, I cry out in blissful relief.

In truth, my prince of darkness possesses every part of me. Body, mind, and soul. Now that I've given myself over to him and stopped fighting how I'm feeling, custody of my entire being is non-negotiable.

He owns me.

CHAPTER 42

Apollo

I have never seen my perfectly composed girl so wholly unbridled before, and I fucking love it.

Drilling my cock into her as I stare at the red marks I left on her perky little ass, I can't help but thrust harder. "Such a tight pussy, Edie. I love feeling how much you need me right where I belong."

She flexes around my cock as she murmurs into the couch, her nails scratching against the fabric on the harder thrusts. Gentle is not in my playbook tonight.

I pull out, all the way to the tip, and right as she rears her head back to protest, I smack her and spear her in one go. The raw moans of pleasure she's making serve only to make me harder. I need to ravage every inch of this woman.

Her walls tense, flickering with telltale signs that she's close. "Don't fight it, *princesa*."

The temptation to circle my finger around her asshole is damn near overwhelming. She's never had anyone there, and the drive to send her over the edge in a wave of unprecedented bliss—but the risk of pushing her too far all at once, of sensory overload, isn't one I'm willing to take.

There's no way she won't feel my presence all day tomorrow, given that she's been perched at the perfect angle for me to handle her ass.

Another smack. Another uninhibited string of noises.

The quivering of her walls intensifies around my cock, and I hiss out a breath, determined not to blow until she's come for me. "Take it, princesa. Take every inch of me." I can't stop staring at the space where our bodies connect. My cock is slick from her arousal, and with each thrust she gets wetter.

I've never questioned if she'd be capable of what I need her to take from me. She's strong, determined, and she hates to fucking lose. But the harder my balls slap against her and the needier her little noises become as she pleads for me not to stop, the surer I am.

She ignites around my dick, gripping me with a force that sucks the breath from my lungs, forcing me over the edge with her. I can't hold back with her silky hot walls gripping me.

Grabbing onto her hips, my body jerks and spasms as I come, spilling into my whimpering girl. Bending over her, I stretch for the discarded panties on the cushion next to her.

As I tease my cock out of her a little at a time, we both hiss. Her legs twitch and jump as the remnants of her orgasm roll through her body.

Using my thumb, I collect the thick creamy cum trickling from her pussy and push it back in before stuffing her panties into her entrance to keep it there.

Sweeping her into my arms, I nuzzle the side of her deliriously sated face, my facial hair grazing against her soft cheek. "You are mine, *princesa*."

Her eyes flutter closed as she gives me a "mhmm. Forever." She sighs, her body sagging against me as I carry her to the bathroom. I pluck out the cum-soaked panties and place her on the toilet while I start the shower.

She yawns, blinking at me through heavy eyes. "But I'm not done yet."

She can barely keep her eyes open, but I love her enthusiasm, her determination. Cocking my eyebrow at her while she pees, she frowns. "I'm not."

When she stands and flushes, she sways on her feet. I was almost convinced. Her leg is still weakened from being in the cast for so long. I finish undressing her, pick her up, and place her on the bench in the shower. Her head lolls back against the tiles as the hot water hits her naked body. When I get onto my knees and pick up the sugar scrub and the shaving foam, her eyes flex wide.

"Wh-what are you doing?"

I wave the razor at her. "Shaving your legs, what does it look like I'm doing?"

Her mouth drops open like it's the most ludicrous thing she's ever heard. "But why?"

Shrugging, I uncap the scrub and squeeze a healthy dollop into my palm. "I want to take care of you. You've had that cast on for months. I figured you'd want to exfoliate, shave, and moisturize. It's bound to be dry and itchy after being locked up for that long."

Her eyes glisten as she nods. She's barely had a trace of hair on any part of her body in all the time I've known her. She grumbled to me last week about how she needed to get to the salon for some *maintenance*. But thus far, she hasn't gotten around to making an appointment. At least I don't think so.

"Did you book an appointment to get waxed yet?" At the stitch between her brows, I hurry to elaborate. "I don't care if you grow the biggest lady bush and never trim or wax it, but I know it bothers you." I rub at her pale calf and shin with the sugar scrub, taking particular care not to put too much pressure onto her leg.

She sighs. "It's really bothering me. I hate being so hairy."

She shakes her head. "I guess I don't hate it, but it's not what I'm used to, what I enjoy."

Nodding, I scrub the other leg a little more aggressively. "I booked you into the spa tomorrow. With Ares's manscaper. Bikini area and underarm, face if you'd like." My body heats. "I have no idea what you usually get. But when you're done getting waxed, I thought we could get massages. You know, glasses of champagne, fluffy-as-fuck dressing gowns, plush slippers, and his and hers baths while we read a few chapters together."

She folds her arms as I lather up the shaving foam gel between my hands.

"What?"

"If I'd known how high you'd level up your game when we became more than friends, I'd have done it years ago."

I'm laughing as I drag the razor down her leg, taking care not to slice her open around her knee, and again around the ankle. Dark red scars stand out against her stark white skin. It's hard to believe that those are the only external marks left on either of us from a night that I was convinced I was going to lose her.

When I'm done shaving both legs to her satisfaction, I'm not ready to stop taking care of her. She lets me shampoo and condition her hair, sugar scrub the rest of her body, and when I'm done patting her dry with a soft towel she lies face down on the bed and lets me cover every square inch of her with lotion.

By the time I'm done, she's snoring. So I climb into bed beside her and stroke her skin until I fall asleep too. I've never been fucking happier.

CHAPTER 43

Edith

(MAY 22ND – DAY 46 POST OP)

My legs shake as I wait to be called for my first PT appointment since my second surgery. I've done everything I was told this time. I'm even wearing my boot sometimes, when my leg feels like it needs that extra bit of support.

Sven calls me back into his office. It doesn't take long before his noises and facial expressions tell me that my ankle isn't moving the way it should. After a series of what he calls diagnostics, he talks about treatment for an immobile ankle, tells me it's like it's fused, even though it isn't.

He says it's not abnormal, that because it wasn't used for months I'll need physical therapy for rotation, flexing, and sideways movement.

He takes my hand when he tells me he thinks I'll get most of the movement back in my foot, but not all of it. He says when I point my toes up and down they're particularly limited—it's just as well I haven't picked a career that involves flexibility in my feet or anything, right?

When I tell him my balance is off, he nods thoughtfully,

telling me that the ligaments and tendons in my foot are going to be weak, then says the dreaded "Be patient."

I want to smash his face in with what's left of my fucking patience.

By the time my session is up, I'm drenched in sweat, my foot throbs with a bone-deep pain, and I'm hoping it's the good kind of pain, the healing kind.

My dance teacher, Miss Smith's words rattle around in my head.

"Miss one day you'll know it, miss a week and your peers know it, miss a month and the audience knows it."

I've missed five months.

I likely couldn't go back even if by some miracle my foot came out of the cast fully mobile.

I wasn't stupid enough to believe I could start dancing anytime soon, or that I'd be landing any major roles on stage, but I'd hoped for... more.

But I'm doing *something*, taking back control, and for now, that has to be enough.

I limp out onto the street. Standing against a lamppost is my prince of darkness, a crooked smile on his face. "How'd it go, champ?"

"What are you doing here?" I thread my arms around his neck and pull him into me for a kiss.

"Came to pick you up. I figured you'd be owie after you got done with PT."

He's not wrong, and his consideration, compassion, and empathy are all wrapping themselves around me like a warm hug. When his arms tighten around me, the hot tears that had been pricking my eyes for my PT session, fall freely down my cheeks.

"Didn't go well?" he mumbles against my head before he kisses my temple.

Shaking my head, I cry harder. "I wish I was David

Halberg. Then I could buy a one-way ticket to Australia to go to rehab for a year." I sob harder against his comforting body right there in the street.

I hadn't truly accepted that I wasn't going to dance. I guess I was clinging to shreds of hope that Sven the physical therapist would say, "Hey Edith, your leg is miraculously better." He'd pat me on the shoulder and tell me to go forth and dance my little heart out.

This fucking blows.

An hour later, Penelope and I are sitting in oversized massage chairs with our feet soaking in water. The warm bubbles tickle my skin. Pen's head is tipped back, her body shuddering with the force of the massage rolling through her body.

"I'm sorry, Pen." Grief and shame clogs my throat, thick and goopy like I've swallowed a whole pot of Jell-O, and it's gotten stuck. I haven't seen her as much as I would have liked recently, or even as much as I should have. I've pulled away from her, and I'm hoping that we can find our way back to baseline for our friendship. I miss her.

She holds up a hand, without opening her eyes. "Nope."

"But—"

"Edith, you suffered an almost life-ending trauma. You survived, and you've waded through nightmares, and therapy, and you're still working through recovery and rehabilitation. You need to mourn, and process, and heal at your own pace."

When did she get so smart?

"If you needed to turtle into your shell and hide away with your tall drink of delicious Dominican water for a while..." She shrugs. "I get it. Our friendship is stronger than a little distance between us."

Reaching for my hand, she cracks an eyelid. "Have you called your parents?"

I swallow again, but the thick wad at the back of my throat doesn't give.

"Edith!"

I shake my head. "Don't. I wasn't ready."

"And then?"

"Then I still wasn't ready."

"Do you even know where they are?"

My face burns. I probably should know that, right? "Tropical island somewhere, I'd guess."

Pen nails me with a stare that tells me she's about to say something I don't like. "Stop trying to be a one woman show and let people in to help. I mean, I know you have God-Boy, but your parents could support you if you let them."

In my defense, though, they haven't called me either. It's for the best. "I don't need the added pressure of getting back to dance before I'm ready, or the constant stress at not knowing what I'm going to do with my life if I never dance again." I sigh. "Mom has always wanted me to be Odette, she won't take it well when I tell her I'm not even going to be a swan."

CHAPTER 44

Apollo

(MAY 30TH – DAY 54 POST OP)

"I was thinking."

"Did it hurt?" Edith barely looks up from her book on the couch to acknowledge my statement. Her still-swollen foot is propped up on a stack of throw pillows with an ice pack draped over it. She cried a lot last night, and when she finally gave in to her exhaustion I did some research.

She's had three physical therapy sessions in the past week. Each seems to be more challenging, more tiresome, more draining on her energy. But her comment about flying to Australia like some guy called David stuck with me.

After some digging around on Google, I discovered a bunch of articles about David Halberg. It was seemingly a huge story in the ballet world a few years ago, and after a year of intensive rehab in Australia, he could dance.

From what I've read, the Australian Ballet is the absolute shit when it comes to injuries. If my girl ever has a chance of dancing again, that's where it's going to happen.

She tips her head to the side, lowering her book onto her lap. "What you got?"

"Let's go to Australia and get you rehabbed."

Her jaw drops open, hangs for a beat before snapping closed. "You're fucking crazy."

"Hear me out. I'm about to wrap up school for the summer, we could go and at least get you evaluated, talk to some people, see if there's anything we can do to increase the mobility in your ankle. I know you'll never get back what you had." I pause, struggling to contain my grief for my girl. "But if we go to the best in the world, there's a chance you could dance for fun, and maybe that'll be enough?"

Her face says "Bless you, sweet dumbass boy," as she gives me a sympathetic smile. "I'm not sure dancing will hold everything it held to me if you remove the competitive element of it, Pollo. But I appreciate the idea, and the thought. It's clear you've done some research."

I nod, but I'm not willing to let her away with it yet. "Will you think about it?"

"I don't want to ask my parents for that kind of money, Pollo." She hasn't been to class in months. I'm not sure if her parents have been notified of her pulling out of spring semester classes and just don't care, or my girl is somehow running interference so they don't know yet. Either way, she doesn't want to involve them.

I frown at her. "You know I'll pay whatever sum of money it takes to get you whatever treatment and rehab you need."

She sticks her tongue out. "Oh, how the other half live." She's scoffing, but her eyes glisten with gratitude. "You can't leave the country over the summer. You need to train, to play hockey, to practice with your team. You need to keep pressing forward so when the fall comes the scouts pick you up and offer you contracts for every NHL team in the country."

My stomach drops. She's not wrong. But if it means she'll consider it, I'd absolutely rearrange my life and go with her.

Her face flickers, she points her finger at me. "No. I'm not letting you trash your hockey career to take me to Australia on a wing-and-a-prayer idea that someone over there can make my busted up foot magically better."

She pauses for a beat. "Not to mention you'd have to *bribe* someone to work with me. Generally the PT staff work exclusively for the company."

"Your story took an unexpected turn, Edie. It sucks, no getting away from that. But don't let your story push you forward. Think about taking back some control, writing your own narrative, pushing the story forward yourself."

She looks at me like I've grown an extra eyeball in the middle of my forehead. "What the fuck rabbit hole did you fall down into on the internet last night when you looked up injury recovery?"

Shrugging, I flash a grin at her. It's true, there were perhaps some inspirational, you've got this, go team type articles I read about mindset, but Edith can accomplish anything she puts her mind to. She just needs to decide.

"Maybe you can't ever compete against other dancers again, *princesa*. But there's nothing to say you can't compete against yourself."

"I'll think about it." She taps her book against her chin. "But."

Here it comes.

"If I decide to go to Australia, it's by myself. I'll go solo, then you can stay here and practice hockey, and skate until your legs fall off. I want to come back to see you with a shiny new C on your shirt."

The fact she's already talking about coming back means she's thinking about it enough to go in the first place. That warms my chest way more than any mention of getting the captain's C. Not to mention, Artemis is a much better leader than I am on the ice. The whispers around the locker room concur. Everyone thinks he'll take over the reins when Justin graduates this summer.

She hasn't dismissed it right off the bat. She's already turning it over in her grey matter because she hasn't reopened the book on her legs. She's staring at it like it might have the answers she's seeking.

I don't want to push her either way. But I've brought her flowers to every, single dance recital she's performed in since she was a little girl. I've seen her light up from within when she dances. She's talked about nothing else for over a decade, and if this is what she needs to be able to get back doing what she loves? I'm all in.

Ares paces back and forth like a caged animal. This is the third sibling meeting we've had in as many days. This time it's at Edith's place, where I've moved in permanently. She's stretched out across the sofa, her feet on my thighs as I rub her recovering foot.

The longer my siblings and I take to reach a consensus on what to do about our cheating father and half-siblings, the more Ares seems to boil over.

It currently looks like someone shook him up like a can of Coke, and we're waiting for something to pop the tab.

Eloise told Athena that he's not sleeping. She's still taking him to meetings, but she said she'd be lying if she wasn't worried about his sobriety.

I get it. He's always been super close to Mamá, and while we don't know that she's aware of Papá's indiscretions, the fact that it has happened at all is enough for Ares. He's a hot head, his blood burns with the Latino passion we're famous for, but his heart is also the biggest I know.

He's caught between wanting to tell Mamá, and wanting to kill Papá. Fueled by rage and the desire for, if not revenge, then at least recompense. He wants to scorch the earth, or at least the family dynamics.

We're split fifty-fifty on how to proceed with our half-siblings, too, which isn't helping the harmony of our group. Ares and Artemis have no strong desire to meet our brothers. Athena has already talked to one of them, and she'd like to meet the others, as would I.

"We need to talk to Mamá." Ares has said this four times in the past thirty seconds. As he spins on his foot to change direction, he rakes his hands through his hair. "We at least need to know if she knows. We've waited long enough. I can't keep this to myself anymore." He grinds his chest with his fist. "We've sat on this for months, and we're no further ahead. We—"

He's cut off by the doorbell. The fact someone got upstairs without us being buzzed by the front desk means it's someone we know.

Athena holds up a hand. "I called her."

"Called who?" Artemis is already moving toward the door. He pulls it open before looking through the peephole. "Mamá."

Edith gasps at the same time my eyes finally catch up to what my ears heard. Mamá walks into the apartment, tugging her scarf off and shifting her shades onto her head. She looks like a supermodel.

Edith moves to pull her feet from me, but I stop her. "I should let you all..." She drops her voice to a whisper. "Apollo it's okay. I can go out for a while." She shakes her phone at me. "I can go hang out with Penelope or something. It's a family thing."

"And you're family." It's not my voice that corrects her, it's Athena's. "We don't expect you to leave." She speaks for all of us, as usual, but my brothers don't correct her, and they don't speak up—my brothers are nothing if not vocal. If they were uncomfortable or unhappy with Edith's presence, they'd say so.

Mamá puts her hands on her hips and surveys the somber room. This isn't going to be a fun conversation for any of us, and now that it's here, in the room with us, my gut weighs heavily at what's about to go down. "Does anyone want to tell me why you all look like someone died?"

"Papá is cheating on you." The words are out of Ares in an anguished burst of speed as he races to throw his arms around her.

Her face twitches—surprise, maybe? —but it's barely perceptible at all. Her face softens as she embraces Ares. *"¡Ay, mijo! Tranquilo."*

If Ares isn't crying, he soon will be. His body shudders in our mother's arms and my heart breaks for him. I have no idea why he's taking this the hardest of all of us—perhaps because he's the youngest, I don't know. Either way, he looks like a little boy in Mamá's arms.

"You already knew." Athena's voice is flat as she speaks.

To her credit, Mamá doesn't shrink or lie. *"Sí, mija.* I knew."

"So why did you stay?" Athena plants her hands on her hips and she's like a time-delayed mirror image of how Mamá looked a moment ago. "Why don't you leave that sorry piece of shit."

Mamá's face darkens, her eyes narrow, and she points a long, perfectly manicured finger at my sister. "Watch your mouth, Athena. That's your father you're speaking about."

Athena doesn't back down. She never backs down. She squares her shoulders, meets Mamá's glare with a judgmental one of her own and shakes her head. "If it was my boyfriend we were talking about, you'd have a different answer." She hooks her fingers into quotation marks.

"Never stay with a cheater, Athena, they'll never stop

cheating, and you deserve better than that." She pauses, barely for a beat before she's back on the offense. "So how come only I deserve better, Mamá, eh? Why don't you deserve better?" Athena's words are rapid-fire, shooting the accusation at Mamá.

Mamá shrugs. "Men will be men, *mija*. I've had a good life. He takes care of me..."

In Dominican culture, rich men cheating on their wives is pretty commonplace. Rich men were always expected to have mistresses eventually.

But this isn't any rich man, and this isn't any wife. Those women stayed with their husbands because they were stay at home wives and had no way to support themselves. But Mamá has her own money. The restaurant is in her name, she has her own car, she never sold her childhood home that Papá bought for her when we were younger. She could leave. She could be by herself.

She just isn't.

My stomach sours as Mamá continues to soothe Ares who seems to be crying in earnest at this point. Artemis hasn't said a single word, but the rage wafts from him in such strong waves that Athena keeps sending concerned glances his direction.

Our twin link seems to be malfunctioning. I can't get a read on what's going on in his head. Is he mad at Mamá for staying, at Papá for being a cheating *cabrón*, at Hen for being so confrontational?

Hard to say.

Athena doesn't accept Mamá's explanation, or defense as to why she's still with someone who very clearly doesn't deserve her. "I've spoken to some of his other children." Her eyes shine with challenge, like she's taunting Mamá, provoking her.

"No." The only word to fall from Mamá's lips.

"Sí. And I'd like a relationship with them. Perhaps with their mothers, too. Considering they're family."

A string of Spanish expletives spew from Mamá's mouth, and if Ares wasn't accidentally providing cover for Athena, she'd have—without a shadow of a doubt—the mark of Mamá's handprint across her face.

"That's enough, Hen," I hedge, softening my tone so she doesn't see me as a threat and launch across the room at me.

She shakes her head, and tears in her eyes glisten under the overhead light. She wears her anger like a mask. It's only on a rare occasion we get a glimpse of what's behind it. When I take a step toward her, she holds up her hand, shaking her head.

"You will *not* meet those... *perras*, are we clear?" Mamá levels each of us with a glare that could melt ice. She pushes Ares back, looking him dead in the eye. "Are we clear?"

"What about the kids? They're our siblings, Mamá."

Her nostrils flare in time with the flexing of her jaw, making her cheeks move as well. "I can't make that decision for you."

Her words say one thing, but the way she's grinding them out, the way she's holding her body, and the way her voice carries that unspoken threat we all learned as children... her message is clear. She doesn't want us anywhere near our father's extra-curricular activities.

But from the determined look on my sister's face, I'm not sure she's getting the message.

CHAPTER 45

Edith

(TWO WEEKS LATER)

Ding dong, the cast is gone.

It has been for a while, but it's still taking time to adjust. It's getting a little easier to remember a time when my leg wasn't wrapped up in a protective layer. It's as though every month post-accident covers an entire year of my life prior.

I'm starting to forget what the marley felt like under my feet as I danced, or the curve of the barre in my palm, the pain in my feet from turn after turn, and the cramping in my hips and calves.

Ugh. Cramping calves from an endless series of relevés are the devil.

I still haven't heard from anyone in my class. It doesn't sting quite so badly as it did a few months ago, but it sucks.

My mother on the other hand...

"Is that her texting again?" Apollo enters our bedroom from the bathroom, a towel wrapped low around his waist. "She seems... enthusiastic?" He flashes me a smile as he towel dries his hair, but all the blood has rushed to my va-jay-jay and any hope of packing for my trip to Australia has gone out the window.

As though he's reading my mind, he points at the opened, oversized case on the bed. "Pack first. I can't fuck you on top of that damned thing." After a beat of shaking droplets from his hair like an oversized German shepherd, he jerks his chin at me. "Your mom?"

Nodding, I sigh. "She finally paid attention to all of the medical bills her secretary was getting. Once she'd come up for air from husband number two and before she found number three. The wedding is next week, and we're invited, by the way." I can't help but roll my eyes. I don't know what was wrong with Dad, but it seems something was wrong with Bernard, too.

"She's getting remarried? Isn't she still with the boat guy?"

"Don't try to keep up, *príncipe de las tinieblas*. It's not worth the effort."

"Did you tell her about Australia?"

I take a tentative step toward my closet. Part of me expects my ankle not to bear weight, that I'll crumple like a Slinky going down stairs. "She knows I'm going, offered to pay, transferred a ludicrous sum of money into my account, offered the use of her name—though it was unclear which one she thought would get traction in Australia..."

"Did she ask how you're doing?"

A lump appears in my throat at my boyfriend's ability to drive a stake straight through the heart of the matter. I shake my head. "You know money equates to affection for my mom." I don't know why I'm defending her.

He steps up behind me as I toss a few shirts into the open case in front of us, threading his arms around my middle and placing his face on the back of my shoulder. "I'm sorry. I know you've always wanted more from her. You deserve more. It's okay to be sad that she's a selfish bitch."

I chuckle at his candor. We've never held back in our friendship, and if anything, we've gotten even more frank with each other since we crossed over into forever territory.

His cock is waking up against my ass so I wiggle but he steps back. "No packing, no peen. That's the rule."

Huffing out a grunt of frustration, I pull out my underwear drawer, upend the entire thing into the suitcase, drop the drawer onto the clothes and swing the case closed. With a shrug and a smirk over my shoulder I announce that I'm done.

He bends me forward over my case with his chest, and the pressing of his cock against me. "*¡Ay!* So sassy, *princesa*. I'm going to miss your smartass while you're gone." His fingers skim across my hips, sending a shiver all the way up my spine, snapping my head back.

Ever the opportunist, he wraps my hair around his hand, arching me toward him and grinds his now fully hard cock against my ass cheeks.

Before I know what's hit me, my leggings are shoved to the floor, and a loud crack rings out around the room. A sharp sting, a flash of heat. I should object, I should shriek and fight and yell and protest but the only noises I can find are deep, guttural, feral moans as I bend farther forward.

The things this man does to me.

Another slap rings out around the room. "I need to make sure my beautiful *princesa* can't sit down for days because of the marks I've left on her perfect ass." He squeezes my ass cheek, kneading the muscle in his firm hand.

Bracing both my hands on the case in front of me, I pop my hips, sending my ass further into the air. "*¡Ay!* She likes it, don't you *princesa*?"

I'm nodding, but I'm not sure whether it's at the fact he calls me *princesa* with such love and adoration, or the fact he's spanking me and making me wet as fuck. Either way, I'm nodding.

Another spank, another moan, another wiggle of my hips.

His fingers catch the flimsy piece of elastic between my ass cheeks. "Are you wet for me, Edie?"

Desperation, that's all that falls from my lips as I squirm and pant.

His fingers coast down the string, humming when I guess he finds it already wet. "I asked if you were wet for me, Edith. Use your words."

I hate him. I hate him. I fucking hate him. But if I don't answer him, he could—and would—do this all damned day.

"Y-yes, Apollo. I'm soaking. You know I'm soaking. I'm always wet for you, always." I place my forehead on the suitcase, rolling onto my tiptoes and hoping that he stops teasing and gives me what I need.

When his fingers kiss my swollen, dripping lips, I growl. The touch is too fast, and way too short. I need more.

"More," I beseech, but his fingers are already gone.

Slurping sounds are the only reply to my plea. "You taste so good, Edie."

Whimpers tumble from my mouth, please, begging, and the occasional swear word as he repeats the process. "So much wetter, princess. Dripping in anticipation."

The fabric of my thong lights up my skin as he drags it down my legs, pushing my panties to the floor. Opening myself to him, I roll my hips. "Please, Apollo."

The blunt end of his cock slides through my pussy, making me purr. "This is the last time I get to fuck my pussy for a while, Edith. I need to savor every moment."

If he savors much more I'm going to shatter into a million pieces and I won't need to go to Australia to talk to a fancy doctor about my recovery.

"Remind me who you belong to, Edie."

The reaction from my body tells us both who I belong to. The pull of my hips toward him, the tension thrumming through my tight muscles, and while he can't see it, I know he feels the lurch of my heart in my chest.

"You, Pollo, it's always been you."

He rams into me with one smooth thrust, palming my ass cheeks as he sinks all the way inside me. I'm going to miss him. I'm going to the other side of the world. We're going to have very little time together with time zones and schedules, and it's going to suck. But it's something I have to do.

I'd never forgive myself if I didn't throw my whole self into my dreams, and neither would he. We both need for me to go, to find out what my options are so I can pick a path and follow it with my very essence.

As the love of my life thrusts into me, whispering promises of forever, of being together as soon as our lives allow it, a sense of peace descends over me that I've been missing for such a long time. Even if my leg never works the way it used to, even if my mother never tells me she loves me, even if I have no idea what the fuck I'm going to do with the rest of my life, I feel whole.

Positivity and determination loosen the tension in my muscles, and hope fuels my heart. No matter what lies waiting for me in Australia, I know for sure that when shit is getting out of my control, Apollo will be there.

My prince of darkness, my love, my best friend will have my back. And we'll face whatever lies ahead together. Forever.

Epilogue

EDITH

(Seventeen months later)

Australia took a little longer than I'd expected. I had told Apollo that I wouldn't be back until Thanksgiving, but as I wait in the stands for the clock to count down to the Raccoon's first game of the season against the Indy Storm, energy sizzles in my veins.

Savannah is on my left. Justin hasn't played on the team for over a year but she supports the guys as often as she can. And she still wears his number on the back of her shirt.

To my right, Eloise stands with her hands clutched against her chest, beaming with pride. Her hot-shot goaltending boyfriend is rumored to be signing a very lucrative deal with a certain home-state based NHL team, and she hasn't stopped smiling since he got the call.

We're right at the front of the stands. First row, at the plexi and ready to scream like we're being chased by a dinosaur as our boys hit the ice. Tori is late, as usual, but she's gotten less reluctant to come to games than she used to be. I guess things changed while I was gone. Yet in many ways, everything feels the same.

A shiver slithers up my spine at the nip in the air, the door to the tunnel opens and Ares steps out onto the ice. Eloise practically leaps into the air as she starts screaming. Tori comes into the aisle, Penelope behind her, fingers in both ears, shaking her head.

"She used to be the quiet one of the group."

Pen hugs me like we haven't seen each other in a year, and it takes all I have not to cry my eyes out right there in the rink. "We'll talk later, okay? When you're ready to share." She gives me an extra squeeze, *that* squeeze. The one that puts you back together when you're broken.

And while I felt broken before I left Cedar Rapids to embark on my healing journey on the other side of the world, deep down, I know I'm not. But it sure as hell feels good to know I have such a strong and stable network of people who have my back.

When Pen pulls back, Tori gives me a quick hug then hooks her thumb over her shoulder. "He still clueless?"

I nod, rolling my lips between my teeth.

"You're going to make our big, bad captain cry on the opening night of the season, aren't you?"

Shrugging, I nod again, searching the ice for my prince of darkness.

Our eyes meet, his stick is poised in the air, ready to shoot the puck at Ares for their warm-up drill. He drops his stick and skates straight to where I'm sitting. Mouth hanging open, he points his glove at me.

"You're h-here," he stammers.

I nod, turning a slow circle so he can see my shiny de la Peña jersey with the C embroidered on my chest. He brought it to me on his visit last year, but I haven't had a chance yet to break it out for a game on home ice.

Artemis has to physically coax Apollo to move from the plexi. Pollo's staring at me like he's seen a ghost. Before he turns back to warm up, his wicked grin appears. "I'm fucking you so hard after this game, *princesa*."

My body hums in response, and I don't even have the decency to be embarrassed. "Score on the ice, score off the ice."

"Goal for goal?"

I can practically see the competitiveness rising in my guy. Knowing he's going to score just so he can fuck me all night, I nod. "Goal for goal."

Penelope groans loudly enough to be heard. Tori fans herself. "So fucking hot."

Savannah laughs so hard her shoulders shake. "I wouldn't like to be the Storm tonight. You've lit a fire under him."

A sharp tap on the glass brings my attention away from the pulsing need between my thighs. I haven't seen Apollo since the summer. My sex drive has only increased in his absence, and knowing he's actively playing with the sole purpose of winning orgasms tonight... well, that's enough to set my soul on fire.

Raffi stands on the ice, a wicked grin of his own in place, head cocked to the side. He's pointing at Tori, who seems to be doing her level best not to acknowledge his existence. Her face is red, really red. I don't know her as well as I'd like to, but her discomfort screams embarrassment, so now I'm curious. Last I'd heard, the extent of Tori's relationship with Raffi was dumping a drink over his head and cussing him out in the bar.

This is an interesting progression.

Things really *have* changed in the last year.

Raffi smacks the glass again, then again, making it particularly difficult for anyone, especially Tori to ignore him. Dude's three seconds away from having an all-out toddler meltdown right there during warm-ups.

When she finally gives in to the fact he's demanding her

attention, satisfaction ripples across his face, but he doesn't seem smug. This whole exchange is fascinating to me. It screams of Raffi being in the dog house. From what I know of her, Tori is a strong woman, a badass, and certainly not intimidated by Raffi, or anyone else on the hockey team. And yet, her cheeks are the color of a Coke can.

He gestures for her to move to the side, waiting patiently for her to acquiesce. When she's far enough away from the net that protects the plexi behind the goal, he flicks her a puck. "For Wyatt."

Welp. There go my ovaries. He doesn't wait for her reply, he pushes off on his skate and rejoins the drills happening on the ice. All eyes on our row land on Tori, whose scowl tells me she's not open to telling me what the fuck just happened.

Eloise nudges my elbow, leaning close. "You've missed a *lot*. I'll tell you all the tea, later."

What the hell have I missed since I've been gone? I talk to Apollo every single day. All of them. There isn't a day that goes by that I don't hear from him in some shape or form. And he didn't think to tell me that something's going on between Tori and Raffi? Something that sings of salacious, juicy, k-i-s-s-i-n-g up a tree? They're very clearly together, even if she hates the public display of affection. Did I miss anyone else hooking up?

I look at Pen, whose cheeks pinken. Shit. I did miss someone else hooking up. She hasn't said anything either. She holds up a finger. "Later."

Damn. The pang in my heart causes my hand to drift to my chest. I've missed this place, these people. While recovery in Australia was important for me, for my entire being, for my core, this place is where I'm happiest, where I belong.

~

At the end of three periods, my prince of darkness has scored a hat trick. I shouldn't be surprised, but the vibrating between my thighs and the moisture soaking my panties has me so on edge that he could probably growl my name at me, and I'd burst into pieces for him.

Each time he scored, he skated over to where I sat and rapped the glass with his stick like he needed to capture my attention. It's like he forgot that he's the only person on the ice that I give a shit about.

That's somewhat of an exaggeration, but I'm captivated by him, always have been. There is no one else. After he banged his stick on the glass, he pulled off a glove and held up a finger, or two fingers, or three fingers. A threat, a promise, a reminder of what was in store for me after the game.

I'm bouncing on the balls of my feet, waiting for the team to get done with the behind the scenes stuff and get out. He's going to be in his tailor-made suit. He's going to look delectable. And he's probably going to make me wait until after drinks in the bar with his team before he fucks me senseless.

Asshole.

He's the first player out when the door opens. I don't know where his kit bag is, but that predatory look in his eyes as he skims the waiting crowd for me, makes my clit tingle.

He grabs my hand, tugging me away from the rest of the girlfriends. "But—" I don't get to finish my sentence because we're practically running toward the door.

"Don't." It's the only word he says until we get outside the arena and next to his car. He waited a year for this sports car to be delivered. A tiny seed of anxiety is buried deep in my chest. He had no idea that I'd be here tonight, and he had no idea that he might need to bring the other car instead.

When his lips crash against mine, everything is right,

complete, whole again. It's the welcome home I've needed since I landed at the airport a few hours ago.

He wastes no time turning me to face the hood of his car. "Hands out, Edie. Brace yourself."

His words pulsate deep in my core, and I almost forget we're in public.

"But... someone might see."

He's already shucking my pants down my legs and kicking apart my feet. "Don't care." His words are spoken through gritted teeth, like he's already on edge, like he might explode before he even gets inside me. It sends a thrill through my body that has me purring. Bracing my hands on the cool metal of his new-to-me car, the tingles in my clit spread.

A firm hand lands between my shoulders and pushes my face toward the hood. It takes him about ten seconds to unzip his dress pants and free his cock, another half a second to slide his dick through my soaking wet folds, and less than half a second to get seated to the hilt inside me.

We both moan with relief. He gives me a beat to adjust to his presence before he lets go. Slams into me with reckless abandon. It's not a romantic reunion, it's a reconnection of bodies and souls. He pistons his hips against mine, the only sounds in the night air are his balls slapping against my body, and the loud squelching with each thrust against me.

I should expect it when he pulls his jersey up to my waist, revealing my ass to him, but when his palm connects with my skin, it's still a surprise. I yelp, then relish the heat spreading across my ass cheek.

"You're holding back, *princesa*." He leans over me, mouth close to my ear as he jerks his hips against mine. "Let me make myself clear. I've missed you. I don't give a fuck who sees, who watches, or who hears me fucking you right now. But I do care that you're holding back. Where's my unbridled princess?"

Something inside me snaps at his words and I wiggle

against his hips that pin me to the car. "Apollo." My voice is raspy, my palms sweaty against the now-warm metal under my hands.

I don't move, I don't chase my own orgasm, he'll take care of me when we get back to the apartment. Right now, I just take. Take every thrust, every grunt and groan, every smack on my ass until my prince of darkness fills me with his cum.

He doesn't wait for me to catch my breath before he shoves something inside me. "These panties you left on my pillow before you went away will keep my cum where it needs to be until we get home."

He pulls up my pants, pausing to knead my ass cheeks on the way up. My legs are unsteady, my hands shaking, and my pussy aches, clenching intermittently with tiny aftershocks from my release. "Get in the car." He's pulled open the passenger door and is already circling the hood to get in the driver's side.

"But the bar—"

He pauses, driver's door open, an intensity on his face that I can't fully see in the darkness, but I can feel rolling off him in waves. "You have two choices. You can go into the bar and put on a special show for all our friends and the patrons. Or you can get. In. The. Fucking. Car. Edith."

He doesn't leave me much choice as he slides into the driver's seat and slams the door. So I do the only thing I can. I get in the fucking car.

If you're not finished with Apollo and Edith, I wrote a bonus scene for you to enjoy. Sign up to my newsletter and get a freebie extra scene.

Not ready to be finished with the Cedar Rapids Raccoons? Book 4, Lighting the Lamp features Raffia and Tori:

. . .

The night she'll never forget is the night he can't remember.

Tori

How dare he act like we've never met?

I thought we connected, but after a steamy one night stand, the hockey hot shot ghosted me, leaving me with nothing but wounded pride and two pink lines on a stick. And not the hockey kind.

Well, not this time, bud. You fooled me once, and I'm never giving you a second chance to fool me again.

We don't need you.

Raffi

She's not a forgettable woman, so why does she insist she knows me?

One look at her son and it hits me like a slap shot to the chest. The resemblance is undeniable.

How can I convince the mother of my child to let me be part of their lives, when I don't even remember her?

Preorder book 4 now!

Also by Lasairiona McMaster

Two for Interference - Minnesota Snow Pirates book 1

Minnesota Snow Pirates books 1-3 Boxset

Freezing the Puck - Cedar Rapids Raccoons book 1

Two for Tacos - A Snow Pirates Novella

www.Lasairiona.com

Author Note

This book... This. Book. It was fractured, broken, (I guess kind of like Edith) when I got space and peace to write it, it flew from my fingers, reasonably formed. But getting that space felt almost impossible sometimes.

Staring down the barrel of back-to-back editing deadlines for May and June, my original confidence that I'd have plenty of time to write two books was scuppered by the fact we got sick. For two whole months we suffered with the lurgy, and some other personal issues made it really hard to focus on the output. It's been a different kind of challenge, and something I'm learning is that no matter how ready you are to write a book, no matter how much preparation and planning you've done, at least one asshole character is going to come along and shit on it.

Edith and Apollo were doing so well until they weren't. They took over my fingers and were like *hey, dumb little author lady, just follow us, we've got you*. Turns out they had, and they got smug about it.

I've known my friend Robynne (Fancy) for a number of years now. Her dedication and commitment to dance, her passion, her flare, and the elegance that drips from her mere existence made me want to write a dancer into a book.

The parallels between the graceful dancer and the grace of hockey players was something I wanted to explore a little. And what would happen if one of them lost their dream forever?

This book has been one of my favorites to write, it truly has. I found myself adoring the prince of darkness and his princess. And I truly hope all y'all do too.

Acknowledgments

Lewis — Every book starts out with the biggest thanks going to my (now nine-year-old) son, Lewis. As with every single book I write, we had a wall of sticky notes for him to tick off when I hit a certain number of words. You keep me right, then grumble that you can't read my words. Your support is unwavering and I'm totally here for it.

Tracie — Sprints were hard in Q1. Some mornings we just didn't get out of bed. That's cool, it's what we needed, but this is another book that wouldn't have been written without you. Thanks for keeping me focused on the goals, not the dumpster fires. Ride or die, boo.

Irene — The only person who cheers harder for me than Lewis is you. Who knew the McNagster would need McNagged? Seems you do, frequently, and you're not afraid to give me a boot in the ass. Love you!

Fancy — Fancy. Fucking. Says. Without you I'd be another ignorant author pissing off the entire dancing community with my Hollywood recollection of what dance is, and who dancers are. Thank you for always having my back, and my facts, and my feelings when Editor Jess's feedback makes me question my life choices.

Karina — For Mondays in the prom. For breakfasts, chit-chat, and holding space for both of us working outside the house. Our Monday time has been invaluable for not only my writing process, but for keeping my bucket full. Can't wait to hold a signed, first edition copy of your first books.

My Alpha readers—Amy R, Katie 'Violence' Wilks y'all

stroke my hair and tell me my words are pretty, and on the days there are no new words you hump my leg and smack me over the head to write them. Thank you. A million thank yous.

My Beta—Erika and **my proofreader** Corinne. I appreciate your attention to details and eagle eyes. Without y'all I'd have 13 chapter 5s, each character would all have the same colored hair, and they'd all be called John.

My editor—Editor Jess, it's like an eternal game of "What's their goal?" Thank you for pushing me to be better, even though each time I'm always convinced I can't be. And then you push even harder.

My cover designer—Kate Farlow over at *Y'all That Graphic* for bringing my boys to life on the covers.

And finally, to my ARC readers, my Facebook reader group *Margaritas, Men, and Mischief with Lasairiona*, and to each and every one of you who pick up this book: a bazillion thank yous. I truly hope you loved it enough to pick up the next one. Tell your friends! And if you're not in my group —come join us, we don't bite (unless you ask us to!)

About the Author

Lasairiona McMaster writes sassy, classy and badassy women and strong, yet vulnerable men. She challenges reader's expectations by openly dealing with mental health issues, often exploring tough-to-handle topics and 'taboos' and books with a whole lotta heart.

She can either be found enjoying a gin and lemonade by the Irish sea, or baking sweet treats in her kitchen while singing at the top of her lungs. When she's 'home' in Texas, and isn't eating fresh-popped popcorn while buying things she has absolutely no need for in Target, she can be found at Chuys eating her body weight in chips and queso and washing it down with a margarita swirl. She loves to make friends out of strangers.

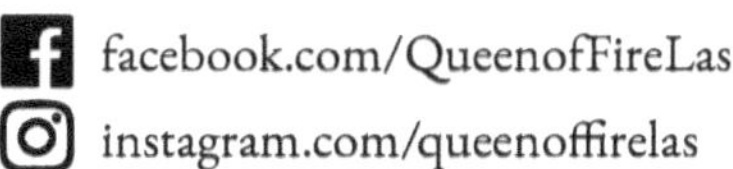

facebook.com/QueenofFireLas

instagram.com/queenoffirelas